THE TRUE BRIDE

Ellen Campbell and her husband, Eric, are cheerfully awaiting the birth of their first baby. She is happy; Eric is devoted to her, her friend Vicky is reliable and her mother has moved halfway across the country to be with her.

Then she notices things going wrong; little things at first, then much more frightening, like her blue shirt cut to shreds, the black car always following her, the telephone messages that make no sense. Soon, Ellen is so distracted by the terrible things happening to her that she fears for her life and that of her unborn child.

Set in the stifling heat of suburban Arizona, THE TRUE BRIDE is an intensely chilling and horrifying story of insanity, the ultimate marriage of love and terror.

Also by Thomas Altman

KISS DADDY GOODBYE

and published by Corgi Books

The True Bride

Thomas Altman

CORGI BOOKS

THE TRUE BRIDE
A CORGI BOOK 0 552 12232 7

First publication in Great Britain

PRINTING HISTORY
Corgi edition published 1983
Corgi edition reprinted 1983

Copyright © 1982 by INK Creations, Inc.

Corgi Books are published by
Transworld Publishers Ltd.,
Century House, 61-63 Uxbridge Road,
Ealing, London W5 5SA.

Made and printed in Great Britain by
Hunt Barnard Printing Ltd., Aylesbury, Bucks.

Turn and peep, turn and peep,
There's blood within the shoe
The shoe it is too small for her
The true bride waits for you.
                    –The Brothers Grimm: *Cinderella*

Part One

The Seventh Month

Prologue

●●

Knife.

Sharp, shining. Your face reflected in a blade. Like a mirror. A fun-house mirror, distorted. Your face.

Your white dress billows and puffs in warm water. You feel it soak through flimsy material, then press against your skin. Warm water seeping through the garment. You look at the knife and you think—

You think of lost things, silenced music, flowers drooping. Violets and carnations and roses.

You think of love and loss and the thought grows and expands until it fills your brain and pushes hard against the bone as though you're falling into a nightmare of pain, bad bad pain. You think: He didn't want the baby. You think: Something might have happened to him. He lost his way. He confused the time. Anything. Anything at all.

Explanations.

You stare at your red lips in the blade of the knife.

Red lips. You open your mouth, push your tongue against your teeth, slide deeper into the warm water. But the pressure builds inside your head and you know you've reached a point where tears aren't answers, where there aren't solutions, and the world tilts away from you in spidery cracks like eggshells tapped by small mallets.

You move a hand, reaching down for your knees, raising the hand upward and pushing the wet dress over your belly. You move your legs and white underwear floats away like a lost thought. You could be drowning. You run the palm of a hand over the belly. But nothing shows yet. Nothing shows. Nothing.

You think love. Poor love, lost his way. Something happened to him. You remember dying music and you stroke the skin of your stomach under water and you remember whispers echoing in a large place and the whispers turn to speech and you put your hands to your ears to stop the noise because you can't think straight anymore; the pressure screams.

3

Noises. You hear voices from a downstairs part of this house and suddenly you no longer remember where you are, you exist only as pressure, the pressure of pain and loss. You take the knife and move it downward. A cut. A slight cut in your thigh but the knife is sharp and a small cloud of pink flits through the water. It would be easy, you imagine, easy to slice the blade across your wrists, but you know better than that. The baby. He wanted you, not the baby. He didn't want the ...

Poor love, you imagine he'll come back, even now you recall the promises and the words and the speeches of love and how love is an undying thing and your memory is filled with the smell of his hair and the way he sometimes smiled and looked down at you after lovemaking and you bring back everything you ever saw in that smile. You won't lose. You won't lose the smile, not ever. You raise your head, look down at your pubic hair under water. Oh love. You know he'll come back. You know he will. His absence is nothing—

And then you wonder why you're lying here in water and why you've swept the white dress up over your stomach and why the knife is poised and angled over your navel. Remember— you make the cut, you make the cut in a line between two points.

You know where to make the cut.

Voices again. From another part of this house. They echo. Where is she? Did anybody see where she went?

You hear movement on stairs. Quick then. You have to do the thing quickly. Make it, make the cut, push the blade into the flesh deep, watch the blood. You press the point of the blade into the navel and pull downward through sudden blood and flaps of skin, downward and downward to a place above the pubic bone, you try to make a line, make a straight line of the gash but then you're blinded by pain, the pain screeches inside you, the pressure is more than anything imaginable, your blood floats across the surface of water, away and away, and the knife—sharp and terrible—the knife goes on tearing through flesh, through layers of flesh and fat, cutting, slicing, ripping at the guts, tearing and slashing, and the pain is fire inside your skull. Light fades, comes and goes, you open your mouth, you don't make a sound, maybe a whisper, but all you want to do is scream aloud—and the knife goes on digging downward through you. Nothing is worse, nothing could ever be worse.

Except the loss of love.

You're blinded, but you look down at your blood spiraling through water and the ragged flaps of your skin punctured by the blade, and the pain is like some javelin thrust directly through your heart. You feel blackness come in. Then light. More light. And finally you see in a dim darkening way—

Where the hell is she? Did she lock herself in the bathroom?

Dim darkening way.

It moves, attached to you, part of you, it moves through mucus and purple blood and streamers of flesh, it moves outward like some misshapen tadpole trying to swim for its life, blind, turning over and over, red and dreadful, in the water, the bloody water, and then you crawl inside the awful darkness of things, sink into the water, feel it entering your mouth, feel yourself choking in your own bloody water, even as the thing floats upward, still turning, dying and dying in its blind and formless way.

You think you hear something at the locked door.

You think you do.

Your head goes under water.

Something banging, rattling.

She's locked in there—

Locked in—

You feel the thing slither against the inside of your leg, go sliding down, no longer a part of you, only another piece of your loss—

And you think: Love, poor love.

Where are you now?

One   July 3

❋❋❋❋❋❋❋❋❋❋❋❋❋❋❋❋❋❋❋❋❋❋❋❋❋❋❋❋❋❋❋❋❋❋❋❋❋❋

It was a crowded restaurant built at the edge of an artificial lake. Across the narrow expanse of dark water Ellen could see the lights of houses shimmer in reflection; docked rowboats moved slightly as if shivered by an artificial tide. If you closed your eyes and pretended, you might think you were sitting near the shore of an ocean instead of the heart of a desert city. A romantic conceit—sometimes you had to allow yourself such small notions. She raised her face from the table, from the plate still covered with half-eaten seafood, and she looked at Eric. A candle burned between them. There was a red rose in a thin-stemmed glass.

Eric laid his fork down alongside the hollow of a baked potato. He watched her a moment, smiling. Then he moved his hand across the table and put his fingers over her wrist.

"You haven't finished your food," he said.

Was he scolding her a little? She shook her head. "I'm stuffed," she said.

"They do a terrific cheesecake here," Eric said. "I've heard of people walking barefoot over the Superstition Mountains just to get their hands on the stuff."

She smiled at him, then looked down at her stomach just as the baby moved inside her. She thought of it turning over and over, a small colorless shape accidentally colliding with the soft walls of her womb. *Cheesecake:* already she perceived herself as a blimp. Somewhere along the way a slender young woman called Ellen had simply vanished, eclipsed by this cumbersome zeppelin. She looked at her husband's face, his expression one of sharp anticipation, as if her acceptance or rejection of the cheesecake were the most important thing in his world right then.

"I can't, Eric. I can't eat another thing."

"You won't try even a sliver?"

"Not even that."

He leaned back in his chair, fidgeting with his napkin, and she glanced out at the dark water a moment. Something moved on the surface, a shadow, nothing substantial. After a second it was gone and the water was very still. A duck, she thought, a water bird of some kind. Eric was reaching for the last of the wine now, holding the bottle over the rim of her glass. She covered it with her hand.

"I don't think Dr. Phelps would approve," she said.

"Why not? It's a pretty decent wine."

"You know what I *mean*. He's always reminding me I'm eating for two people now. He's never said anything about drinking for two." She raised her glass, sipped, realizing that the little she'd drunk had already gone to her head: it was as though a light rainbow-colored bubble floated inside her skull. A pleasant feeling, a warm one, romantic. *Two more months*, she thought. Seven down and two to go.

She watched Eric drain the wine bottle into his glass. For a time he looked pensive, then he raised the glass in the air and smiled at her: "To us," he said. "To the three of us."

"The three of us." She clinked her glass against his. *The three of us*. It was a strangely wonderful phrase, like some new discovery of language, a restructuring of old words in bright forms. She looked at her husband, she felt the child move slightly, and all at once there seemed a conspiracy of romantic elements—the candle, the rose, the shudder of lights on the water, the expression on Eric's face. A world of warm prisms, a world of shining things in which you were willingly ensnared. Even the sudden swift pain caused by the baby, which might have been stretching an arm, moving a leg, was still another aspect of the same shadowless place. Love, loving, she thought—there wasn't anything else.

She put her glass down and watched Eric finish his drink. He said: "You know what? You look terrific. You look great."

Terrific, she thought. How could he say that to her with such obvious sincerity? She was bloated and plump and her ankles were swollen and her breasts enlarged—and yet, for a moment, she could imagine she was slim and lovely and delicate.

"It must be the clothes I'm wearing," she said.

"Clothes have nothing to do with it," Eric answered. "It comes from inside."

"You sound like Mr. Rogers."

"Even Mr. Rogers has his moments, love."

She smiled and stroked his hand and noticed that her wedding ring seemed tighter than before, cutting into the finger; God, had her hands swollen as well?

"I like your blouse," Eric said. "Is it new?"

"Sometimes I think you go through life with your eyes shut, Eric. You were with me when I bought it. Don't you remember my saying it was the first decent maternity blouse I'd seen? At least it doesn't feel like a tent. You even said you liked it at the time—"

"The color suits you."

She touched the narrow cuffs of the blue blouse. The color *did* suit her; it created a dark frame for her paleness. She liked the silky feel of the material. And the cut, which disguised her pregnancy as much as anything might.

Eric was running his index finger round the rim of his glass. She looked past him for a time at the rest of the diners:

it was odd somehow to realize that you were the only visibly pregnant woman in the room—it made you feel like a member of some minority group, a disappearing clan.

"I still think you should have a little more wine," Eric said.

"Phelps—"

"Phelps," he said and smiled. "Phelps is on the old-fashioned side. I sometimes think he secretly wants to belong to that defunct species—the general practitioner—and go around making house calls."

She remembered now the awkwardness with which Phelps had discussed the sexual needs of expectant parents, and how they had laughed over the booklet Phelps had given her, reading it together in bed.

Now she raised a hand to her mouth, stifling a yawn. "I think the wine's made me tired."

"Do you want to go home?"

She nodded. "I enjoyed myself. I really did."

"It was time to celebrate," Eric said.

"Celebrate?"

"All expectant mothers should be celebrated now and then," and he leaned across the table and kissed her lightly on the lips. When he drew back she saw an expression in his eyes that was pure adoration. He helped her out of her chair. Adoration, celebration, attentiveness, consideration—it was almost as if these elements could form a protective shield around her, a talisman against all misfortunes.

Outside on the terrace they looked at the lights on the lake: the desert sky was cloudless, the stars singularly brilliant. Here, even if only for a moment, you could ignore the dry summer heat that pressed through the night. They walked toward the parking lot. Eric opened the door of the Datsun for her, helped her get inside. He went around, his shadow against the windshield, and opened the door at the driver's side. He turned the key in the ignition and slipped the car forward—

And then everything happened so suddenly she wasn't aware of danger, she wasn't conscious of the possibility of a collision until later. Across the parking lot the bright beams of a car blinded her abruptly, growing in intensity as the car came forward at speed, as it came forward as if the driver were drunk or sightless or imagined no obstacle in the way. Eric slammed a foot on the brake, the Datsun stalled, and the other car, at what seemed the last possible moment, swung away to the left and screeched out of the parking lot, taillights burning a fiery red.

"Jesus Christ. I can't believe..." Eric let his sentence go unfinished.

She clutched her stomach. She felt slightly sick from the sudden braking of the Datsun, the abrupt lurch of the car. She rolled her window down but the hot air of the night was no help: she was sweating, she could feel perspiration slide from the roots of her hair, roll down her forehead. The baby inside her was still. You slept through near-disaster, she thought. You slept through what might have been a calamity.

Eric said fiercely, "There's a word for that kind of driver."

"More than one word," she said. She realized now that she was trembling. She could feel various nerves work inside her body like tiny berserk pulses. A crash, a collision, a moment of madness, and everything comes to a bloody end—she shut her eyes but she could still see the bright beams of the oncoming car behind her eyelids, stamped there like indentations made by a branding iron.

"Maniac," Eric said.

"That's the most charitable one that comes to mind," she said.

"You sure you're okay?"

"Fine."

He sighed again and turned the key in the ignition.

"Some people out here still think it's the wild West," Eric said.

Something woke her.

At first she thought it was the sound of the air conditioner blowing passages of ice through the apartment, but the unit was silent. And then she wondered if the baby might have kicked or twisted in her womb. But she couldn't feel any movement.

She sat upright on the edge of the bed and pushed her fingers through her hair. The strands felt dry. Stepping out into the hallway she looked in the direction of the kitchen. A thin light burned above the stove.

She was thirsty suddenly and filled a glass with water. It was tepid, chemical-tasting; how could the citizens of this great desert state drink this rust-flavored water anyhow? She carried the glass into the living room and sat down on the sofa, gazing absently across the room, making out the vague shapes of furniture barely illuminated by the light from the kitchen. The metal frame of the Gorman print caught her eye. (Eric's present to me on the day I told him he was going to be a father, she thought.)

She yawned, wondering what had awakened her, wondering how she could get back to sleep. Dr. Phelps had told her she should stay away from sleeping pills and tranquilizers. *Even if insomnia is driving you up the wall, Ellen, no needless chemicals. Besides, some women in your condition can't sleep because they worry over their unborn children. Perfectly natural worries too, Ellen. Is the child going to be deformed? Stillborn? Just relax. Just follow the exercise procedures in the manual.*

Exercise procedures.

She yawned again, then walked to the glass door that led to the balcony.

She tugged the cord, drawing the drapes back.

Open. The sliding glass door was halfway open.

She put her hand up to her throat as if she were frightened by something. Why was it open? Had Eric forgotten to close and lock it? Had she left it open herself? She moved out onto the balcony and stared down at the dark parking lot of the apartment complex. There was a full moon, a yellow desert moon, creating shadows between parked cars. She could see the outlines of palm trees around the swimming pool and the flicker of a blue underwater light.

No wind. No motion. The night sky cloudless.

Only the tenacious heat. Go back inside, Ellen. Drink ice water and turn the thermostat down to sixty-five and get back to sleep.

But she didn't move.

There was something at the edge of her vision.

She turned her face to one side. A slick of sweat slid into her eye, stinging. She rubbed the eye with her knuckles, then blinked as she looked back in the direction of the pool.

A movement of white. Something white that passed along the wire grids of the swimming-pool fence. A blur that might have been the flash of a prowling cat or a piece of newspaper blown in a wind—but there isn't a wind, she thought. The night isn't moving. The night is locked into this silent heat, the palm trees are still—

She leaned forward and stared.

It was a person. Somebody going in the direction of the pool. Somebody in white. She blinked again. The figure had paused beneath a tall palm, masked from moonlight, indistinct in shadow. It wasn't possible to tell the sex, the height, it wasn't possible to tell anything except for the vague suspicion she had that the figure had tilted its face upward and was staring in the direction of the balcony.

No, Ellen thought. Nobody is looking up at me. Nobody is standing under that palm and staring.

Staring.

She shrugged and went back inside, sliding the door shut and locking it. The entire surface of her body was covered in perspiration.

She walked into the bedroom and heard Eric's voice. He was sitting up, his face little more than a shadow against the white pillow.

"Couldn't sleep?" he said.

She sat on the edge of the mattress. "I want to know why it doesn't cool down at night like it does everywhere else in the world."

She heard him laugh. *Eric,* she wanted to say—*Eric, why did you drag me to this godforsaken desert city when I was perfectly happy in frigid old Maine?*

"I went out on the balcony for air and I couldn't find any," she said instead. "The balcony door was open." Why did this trivial fact continue to bother her?

"Was it?"

"Did you forget to lock it?"

He was quiet for a time. "I don't think so. I don't even remember going out there."

"It must have been me," she said. She shut her eyes and laid her face against Eric's bare chest. The light hairs tickled her. For a moment she retreated into him because there was warmth and sympathy in his physical presence, a sweet sense of security at the center of which she could lose her fears and worries. Deformed, stillborn. *The fears are worst the first time around, Ellen. Every time the baby moves you imagine it's going to drop straight out of your body.*

She moved, tried to find a comfortable position.

"I feel so fat," she said. "I feel like a balloon sometimes. I'm swollen up and my ankles are like tree trunks and my nipples leak and those shapeless clothes don't help—"

"Hey, what brought this on?"

"I don't know. I get a little scared sometimes. I'm scared of the pain of giving birth; then I start thinking maybe the kid will have webbed feet or be blind in one eye, you know?" She was quiet for a moment. "I even imagined I saw somebody when I was out on the balcony. Somebody just looking up at me."

Eric laughed quietly. She understood he was simply trying to ease her tensions, calm her, mock her absurd fears. But they couldn't be shaken loose lightly. Pain of birth, webbed feet, someone in a dark parking lot just looking up at you— these all seemed to belong together, separate layers of the same anxiety. Eric took her hand. His long fingers enclosed her knuckles. She thought about his patience, his kindness: it was almost as if he had some magical quality that absorbed her flaws and turned them into virtues. She pressed her face against his chest in gratitude—he was the center of things, the core; without him, the props would be kicked away and everything would collapse into chaos. Now he was stroking the back of her hand.

His touch seemed to enervate her, reminding her of how it had been to make love in the past and how clumsy their physical contact was now. My fault, she thought. Not his. How can it be his fault when I don't find myself in the mood? When my shape alone conspires against love?

"Sex," she said. "I seem to remember how we used to enjoy sex."

"Relax," he said. "I don't want you to start getting uptight about that right now."

"But what about you?" she asked.

"What about me?"

"You must get frustrated—"

"You get over that, love. Don't ask me how exactly. The urge seems to evaporate. I can't really explain it."

She remembered Phelps's telling her once that for some women pregnancy was a time of sexual urgency, while for others the act was impossible. And she also remembered the last time she and Eric had made love and how afraid she'd been of his penetration, recalling her discomfort and panic, the imagined catastrophe of the child aborting. She wondered if he were being entirely truthful about not feeling frustrated or whether he was simply working hard at being patient.

She said, "In another couple of months—"

He pressed a finger over her lips for silence. "In another couple of months we'll be back to normal, kid."

Normal: she'd almost forgotten what that felt like.

It was a sharp kick from the baby that woke her in the first light of dawn. The room was warm now: the moon had gone and the sky was flaming. Another infernal day, she thought. Another blast from the furnace. She walked to the window. That goddam balcony door—why couldn't she remember leaving it open? Maybe amnesia was just one of the little drawbacks of pregnancy; maybe you just forgot trivial things because your whole life was in orbit around your belly.

She had just turned from the window when she heard Eric moan.

God, no. No.

He was twisting this way and that in the bedsheets, curling them around his body. Dear Christ. He was covered in sweat, she could see it gleam on his chest, arms, on his upper lip. And the moaning sound, so filled with a dreamer's anguish, was rackingly familiar to her.

The nightmare, the recurring nightmare, the dream that periodically haunted him, the images he could never remember in the morning. Sometimes in the middle of the dream, when he moaned and sweated and shivered, it seemed to her that whatever illusions his brain created were tearing him apart.

It always frightened her. A bad dream. Something wicked. Something carved by the mind in a mad sculpture. And dreams were so private, the dreamer so locked away in his own reality—how could you ever *really* intrude? She went down on her knees by the side of the bed and stroked his brow.

Jesus. Let him wake. Let him move out of this horror.

He turned again and again, as if there were an entity he wanted to escape, a monster filling his sleep and throwing black shadows. *Please, please let it pass, whatever it is.*

A nightmare—but why did it come back time and again like this? He never remembered any of it despite the number of times she'd asked. Maybe it was something he *needed* to go through, some wild release of the brain. Maybe. With the edge of a sheet she wiped sweat from his face.

He rocked, twisted, his hands bent in a spastic way.

She wanted to hold him. Save him from his own specters.

Save herself from her own terror—that he was a stranger to her, a man imprisoned in a cell she could never see.

Please wake. Please wake.

She leaned forward and kissed him lightly on the lips.

He opened his eyes suddenly and stared at her with a lack of recognition that was worse than the dream. For a long time he said nothing.

"Did it happen again?" he finally asked.

She nodded. "Don't you remember anything? Anything at all?"

"Nothing. How the hell can I have a nightmare I don't even remember?"

"I don't know, Eric." She wanted to pass it off as a joke somehow, relegate it to the category of the unimportant. But it happened too often that he woke this way, drenched in sweat and weak.

"Is anything troubling you? Something at work, maybe?"

"I can't think of anything," he said.

"The baby? Are you concerned about the pregnancy?"

He looked solemn for a time. "I just know something happens and I get this feeling of fear. I don't remember details. I don't remember any pictures. I just recall being scared to death. Christ, it's infuriating."

She thought: It's like some other Eric exists, someone whose life is a galaxy away. Now she desperately wanted to change the subject—talk about anything, leave the nightmare alone. "Your offspring kicked me awake. He really socked me," she said.

"He's impatient to make his debut," Eric said, then coughed into his fist. He looked pale, exhausted.

"*His* debut?"

"I have a gut instinct it's a boy tucked away in there."

"We'll just have to wait and see, won't we?"

She watched him a moment longer, then she stepped out of the bedroom and into the hallway.

In the kitchen she filled a kettle with water and placed it on the stove. A boy, she thought. I don't care if it's a boy *or* a girl, so long as it's healthy. And suddenly, as if she could see the child, as if she could touch it and cradle it in her arms, she was filled with an extraordinary sense of love. Like the flow of blood, like something warm coursing inside her, she could feel it spread out from her heart and move, glowing, throughout her body. A place beyond nightmare, a feeling no nightmare could touch.

Two more months, she thought.

Two more months.

Two *July 6*

❀❀❀❀❀❀❀❀❀❀❀❀❀❀❀❀❀❀❀❀❀❀❀❀❀❀❀❀❀❀❀❀❀❀❀

July in the desert: the sunlight was a static burning sheet; it lay over everything, blinding fire. It ricocheted from the surfaces of buildings, turned the fronds of palm trees white, glared from the still blue waters of swimming pools. It created an atmosphere in which otherwise solid citizens might claim they had seen unidentified flying objects in the sky: a quality of illusion where only the swollen sun seemed near. To Ellen it was intolerable. A form of hell, she thought, a hell where your pores just opened and you disintegrated like some misshapen wax figure. Even as she drove through the streets of downtown Scottsdale she realized that no air came through the open window of her Opel; summer was suffocation, the intense suffocation of a dream of drowning.

She drove north, marveling as she always did at the sheer pioneering tenacity that had hacked cities from such a hostile environment, astonished, as ever, at the fact that this same tenacity had been accompanied by a dismal lack of taste. A city springs up looking like the collective architectural nightmare of car salesmen and chamber of commerce types who'd spent a couple of nights in some Mexican border town—then you had used-car lots reminiscent of grandiose funeral homes and buildings suggestive of Mexican ranches. Even the names of apartment complexes had been rendered in Neanderthal Spanish. The place where she and Eric lived was called, for example, the Casa Manzanita: you might nod to Pancho Villa as he went for his morning dip in the pool.

To her left she saw a vague pall hanging around Phoenix, a city to which Scottsdale seemed like a curious adjunct, an afterthought. Why, when she thought of Phoenix, did she imagine some desert hooker winking in the dark? Sweating, she reached for the air-conditioning switch on the panel and flicked it. Useless, broken; she would have to remind Eric to get it fixed. She would also have to remind Eric sometime that she had no intention of spending the rest of her life in this arid landscape, that she found it a travesty of nature to live in a place where people played tennis at midnight under floodlights or had back-yard barbecues on Christmas Day, where snow was as rare as a camel in Vermont.

She reached the outskirts of Paradise Valley, a self-proclaimed "township" to the north of Scottsdale. Here was the place that typified Arizona wealth for her. The landscaped gardens, the two-bedroom houses that exchanged greedy hands for three-quarters of a million dollars, the stylized churches with their bulging collection plates: here was the true squalor of new money. It was the land, as Eric called it, of the desert debutante, those girls of rich families who had the thorazined look of mindless clones, who had had their teeth straightened and their yellow hair teased, who were given Corvettes or Thunderbirds on their seventeenth birthdays. The land of the two-piece powder-blue leisure suit, turquoise jewelry clinking on wrists, flowered shirts slashed to deep navels, expensive belts that matched the patent leather slip-on shoes.

She turned the car along a rutted road that led to a fence of wrought-iron elegance. The house beyond was low-slung and ranchlike and the arched doors created a Mexican illusion. She parked the car alongside a vintage Bentley, a shimmering maroon vision trapped in the wild sunlight, and walked as quickly as she could toward the shade of the house. She felt sweat cover the whole surface of her skin, moisture gathering in her armpits, her inner thighs, her scalp—between her toes, welding her feet to her open sandals. The baby moved as she hurried. It twisted inside her, like some miniaturized Houdini seeking an escape hatch, and there was a sudden flare of pain seeming to burn through her spine. *Baby, baby: please be still.* The shade itself must have been more than a hundred degrees. She saw the door open in front of her and Hattie Dalrymple stood there in black satin pants and a fiery pink blouse. Her spectacles hung from a chain around her thin neck. Ellen managed a smile and stepped past Hattie into the dark cool of the house.

"It isn't the weather for pregnancy," Hattie said.

Right on, Ellen thought. She felt as if she'd been hauling a ball and chain tethered to her ankle. She sat down in an armchair and spread her legs. The thin cotton of the maternity frock stuck to her thighs.

"How are you anyhow?" Hattie asked.

"Just wonderful," Ellen said.

"You look it." Hattie frowned. It was hard to guess Hattie's age: Ellen estimated it at somewhere around forty—maybe a little over, a little under. There were lines spreading deeply from the corners of the eyes: they might have been the marks left from some old sorrow, some aspect of her past Hattie never mentioned.

"Your mother isn't awake yet. She decided to have a nap after lunch. She naps too much, if you ask me."

Ellen laid the palm of her hand against her forehead. She felt suddenly faint. She stared across the tiled floor of the living room. The upraised lid of the piano reminded Ellen of a vulture's wing.

"You want something to drink?" Hattie asked.

"Please. Water would save my life right now."

Hattie, her crisp white tennis shoes barely touching the floor, turned and went out of the room. Ellen watched her go, her small-boned body moving lightly as if years ago she might have taken dancing classes. But Ellen knew very little about Hattie's past, save for the fact that she'd entered her mother's life some six months ago as a live-in companion, one in a long line of such companions employed by Ellen's mother after she'd been widowed ten years previously. You'd have to be something of a masochist, Ellen thought, to stick around as my mother's companion. She closed her eyes a moment and when she opened them Hattie was standing over her with a glass of ice water.

"Thanks," Ellen said. She took the glass, sipped.

Hattie stared at her, her look one of curious concentration. Her mouth was tight, the lips drawn. And then her eyes moved down to Ellen's stomach, where they remained. All at once Ellen felt self-conscious. But what was the use of that? You could hardly pull in your stomach, could you? You could hardly pretend you weren't carrying a baby around.

"It must be terrible in this heat," Hattie said. "I don't think *I'd* like to be pregnant in this kind of weather. I'm not sure I'd like to be pregnant in any kind of weather." Hattie emitted a nervous little laugh, high-pitched.

Ellen glanced at the woman, wondered at the sharp edge

in the sound. Maybe there was a bad marriage locked away in
Hattie's past—a bad childless match. Pure speculation, she
thought.

"I just never took to the idea of having something grow
inside me," Hattie added.

"You get used to it," Ellen said.

"I guess." Hattie drifted absently to the window and a band
of sun, a shaft of theatrical light, struck her head, seeming to
make her brown hair catch fire. Then she turned and the fire
died. "How is your husband?"

"He's fine," Ellen said.

"He never comes around here. We never set eyes on him."

Ellen was quiet for a time. There was a slightly forlorn note
in Hattie's voice. *It's simple,* she thought. *Eric doesn't come
because he knows he isn't welcome.*

"This godforsaken heat," Hattie said. "If your mother
hadn't wanted to be near you in your present condition, we'd
still be home in Maine. I don't like it here. I don't like this
house either. I don't know why she didn't rent instead of
buying."

"You know my mother, Hattie. Every empty house is a
potential investment."

Why had her mother trekked all the way down here
anyhow? At first it had been under the pretext of "looking
after some business"—but when that sham had been played
out she'd declared her real interest as that of her daughter's
welfare. *I don't need her help,* Ellen thought. *I'm a big girl,
I'm twenty-seven years old.* Why didn't her mother ever
recognize that fact? Some parents couldn't let go, that was
all—they couldn't come to terms with the prospect of their
kids growing up; maybe it reminded them of their own aging.

There was a sound at her back, the tapping of rubber on
ceramic. Ellen swung around on the stool. Her mother
moved in the doorway, pushing her gray metal walker—like
some small protective cage—in front of her.

"Ellen Ellen Ellen," her mother said, then paused to catch
her breath, as if she wished to project the burden of her life.
The martyr idiom, Ellen thought. The arthritic legs that need
the support of the walker.

Ellen rose from the stool and went across the room to kiss
her mother. The side of the older woman's face was cold, the
skin had the texture of rice paper recently removed from a
refrigerator. She was, as always, immaculately made up,

cheeks lightly rouged, lips neatly pink, a faint smear of mascara around the eyes.

"This heat, dear. This awful heat. Give me a hand, will you?"

Ellen helped her mother to an armchair by the window. With a great effort, the older woman sat. Ellen watched her for a time, conscious of the fact that Hattie had somehow silently transported herself from the room. Her mother took a small cheroot from the pocket of her cardigan and lit it; it was one of her cultivated eccentricities, like playing ragtime music on the piano, like hassling the IRS every year into auditing her, like collecting vaguely pornographic Japanese prints. It was the kind of eccentricity that depended on wealth and the sense of cussedness that came, quite naturally, from being rich.

Ellen asked, "How have you been?"

"As you see. Some things don't change. The walker and I form the perfect couple, dear. How have *you* been?"

"I can't complain, Mother."

"You're not trying."

Ellen smiled and sat on the arm of her mother's chair. "I have my ups and downs. Some days are pretty good. Some days are the pits."

The older woman held her cheroot at an angle, staring down its length: "And how is Eric?"

"He's fine. He works hard. He seems to like living in all this sunlight."

"Is he still doing the same kind of thing? Raising money for charities?"

"The same thing," Ellen said.

Silence. Ellen watched her mother frown: she understood that Eric had never been entirely accepted, that in her mother's somewhat quaint sense of world order Eric came from the wrong side of imaginary tracks, that he had no particular bloodline to recommend him. She also understood that it would have been the same with any man who'd married her—this faint distrust, this frail but unspoken suspicion. *No man could possibly be good enough for* my *daughter, dear.* Ellen sighed: there were limits to maternalism. Her mother had long since passed them.

"You still get along?"

"Of course we do," Ellen said sharply.

Ellen's mother stubbed out her cheroot and was silent a

moment before changing the subject. "Tell me about this doctor of yours."

"Phelps? What about him?"

"Is he good? Is he competent? Is he looking after you?"

"He's fine—"

"In my day, dear, a doctor was a doctor. They weren't all specialists trapped in their own little worlds, you know. Save us from specialists. I still wish you'd gone to the man I recommended—"

"Mother, Phelps is okay. Really."

"Still..."

Ellen turned her face away. This wild protectiveness, she thought—I won't be this kind of mother, I won't interfere in my child's life, I won't harness and hinder and try to impose my judgments.

"It's only because I worry about you, dear. That's all. You'll find out soon enough that even when your children are grown you're not any less a mother. In some ways you're even more. Out there..." And she hesitated, became silent, leaving the monsters out there to Ellen's imagination. Razor blades in Halloween apples, raincoats buttoned over flesh about to be flashed, thin-lipped men standing amongst shrubbery with candies in their fists. The woman's world was filled with sharks.

Ellen rose from the arm of the chair and walked to the window. *I approve of my doctor,* she thought. *I love my husband. I want this baby. I'm doing just fine, Mother. Can't you see?*

The baby—suddenly she was conscious of the stillness of the child in her womb, sleeping, resting, floating in the security of the amniotic sac. And she imagined its face, for the first time she saw this child's face, the softness of eyelid, the blue of eyes, the fleshiness of cheeks and lips. She laid the palms of her hands over her belly. For seven months I've carried you, my love. And I adore you even before I've set eyes on you.

She turned her head when she heard the tap-tap of her mother's walker. The older woman was moving in the direction of an antique desk near the piano. She opened a drawer, took out a manila envelope, and held it toward Ellen.

"These are the papers you have to sign, dear."

Ellen took the envelope and opened it. Legal papers, the gobbledygook of men and women who sat in rooms of mahogany, designing hieroglyphs that none but the initiated could read. Ellen put the papers back on the desk and, without reading them, signed her name. Twice a year there were papers to be signed: it was all a part of the legacy, the twisted series of trust funds and tax shelters and general chaos her father had left behind.

In the silence, Hattie Dalrymple appeared in the doorway.

"Are you staying for tea, Ellen?"

"I don't have time. But thanks."

Ellen's mother said, "You rush around too much—"

"I don't rush around at all, Mother."

"Everybody hurries these days, Ellen. And you are no exception. Thanks for attending to the papers."

Ellen shrugged, kissed her mother, and walked to the door. "I'll come again soon."

There was no answer. The older woman began to play the piano: a spasmodic ragtime rhythm that pursued Ellen as Hattie opened the front door for her.

The heat struck with the force of an unexpected coronary. Even before Hattie had closed the front door, Ellen was sweating. She stared across the front yard to where her Opel was parked. For a moment the car seemed to float in midair, raised by a trick of light as she moved toward it.

The door handle was pure heat. She had to wrap the hem of her dress around it before she could touch it. She got the door open and sat down behind the wheel.

A bad mistake.

The leather upholstery scorched the underside of her thighs with such violence that she wanted to cry aloud. She reached for the wheel so she could raise herself from the seat but the wheel might have been freshly forged metal, and she had to pull her hands away, gasping. Sweat streaked her face, she could taste it. She fumbled her key in the ignition and listened to the engine click into life. Barely touching the wheel, she began to reverse out of the driveway.

Then she stopped.

There was a small black car blocking the driveway. It was idling. Because of the light Ellen couldn't see the driver, couldn't even tell if there was a driver: the windshield was on fire. She waited. The black car didn't move. It remained stationary and—what was the word? how would you describe it?

Menacing.

She shook her head. Menacing. Only because you rarely saw black cars in this sunshine state. They trapped the heat, as Eric had once explained to her. They held the heat like misers. Why didn't the goddam thing move?

She continued to reverse until she could go no further without striking the other car. Move, move, dammit.

The car remained still. Its exhaust emission shimmered behind it. Ellen tapped her horn lightly. Move, for Christ's sake.

And then it *did* move, slowly, seeming to drag as if it were hauling a terrible weight. It swung away, made an arc, then puttered along the road in a wake of its own fumes, a sudden gray pall. Ellen backed the Opel out of the driveway. Damn stupid desert driver, she thought. They had the world's worst drivers in this state. Then she remembered the lunatic in the parking lot the other night. The world's very worst.

She shoved the Opel into first and revved it.

As she drove she looked up at the sky, blinded by its harshness. The sun was a solitary malevolent eye. And she realized that what she longed for wasn't rain, frost, or even a simple chilly morning: what she longed for was a total eclipse.

You saw her again today. You saw her and you were filled with something more than hatred, something black and blind, a deep dark feeling churning at the heart of you. More than hatred.

You saw her and you thought—

It's a mistake. A lapse of the heart. A kind of emotional amnesia.

He doesn't love her. You know that.

How do you know it? Because—because he could never love anybody other than you.

You sit in your darkened room and you look at your hands lying in your lap and you hear the sound of traffic moving through the night and sometimes the sound rises like a babble of whispered voices that grows and grows until you want to deaden your brain.

But the voices go on and on. Wicked, spiteful, hurtful.

He never really loved you. He only pitied you. Just pity. It was wrong from the very beginning.

No, you know that's not true, you know he loves you, he's always loved you.

You rub your scarred stomach. You rise from your chair

*and pull the blind back from the window. A dark desert
night. You smile suddenly and the voices stop accusing you.
You will put everything back together again.
You will put it back together almost the way it was before.
My love, you think. My sweet love.*

Three   *July 8*

She was reading *The Book of Names*. It was a difficult
business choosing the right one for the baby. There was the
mystery of sex, for one thing. You might settle on Gregory,
you might be enchanted by the sound of that name—and a
girl would turn up. She wished there could be a different
arrangement; the baby might be born, say, with its own
choice of name on its lips. *Hi, Mom, I'm Tracy.*

Across the room Eric was hidden behind a copy of the
Phoenix Gazette.

"Will we ever go back East?" she said.

Eric remained hidden behind his newspaper. "Do you
want to?"

"Sometimes. I don't want to get accustomed to living here,
I guess. I don't want to be seduced by this place. It's like I
don't really belong here, if you know what I mean."

He put his paper down. "It's cold back there—"

"Yeah, I know—"

"Do you remember using credit cards to scrape ice off the
windshield? Do you remember having to dig your way out of
the house in the morning? What about the day we lost the
postman in the drifts?"

"I don't remember losing any postman," Ellen said. "What
I do recall is how beautiful the summers were—"

"They were humid and you sweated your ass off—"

"And the falls. The falls were always terrific—"

"As a brief preamble to the sheer terrors of winter, sure."

Ellen shrugged. She closed her eyes and remembered the
time they had driven through New York State in the autumn
before their marriage—the dying lushness of the Adirondacks,
the incredible sequence of colors in the Thousand Islands, a
blaze of rusts and yellows and golds that might have been

spilled from the palette of a mad artist. She remembered the
strangely sad feeling she had experienced all the way up the
St. Lawrence to the Canadian line—almost as if that particular fall might elude both her camera and her memory and be
lost to her forever. Romantic notions, she thought. What she
always associated with that kind of autumn was the dizzying
sense of being in love with someone, the curiously possessive
feeling of wanting to be close to him for the rest of her life.

But she and Eric were no longer a couple, a twosome, a
pair; she had begun to think of them as three, a family unit.
Expectations. She touched her swollen stomach lightly, and
suddenly experienced a moment of great tranquility, a moment of love and loving. If she could have preserved the
feeling in amber and passed it down as a family heirloom, she
would have done so.

Then a slight pain played along the base of her spine. She
hooked her finger inside the strap of her supportive bra and
loosened it. Baby, she thought—all the terrifying responsibili-
ties of a baby: and the little devil in the womb didn't
understand any of them, didn't know about the lists of
recommended vitamins, the abstinence from tobacco and
alcohol, the wretched exercises that had to be undertaken
religiously—as if she were preparing for an Olympics restricted
to pregnant mothers. The Neck Stretch, The Stretch and
Flop Over. The Hip Roll. The Kegel Exercise. *Don't forget to
do your Kegels, Ellen. They're important for your pelvic floor
muscles*. The list of forbidden or suspect drugs that was
tacked to the kitchen wall.

Chloromycetin.

Streptomycin.

Dilantin.

Compazine.

According to the chart Phelps had given her, some drugs
could produce a kind of jaundice in the newborn that meant
brain damage.

Brain damage, Jesus.

Eric smiled at her, let one hand brush lazily against her
hair, then turned on *Star Trek*. She thought of how he had a
whole library of *Star Trek* books—not the novelizations he
called sleazy and childish, but the compilations that concerned the making of the series, the filming of the movie,
even the fictitious star-charts which purported to describe the
voyages of the *Enterprise*. A Trekkie, she realized: I'm the

wife of a goddam Trekkie. Maybe it was something nostalgic, a yearning for the past that made him a slave to the stuff. Maybe he was looking over his own shoulder for a ghost.

She propped herself up. Then, stiffly, she rose. "I guess it's time for me to do my Kegels," she said.

He didn't seem to hear.

"I'll be in the bedroom," she added.

He watched the screen without answering.

The exercises tired her now more than they usually did. Her arms and legs ached; her abdominal muscles were sore. When she'd finished she lay down on the bed and looked up at the ceiling. The baby was quiet inside her. How could it have slept through all the motions of the exercises? The twistings, turnings, the muscular tensions? Contrary little thing, she thought—you spring to life when I'm trying to relax but you don't even budge when your house is shaking.

She turned on her side now. Her eyelids were heavy, flickering, pressing against the surface of her eyes. She found herself squinting at the glass cabinet set against the far wall, at the faces of the dozen antique dolls that sat in a frigid unblinking way, as if they were forever scrutinizing the confines of their tiny world. They had gentle sculpted faces, perfect mouths, delicate lashes; they wore lacy Victorian clothes. Innocent, she thought—with expressions of some terrible serenity on their porcelain lips. She didn't like the dolls because they suggested embalmed creatures to her, living things that had been stuffed by some taxidermist in an insane fit. But they had come from her mother, who had inherited them from *her* mother. *Heirlooms, Ellen—but more than heirlooms, dear, they're an investment, even as they sit there they're growing in value*. Someday, she thought, I'll sell the whole congregation of them.

When she woke a few hours later the bedside lamp was unlit and Eric lay asleep beside her. He was snoring slightly, lips parted. She raised herself on one elbow and watched him. Peaceful. At rest.

A light was burning in the living room and she moved slowly toward it. Strange—Eric had left the TV on. It was something he never did. She stared at the silent test pattern a moment before switching the thing off. Only as she sat on the sofa and looked around the room did it occur to her—a perception out of nowhere, a vague recognition—that something wasn't quite right, something was out of place. But what? It was more an intuition than a particular realization, as if she'd entered a room somebody had just left, caught some trace of an absent stranger, a departed trespasser. She stood up, walked around. Nothing. The furniture hadn't been moved. The same prints still hung on the walls. The books on the shelves were orderly. She absently touched the spines of a couple, noticing faint dust adhering to her fingertips. *The First Nine Months of Life*. *Diet For A Small Planet*. *The World of Star Trek*. What was wrong then? What was it she'd felt?

She moved out to the balcony, sweating. The clothes she'd fallen asleep in—loose jeans, loose print blouse—were damp against her skin. Outside, the night sky was a riot, vast and starry. It made her feel dizzy and small. She gripped the balcony rail and looked down into the parking lot. Silent.

And then it came to her suddenly and she wanted to laugh at herself, she wanted to laugh at the feeling she'd had indoors, the sensation of something being out of place. The laundry, it was nothing more than the laundry, the fact that she'd forgotten to take the clothes from the dryer in the laundry room, where she'd put them just after supper—nothing sinister, nothing had been touched or changed or shifted by an unseen hand. No gremlins, no shadows. Just a breakdown in the patterns of memory. Maybe your memory, like the rest of your body, is just getting out of hand, kid.

Wrinkled shirts. Nothing more than a simple domestic inconvenience.

She left the apartment and walked downstairs, moving in the direction of the laundry room. The courtyard of the Casa Manzanita was leafy, surrounded by the four buildings of the complex. At its center was a pretentious fountain lit by a garish blue light. She took her key from her jeans and unlocked the door of the laundry, a room that was white and gleaming and intolerably hot even at this time of the day—why hadn't they air-conditioned this room?

She found the dryer and unloaded her clothes—Eric's shirts mostly, one of which he'd certainly be looking for in the morning. She folded them neatly under the stark fluorescent tube that lit the room and was going to leave when the door opened and a girl of about eighteen came in. The girl, tossing her yellow hair back in a gesture that was almost arrogant in its carefree way, returned the smile and set her basket on the table.

"I like this time of night for doing my laundry," she said to Ellen. "It's quiet and you don't get the hassles you get when the place is crowded."

Such white teeth, Ellen thought. Such white teeth set in shiny pink gums. Perfect legs, the thighs clasped by tight white shorts. A pink tank-top, large breasts. Tiny blonde hairs glistened on the bare arms. A splendid desert specimen. Ellen turned her face away from the sight of the trim body.

She said, politely, "I've never been in here at this time of night before." *God, I envy this kid. I envy her slimness.*

"You'll like it if you get used to it." The girl stared at Ellen for a moment, smiling still. Ellen noticed the eyes were red—the stoned red of the doper. So: a world of marijuana, late-night munchies, and grooving on the beauty of empty laundry rooms. *Far out.*

"When's it due?" the girl asked. She was gazing at Ellen's stomach now. Is that look critical, disapproving, or what? Ellen wondered.

"September," she answered.

"Hey, that's great," the girl said. "I'd like to have babies one day, you know? Only marriage is such a drag."

Ellen said nothing. She stared at the pile of Eric's shirts.

"I guess it works for some people, though," the girl added.

"Sure."

The girl smiled—and there was something almost patronizing in the expression. Then she said, "I'm Anna by the way. Anna Rosenberg. I know it sounds Jewish. It always makes people kinda laugh, you know, when they've only talked to me on the telephone and then they meet me in the flesh—*you don't look Jewish with that hair and those blue eyes.* It's funny. People jump to the weirdest conclusions, don't they?"

"I guess," Ellen said.

"What's your name?"

"Ellen."

"A nice name. Sounds peaceful. I dunno."

"Thank you."

"I get off on names. I like to imagine people somehow *fit* their names. What's your last name?"

"Campbell."

The girl was silent for a moment. From the pocket of her

shorts she took out a candy bar—a Marathon—and unwrapped it. She stuck the end of it in her mouth and began to suck. Ellen watched this a moment: She's into a thing with her candy bar, she thought. She's got an oral relationship going on.

Anna Rosenberg took the Marathon from her mouth and gazed at the end of it. "Say, is your husband that kinda tall good-looking guy who drives a red Datsun? The guy, with black hair?"

"He drives a red Datsun," Ellen said. Eric: how would this young thing know about Eric?

"I've seen him around. I'm pretty sure I have."

"I guess you must have." That chill, that little touch of permafrost—could she keep that out of her voice?

"What's his name?"

"His name?" Ellen, who had been gathering up the shirts, turned to the girl. Why can't I just come out and say, *Mind your own damn business?* Too polite, too mellow, too well-raised.

"Yeah, his name. I mean, if you don't mind saying."

"Eric," Ellen answered.

"Er-ic," Anna Rosenberg said, as if the sound of it were a broken lozenge in her mouth.

Ellen picked up the shirts and moved toward the door. She hated herself; what weakness was this anyhow—just handing your husband's name to an attractive young girl who found him good-looking? At the door she turned around. Anna Rosenberg was sucking on her Marathon bar again, watching Ellen in a slightly glazed way.

"He's real cute," the girl said.

"I'm glad you think so." The ice, keep the ice out of your voice, Ellen.

"I often figured if I was going to get married one day I wouldn't marry anybody too good-looking. I wouldn't want other women trying to get their hands on him," the girl said.

Ellen didn't know what to say. She looked at the girl and wondered if there were perhaps some mischief, some hint of malice, in what she was saying. *You're fat and pregnant, Ellen, and maybe you turn your husband off, so you'd better keep an eye on him*—was she saying something like that?

"I don't really notice his looks," Ellen remarked finally. "I see something beneath the skin." It wasn't meant to sound pompous, smug, but she was afraid that was how she came across.

The girl sucked on her candy for a moment. "Maybe we'll run into each other again, Ellen."

"It's a small world," Ellen said.

She stepped outside, moved back in the direction of her block. She realized she was walking too quickly, the weight of the baby dragged at her, and she stopped by the fountain to catch her breath. She thought: My God, you're jealous. You're just jealous. Because you're plump and shapeless and confined to the inelegant quarters of cavernous maternity smocks you let some stoned-out, wasted little desert teeny bopper get to you. You let her hit you with a passable replica of the old green-eyed monster. You idiot, you allowed her to make you feel jealous!

Jealous. It was just the way Phelps's nurse, Grabowski, had once said to her: *You feel fatter than you look, Ellen. You feel more gross than you really are. And you think your husband is watching every skinny little thing that comes down the pike. One of the worst side effects of pregnancy is raging insecurity.*

No way, she thought. I won't be insecure. No way at all.

Breathless, she climbed the stairs. Inside the apartment she locked the door. She went toward the living room, let the shirts fall to the rug. Two more months—how could two short months take on the uncomfortable feel of an eternity?

In the bedroom Eric was still asleep, still in the same position as before. She took off her clothes and crawled into bed beside him. Jealousy, she thought: what a pain in the ass. What a drag. Eric is loyal. Eric wouldn't be interested in another woman and certainly not in a child like Ms. Anna Rosenberg. Hadn't he once said, in a sentence you've never forgotten, that trust was the only true currency of a relationship? *I don't lie, Ellen. Liars need memories like computer banks. I'll never lie to you.*

She put one arm around his shoulder.

Love you, she thought.

Love you.

Vicky said, "The one thing I really hate about visiting with
you at this apartment is the way you always stare through that
wretched peephole before you open the damn door. It makes
me feel like a goldfish or something."

Ellen smiled as she shut the door behind her friend:
"Eric put it in, you know. For my own safety, he said."

Vicky moved along the hallway, taking off her blue denim
hat and shaking her long hair as she went toward the living
room. Such long strides, Ellen thought: always in a hurry.
How the hell can she expect me to keep up with her?

"Safety is an illusion, kid," Vicky said. She was already
seated on the sofa. From her purse she took a cigarette and
fitted it into a short holder designed to make you cut down on
nicotine. "Tell me who's safe in this world of ours? You know
anybody *really* safe?"

"Is that a rhetorical question or do you expect me to
answer?" Ellen asked.

Vicky puffed smoke quickly, vigorously. "Bear with me. It's
just my mood this morning. I had a letter from my late old
man, Stan, in which he politely informed me that he wants to
keep our daughter for two weeks beyond the legal period. I
wonder why the hell we went through that court battle when
he takes it into *his* mind to extend his visitation rights. I
should sue his fat ass off."

Ellen sat down facing Vicky. The other woman's entrances
were always accompanied by some new energetic outburst, a
flash of words, a glitter of turquoise, a gleam of belt buckle, a
cloud of tobacco smoke. At times Vicky gave the impression
that she was going to burst through into some undiscovered
dimension, sweeping you along with her. She had a beautiful
face, square chinned, the cheekbones high and dominating.
Her dark hair fell thickly to the shoulders of her white
western shirt; her blue jeans were tailored and tight.

"He misses his daughter," Ellen said.

"I miss her too," Vicky said. "Basically, I don't approve of this little hippie girl Stan's taken up with. I just don't like the type—she's only about eight years old, if you ask me, and she thinks she's one of those godawful earth mothers who wants to go on and on having babies and live in a mountain of granola baby food."

Ellen shrugged. She thought she detected a faint undertone of jealousy in Vicky's voice.

"You shouldn't let it affect you like this," Ellen said.

"I miss Kim. I want her back here with me. I don't like her tripping around some hippie commune or wherever it is Stan lives. But that's enough about me. How's it with you? How's the baby?"

"We're struggling along."

"And hoping for the big day, right?"

"Hoping. Fearing."

"There's nothing to be afraid of. I keep telling you. A good healthy girl like you with that nutritious New England background—you'll come through it with flying colors. Believe me."

Ellen smiled. "I hope so."

Vicky lit another cigarette. "How's Eric?"

"He's fine. I think he imagines spending the rest of his life in this town."

"Why?"

"I guess he likes the heat," Ellen said.

Vicky was silent for a time. She stared at Ellen; she seemed to be on the edge of asking another question about Eric but didn't. "Is the good doctor Phelps treating you well?" she asked instead.

"He's pretty old-fashioned, but I like him."

"Old-fashioned? I remember that. He sent me a pamphlet on prenatal sex."

"I got the same one."

Vicky laughed. "Is it the one that suggests you perform oral sex on your husband only after you've lined your mouth with a Baggie?"

Ellen smiled. "Pretty close. I'm going to make coffee. Want some?"

"Sure. I'll keep you company in the kitchen. I'll waddle along with you."

"Thanks. I needed that."

Ellen plugged the coffee maker into the wall and Vicky followed, trailing a line of tobacco smoke. Ellen asked, "How is the real estate business these days?"

"Times are tough," Vicky said. "I still resent the fact that you and your old man never bought that perfectly suitable house through me. I don't think I can ever forgive you for that."

Ellen smiled. "You roll with the punches."

"Even if they're very low ones," Vicky said. "I'll never understand why you didn't buy that home. A good price, neat location. It pissed me off when one of my competitors stepped in and sold you this apartment right under my nose." Vicky was quiet a moment, then she said: "Still, the rewards have outweighed the disadvantages. We're friends, after all. In a world like this one, what can you count on at the end of the day but a few good friends?"

She reached out and impulsively hugged Ellen briefly. When she stepped back, arms at her side, she was smiling—and Ellen wondered why she'd felt mildly embarrassed by the embrace. Some of that New England stiffness in the soul, maybe. Some traces of Yankee chill in the blood even now. She watched the water begin to drip through the basket of the coffee filter. A few good friends at the end of the day, she thought: Vicky was her best, perhaps her only, friend in all of Arizona. She folded her arms under her breasts, conscious of their size and weight. Vicky was wandering round the kitchen; the heels of her cowboy boots tapped noisily on the tiles.

"So tell me about your social life these days," Ellen said.

"Funny you ask. I've been seeing this guy who sells weight-lifting equipment. He's got biceps the way Dolly Parton has mammaries."

Ellen looked at her friend. There was a whole unhappy history floating around her: ever since the divorce from her husband Vicky had embarked upon a series of casual affairs with married men. Eric had once said it was obvious she chose married men because she didn't want any attachments. Attachments—it made a person sound like a vacuum cleaner.

"Can I assume he's married?"

"What else is new?"

Ellen began to pour coffee into cups. "I sometimes wonder—if you don't take this as a criticism—why you bother with men who're married, Vicky. The relationships never seem to go anywhere—"

Vicky dropped the butt of her cigarette into the garbage disposal and ran some water from the faucet into the unit. She flipped the switch and for a moment there was the sound of blades grating viciously. "Do I detect a slight tone of disapproval, Ellen?"

Ellen shook her head. "Of course not. I'm not a judge, for God's sake. It's just that the things you get yourself into never seem to amount to anything. And I think you deserve better."

Married men, she thought. A world of married men. And she turned her thoughts to Eric briefly: What would you do if you found out Eric was having an affair? If you discovered he had something, as it were, on the side? She liked to think she'd be understanding and forgiving, she enjoyed the idea of being generous—but there was another side to this she'd never contemplated: the jealousy, the shot of envy, the adrenalin of hurt, the visual reconstruction in her imagination of Eric making love to another woman. (Anna Rosenberg. Why did that empty-headed child come back to irritate her suddenly? Why didn't she have more control over her own mind?)

"The real reason I stopped by," Vicky said, "was to take you to lunch. Even if I have to *drag* you out of here."

"Drag me? You don't have to do that. Just give me a few minutes to change."

Ellen walked through to the bedroom. She opened the closet door and stared, somewhat gloomily, at the dresses and pants she could no longer wear; they hung together at one side of the closet, as if they had been pushed, like fattening tidbits set in front of someone on a starvation diet, out of sight. The maternity clothes were drab and frumpish by contrast. She took out the blue blouse she'd worn to dinner with Eric then replaced it. Keep it for another celebration, she thought, and settled for a wine-colored dress she hated. Turning away from her own reflection, she brushed her hair quickly, then slipped into a pair of open sandals. Okay, she said to herself, time to face the Arizona heat.

In the living room Vicky was standing by the bookshelves, flipping through the pages of one of Eric's *Star Trek* books.

"I'm ready," Ellen said.

"I'll use your bathroom before we go," Vicky said.

Ellen watched her friend move along the hallway toward the bedroom. There was the sound of a door closing, followed by the rattle of running water, a cistern flushing. And then—

then there was a long silence. Ellen waited, impatiently tapping a foot on the rug. What was keeping Vicky? How long could it possibly take to go to the bathroom? She went to the bedroom just as Vicky was emerging.

"Those dolls must be worth a fortune," Vicky said. "I was just looking at them—they must be ancient."

"You interested in buying them?" Ellen asked.

"Me buy dolls? Didn't anybody ever tell you? Big girls don't play with dolls anymore."

Vicky drove with a kind of calculated insanity, swerving in and out of the midday traffic as if it were simply a series of metallic inconveniences with no right to be on the same street as she. Sometimes Ellen would lean forward and grip the dash with her hands—behavior that Vicky never seemed to notice. When they reached the restaurant, Vicky swung the Mustang crazily into the parking lot, bumping the car over the speedbreak. Ellen felt the baby leap inside her, a flashing moment of pain, an image of the fetus splashing inside the amniotic sac like driftwood rising on an urgent tide. She groaned as Vicky parked the car.

"Sorry, kid. I forget who's in the passenger seat, that's all. You okay?"

"Fine," Ellen said. She knew without looking in the mirror that her face was white all at once. "But I have this desire to give birth in the safety of a hospital. I like your Mustang but I don't see it as a suitable maternity room, you know?"

Vicky patted the back of her hand. "I'm clumsy sometimes. Forgive me."

"You're forgiven." Ellen stepped out into the dense heat of the parking lot. Within seconds she could feel concrete baking through the soles of her sandals. She moved toward the shelter of the restaurant as fast as she could. Vicky came rushing behind. And then they were inside and cool in a large room filled with plants; through tiny stained-glass windows the sun was mercifully splintered and diffused, heat and glare stolen from it by the colored panes.

Ellen studied the menu. Her appetite, such as it was, had evaporated. When the food came she barely picked at it—whether or not she was eating for two—mostly passing time watching Vicky devour her burger and fries. She ate the same way she drove, with an amazing indifference.

Later, when the food was cleared away and they were drinking espresso, Vicky lit a cigarette and said, "Not hungry?"

"I just don't seem to want to eat much these days."

"I had the same thing with Kim. My appetite faded. I had other appetites that faded even quicker, though. Like any urge I might have had to sleep with Stan."

Ellen stared at the surface of her coffee. She was never sure she wanted to hear the intimate details of Vicky's life, but Vicky appeared to enjoy recounting them regardless. She raised her cup and sipped just as Vicky said, "During the last stage of my pregnancy Stan took it into his head to be unfaithful. He had the perverse decency, God bless him, to tell me about it all when I was one week from confinement. Nothing was the same after that."

Ellen gazed at her friend over the rim of her coffee cup. A nerve tightened inside her.

Don't, she thought. You don't have to go in that direction. Eric.

Eric wouldn't. Eric wouldn't ever do a thing like that. If you didn't have trust and confidence you didn't have a goddam thing. The marriage was intact. There was love. Nothing was going to stray outside that boundary. Nothing ever.

"What the hell," Vicky said. "If I'm realistic and true unto myself, I guess we were on the rocks long before the baby."

Ellen said nothing. Confessions. Baring the soul. Why did she always feel the same lingering uneasiness when Vicky trotted out the facts of her life? She found herself suddenly being defensive and, almost against her will, said, "Our marriage is fine. We love each other." Smugness—had some momentary smugness crept into her voice? She hoped not.

"Then you're lucky," Vicky said. She fidgeted with her cigarette filter. Then she called to the waiter for the check. "You're really lucky."

Lucky, Ellen thought. She felt herself blush all at once, a sensation of hotness that spread across her cheeks. It wasn't a bad feeling—and even the discomfort she experienced now, from the peculiar angle the baby had assumed in her stomach, was a minor thing. *Luckyluckylucky*. More than that. Much more. She pushed her chair back, starting to rise.

Vicky said, "Something I've always wondered—"

"What?"

"Do you have tutorials in blushing at those fancy private schools back East? Or is it just natural?"

Ellen made a ball of her paper napkin and threw it gently in Vicky's direction. Her friend ducked; the missile just missed an approaching waiter.

"Next time," Ellen said. "I'll get you next time."

"You'd have to be up real early to do that."

And Vicky smiled.

You go to the window, pull back the blind, stare out into the dark of early evening. The sun has left a single streak of rose-red low in the sky. You watch it for a while until it disintegrates and the darkness is total. The scissors feel light in your hand. Sharp and light.

You wonder now if the superintendent saw you, if he felt you were watching him when he stepped out of his office and crossed the courtyard, passing the fountain. If he saw, from the corner of his eye, your shadow move toward the open door of his small office. If he noticed the missing key. What would he think if he had noticed it anyhow? Nothing. He'd imagine he lost it, misplaced it. You understand you don't have to worry on that count. You understand that.

You don't have to worry about anything except waiting.

Waiting for the right moment. The opportunity.

You close your eyes. Your forehead touches the warm glass of the window. The heat seems trapped inside the pane. You close your eyes and you dream you see his face, you imagine him opening the door now, coming into this room, your room, crossing the floor and putting his arms around you and kissing you. You imagine all this in one wonderful sweet moment. And you think: Soon, soon, soon, my love.

My love.

My Eric.

You turn the scissors over and over in your hand.

Five   July 12

❦❦❦❦❦❦❦❦❦❦❦❦❦❦❦❦❦❦❦❦❦❦❦❦❦❦❦❦❦❦

He was late returning from the office. It wasn't like him—when he was going to be delayed he always called to tell her—but tonight the telephone had been silent. She'd begun to prepare one of his favorite meals, and even if her heart wasn't in it, even if the idea of actually eating it herself appalled her, nevertheless she spent considerable time beating cutlets of veal with the back of a wooden spoon and marinating them in a mixture of soy sauce and garlic. Now, though, the cutlets lay in the oven, curling and darkening and turning—as if through a process of alchemy—from something edible to something a dog might disregard. Where the hell was he? And why hadn't he called?

She sat in the living room and gazed at the flickering lights of the two candles she'd lit on the table. Wax sizzled. Drops slithered down the stalks and hardened on the linen. Her sense of impatience gradually changed to concern. What she envisaged was a gritty newsreel photograph of an automobile wreck on a freeway—firemen hacking at the crushed steel of what until recently had been a car, the lights of cop cars flashing, warning flares lit on the pavement. She walked up and down the room, going now and then to the balcony door to look for a sign of the Datsun. *Nada*.

She was beginning to feel a certain weariness, a nervous fatigue, and she sat down once more, trying to find a position in which she might be comfortable. Think the worst thing first, she thought. Imagine he's dead in a car wreck. *Somebody would have telephoned to say so*. A cop would have called, right? Maybe so. *Excuse me, Mrs. Campbell, how does it feel to be so recently widowed?* Dear Christ. How could she even entertain any levity? Bad news travels quickest, don't forget. Okay, if there hadn't been an accident, then it had to be work-related. Go back to the office emergency. What could have turned up? An extraordinary meeting of the board? A sudden influx of auditors who'd found something doubtful in the books?

A bad taste rose in her throat. No accident. No office emergency. What then? Just what?

For no apparent reason she found herself remembering the time he'd proposed to her. Snow, bitter winds and falling mercury, the wild Atlantic dumping a storm across the coastline of New England: they'd been drinking wine in a restaurant when Eric had suddenly leaned forward across his glass—almost spilling it, she recalled, making it spin and almost toppling it—and placed The Question in front of her.

We don't really know each other, Eric—

What more do we need to know? We're good for each other. We're good together. What else do we need to know? I love you. Don't you love me?

She remembered staring into her wine, feeling unbalanced, removed from the physical space of the restaurant. She remembered looking at the window, the great pile of snow pressed against the glass. She'd imagined a longer process somehow, something less spontaneous: a long engagement, a traditional wedding coming at the end of a suitable period of time. *Traditional, suitable, a long engagement*—what was she thinking? These were the kinds of words and terms her mother might have used. It was as if she'd involuntarily stepped into her mother's way of looking at life. Conditioned reflexes, learned behavior. *I'm not marrying my mother,* she had thought.

I love you, Eric.

I hear a but someplace in there.

I don't mean there to be one . . .

There was a long pause then, a fevered space in the conversation. She'd had a good job with an insurance company in Bangor. Her own apartment. A new car. It was as if she'd come to consider these things, the things she possessed, as defenses against dependency, ways of escaping from her mother's fortress. What would happen if she accepted Eric, if she gave up these defenses?

Love. The force of love. It was as intangible as any wind, unpredictable as the waywardness of a hurricane. It was love she kept coming back to during the silence. Love defined, drew outlines, gave form and substance. It filled in the blank spaces. She had reached across the table and held his hand. Then she'd whispered what he wanted to hear. Snow, red wine, a proposal, an acceptance: down to the sound of brittle logs burning in the fireplace, the details might have been plagiarized from an old romantic movie. *Yes,* she'd said—and then for some reason she'd started to laugh, she laughed until her eyes were moist. She'd gone to the bathroom and looked at herself in the mirror. *You're laughing because you feel good. Because you feel so* damned *good. Because in a single moment, in the sound of a single word, you're elated beyond all the rigid controls of flimsy earthbound emotions. You're really free, free and in flight.*

After that Eric had gone away for three days to see his parents, to tell them about the marriage. Those days had been filled with the most acute emptiness she'd ever felt. He didn't call. He didn't write. She'd stayed home in her apartment and waited for the telephone to ring. When he returned he didn't talk much about the visit. She hadn't asked many questions either—she simply assumed that, for some reason, they were unhappy about the match. Maybe it was too much of a surprise for them, maybe they had nurtured other ambitions for him; how could she know? She hadn't ever met them, hadn't seen any photographs, and Eric never talked about them. They fell into some mysterious corner of his life and she didn't pry. In any event, they hadn't come to the wedding. Nor, for her own miserable reasons, had Ellen's mother.

Now, as she thought about the past, the sharp emptiness of the apartment assailed her. She stared around at familiar objects—the prints on the walls, the stupid macraméd owl, the TV, Eric's expensive stereo—and she realized they had lost some of their familiarity, they had become strange. *They don't mean anything when he's not here,* she thought. *They lose their significance.* She rubbed her hands together nervously. Her wedding ring seemed dull. Even the baby in her womb didn't feel a part of her.

When she blew out the candles, the smell of burning wax was bitter. She looked at the salad, limp and dry in the bowl. Where the hell was he? (*Dead? He can't be dead. Eric can't be.*) She picked out a sliver of wilted lettuce and let it drop back into the salad. The baby moved. It seemed to turn over inside, twisting itself in the umbilical cord: she imagined an astronaut floating in space, attached to the mother capsule by a slender lifeline. Not now, she thought. Don't act up now. She went inside the bedroom and from there to the bathroom. Although Phelps had advised her against it, she took out a prescription bottle containing 5m Valium and swallowed one drily. Relax. Try to relax. There's some good reason for his absence.

She walked back to the living room.

Panic. It was odd how slowly it began, how it started in such a minuscule way and then, like a blimp being filled with helium, grew and grew. Panic—always elusive, always dominating. She shut her eyes and waited for the Valium to work on her. There was a blunt-edged pain around her heart, an ache that suggested indigestion. If I could sleep, she thought. If I could just sleep the time away until he gets back.

This is silly. This is really absurd. You have to pull yourself together. The man is about two hours late and already you're imagining yourself going to the morgue and identifying the body. Silly, theatrical, giving in to a preposterous panic like this. She watched the headlights of cars cross the parking lot below. Then she opened the balcony door and stepped out. The heat of darkness was stifling. Beyond the pool were the high floodlights of the tennis courts, stark and brilliant in the sky. She could hear the sound of a ball being knocked back and forth, then the indolent laughter of a girl. (Anna Whatsername. Somebody like Anna would play in this heat, looking good no doubt in one of those idiotic floppy hats. Her brown thighs would shine under the glare of the lights.)

ERIC CAMPBELL LEAVES A WIDOW, ELLEN, 27, AND AN UNBORN CHILD. Pages of a grim obituary, the statistics of death, the face white on a marble slab and the cold facts distilled in unfeeling print. God damn you. She could feel sleep move in on her now, but she wanted to fight the sensation. How in the name of God could she sleep at a time like this? The drift of medication. The sense of floating out on some placid sea. The muscles turning to tepid water. She struggled into an upright position, sat up, swung her legs around.

She heard something now.

A key turning in a lock.

A door opening. Closing.

The sound of someone whistling softly.

Eric.

As if he weren't late, as if he hadn't put her through all of it, he stood in the doorway and smiled and set his briefcase down on the rug. In spite of herself, she smiled back: recrimination would have to take second place to relief. He crossed the floor and put his arms around her. For a long time she said nothing. She simply held him. She held him tightly. And then she realized she was crying. When she pulled back from him she saw his face as if through frosted glass, a blur.

"Hey," he said. He put his hand beneath her chin. "Hey," he said again.

"There are telephones. They take a couple of dimes. You've heard of them, I guess."

Eric sighed. In a kneeling position beside her, he rocked a little on his heels. "I know, I know."

Don't interrogate him, she told herself. Don't be the

Nagging Wife. The Worried Hausfrau. Don't lay a trip on his head, for Christ's sake.

"I mean—you could have been dead out there, for all I know. You could have smashed up the car. You could be lying in some goddam hospital emergency room, Eric." She heard her voice rise and rise. She wanted to stop herself, to silence the edge of hysteria. But she couldn't. "How the hell was I supposed to know? I'm not psychic! I'm not gifted with any sense of clairvoyance! I just sat here and worried my brains out. That's all I did. Worried my goddam brains out." *You're whining*, she thought. *Whining and bitching and complaining. Let it go, just let it go.*

He began to rub her shoulders. "I should have called, I know—"

"Damn right."

"I just didn't get the chance, Ellen."

"It doesn't take much, does it? I mean, you've only got to press a few buttons and speak a few words, Eric. It doesn't take much to make a single phone call."

Eric got to his feet. "I was sitting in the office at approximately two minutes to five, okay? I was just getting ready to come home when suddenly who should appear but Himself. He wants to discuss a whole new strategy of fund raising. *At two goddamn minutes to five*, remember. He has no rush to get home. He doesn't have a wife, never mind a pregnant one. He can sit there with his feet up on his desk and babble for days. *Your* husband *has* to sit still and twiddle his thumbs and fidget while he's growing increasingly worried about you. Meantime, Himself is still muttering."

Himself was Eric's name for the director, Ralph Houseman. "Okay, I can see that," she said. "I can see all that. But you could have excused yourself and called, couldn't you?"

"And interrupt Himself? I'd rather blaspheme. I'd rather go inside a church and spit on the altar, love."

"Okay, I can even see *that*. But when you left you could have made one quick call, no? I only wanted to know you were all right. That's all I wanted to know. Does that make sense?"

"It makes sense, sure. But by then I was in a hurry to get home. I drove like I was being pursued by the Furies."

"The point is—"

"The point is, I didn't call." He reached for her hand, held it, kissed the side of her face. "I'll remember in the future. If it happens in the future. I won't upset you again. I promise. I *swear* that."

She raised his hand and clasped it between her own, staring for a long time at the faint dark hairs that grew along the backs of his fingers.

"How can you put up with a fat old whiner like me," she asked.

"Piece of cake."

"Is it?"

"Sure it is."

She laughed—there was calm now, the disturbance gone; she felt she was looking at a landscape recently violated by a freak storm. Calm, peace, a sense of contentment. "How do you feel about two completely dead veal cutlets?"

"I don't think I have any feelings."

"I could do an omelette. I could whip up some eggs."

Eric shook his head. "I've got a better idea."

"Like what?"

"I could take you out to eat. You remember that place round here that does fondues?"

She nodded. "Fine. Give me a few minutes to change, will you?"

"You look good the way you are—"

"I feel ugly the way I am."

He smiled and sat down on the sofa and looked at her. His expression—how would she describe that? He appeared to be beaming at her, as if he were proud of what he saw. *My wife*, she thought. *My family. The three of us.* That's what his expression was saying.

She sat down in front of the dressing-table mirror. From the corner of her eye she was conscious of the dolls gazing at her; she turned, glanced at them, hating the sight—lined up like deceptively cute but heartless androids. Lifelike, but in a perverse way, suggesting some travesty of existence. Next she stared at her face in the mirror. Pale, she thought, pale as one of those porcelain dolls. There were dark circles under her eyes, a color between ink-blue and violet. She clasped her hands together. Then she rose and went to the closet, unzipping her skirt as she moved. She took off her blouse and glanced down at the upraised veins in her breasts and she imagined blood coursing through her body, traveling the intricate network of arteries and veins, pumped by the heart for the miraculous purpose of sustaining two lives.

She opened the closet door and stared at her clothes. Slowly she began to sift through the hanging garments. How wide they seemed, how baggy, uninviting, how singularly drab despite the brave attempts of designers to infuse their shapeless offerings with wild splashes of bright color.

One blue blouse with puffy sleeves and modishly narrow cuffs.

Where was it hiding? Come out, come out, she thought. Where the hell was it?

When she couldn't find it she thought it must have slipped from the rack to the floor so she bent down to look, rummaging through various boxes of shoes, paper bags, shirts in their cellophane wrappers. Nothing. No sign of the shirt. Hell. She rose, moaning a little, tiny spots moving in front of her eyes. She checked the rack again. No blue shirt.

She turned when she heard Eric come inside the bedroom.

"I was about to send out a search party," he said.

"I'm looking for my blue blouse." Where could it vanish to?

"Can I help?"

"Blue blue blue," she said. "Almost brand new. I wore it at dinner the other night. Do you remember it?"

"Sure." He approached the closet. "I don't see it."

"I'm pretty sure it was hanging here yesterday," she said. She fingered her way through the rack again. Zero. Then she turned to Eric. "Did I send anything to the laundry today?" Why couldn't she remember?

"I was at work," he said. "I wouldn't know."

"Then how can a shirt just vanish into thin air?"

Eric was humming a tune to himself, withdrawing from the situation: a missing shirt was no big deal, a thing of no consequence. He said, "It'll turn up. Everything turns up eventually."

"I guess." She hauled a dark red cotton thing from the rack and struggled into it.

"In the meantime, I'm starving," he said.

They ate fondue on a terraced restaurant. She dipped pieces of celery into melted cheese and managed to swallow a number of them. Eric ate ravenously and when he'd finished he lit a cigarette and tilted his chair back, looking up at the night sky. She was tired, tired from the effects of the Valium and the strain of recent anxiety.

"What are you thinking?" Eric said.

"Names," she said. She looked down at the strands of hardening cheese that had fallen across her plate. "They're such a problem."

She stared across the empty tables on the terrace. You'd have to go through the alphabet for names, beginning with A—and then she found herself thinking about Anna Rosenberg. The mind has a mind of its own, she thought. I don't need to think about Anna Rosenberg, do I? She smiled and leaned forward against the table.

"Incidentally, do you know you have an admirer living in the apartment complex?"

He said nothing.

"A pretty young blonde number. I ran into her in the laundromat and she was saying how handsome she thought you were."

"She has good taste."

"I agree. I don't know whether to be flattered or suspicious." Keep it light, Ellen, she thought: keep the tone light, bantering, a vague edge of mischief.

"Be flattered. It's easier to deal with."

"You've never seen her? Anna somebody or other."

"I'd say there were about twenty Annas living around the complex. They go to bed at night numbering only ten, then by some mysterious process they multiply in the hours of darkness. They wake up and suddenly there are twenty of them."

"I just thought you'd like to know you were admired."

"I'm really interested only in your admiration, Mrs. Campbell."

I love you, she thought. *I love you beyond life*.

The breeze came again, tugging at scraps on the floor, flapping the edges of table linens. Eric stood up, helped her to her feet. He put a hand to his mouth, covered a yawn.

"It's been a long day," he said.

A long long day, she thought.

She closed her eyes as he drove back, drifting in and out of light sleep. When she opened them again he was easing the Datsun into its parking slot. He got out, helped her struggle from the seat.

"You know what would be nice?" he asked.

"You want to sit by the pool," she said.

"How did you guess?"

. He led her around the wire fence with its grids lit softly, diamond-shaped in the dark. The tables around the pool were unoccupied. The candles flickered inside their red jars. They sat down and stared in silence at the underwater lamps and the occasional ripple along the surface: it was as if an invisible hand dropped an invisible pebble into the pool from time to time. Hypnotic, generous, calming. She wanted to dip her hand in the water, cool her fingers and wrists. But she didn't move, only gazed.

"It's like a liquid fireplace," Eric said. "It has the same effect as looking for things in an old log fire, you know?"

She nodded.

"When I was a kid..." He stopped.

"When you were a kid what?"

"We used to have these great fires. We always had good burning wood, logs. I'd almost forgotten that."

"You never really talk much about your past," she said.

"I didn't exist until you, did I?" He stared at her; his eyes reflected the softness of the candles. He was smiling—and she realized she hadn't seen quite that look of tenderness in his face for some time. She reached across the table for his hand. She wanted to ask more but she had the sense, somehow, that the time wasn't right. And something else circled her mind, an intuition of some past tragedy in his life, an event that had touched him—perhaps long ago—and one he kept locked inside himself. She liked the faint sense of mystery. She liked the prospect of his telling her suddenly one day. Romantic, she said to herself. You're a terminal romantic.

She smiled back at him and turned her face toward the shallow end of the pool.

It floated like a shapeless jellyfish, a dark relic of the deepest sea. It floated quietly back and forth against the shallow end. Billowing, puffed by water, it moved in a gentle way as if chided by the whisper of some reticent tide. She stared at it, puzzled at first. A large piece of darkened newspaper, a small animal, she wasn't sure what. Very faintly, it seemed to slap against the blue tiles. She nudged Eric, pointed, said nothing. The object, pinned by light, bloated by water, appeared to sink under the surface and then emerge in a different shape, changed by the quiet motions of trapped water.

"What is it?" she asked.

"I don't know," Eric said.

She stood up and went toward the thing. Halfway between the table and the shallow end she realized she knew. She understood what it was that lay against the tiles. All at once the candles on the tables seemed to glow more brightly, blindingly. How? How in the name of God? She walked quickly now, standing on the first step above the water. *She knew.*

On the second step she felt tepid water stroke her ankles. When she was on the third it lapped her knees and soaked her dress and made it cling to her skin. The thing, tantalizing, teasing, seemed to float away from her. Her feet touched bottom before she realized what she was doing, why she was doing it, and then she was conscious of Eric's footsteps coming along the side, the sound of his voice calling her name. She waded toward the object. A dream, she thought. A dream. How could this happen? She felt the water press clammily against her skin. When the thing was about a foot from her she reached out, slipped, felt herself falling facedown, saw the underwater lights explode all around her, saw the thing float inches above her. She struggled to regain her balance: chlorine stung her eyes, choked her nostrils, her hair was plastered flat against her skull. She reached forward again and gripped the material of the object and dragged it toward her, barely realizing that Eric was in the pool now too, his hands gripping her beneath the armpits. *For Christ's sake, for Christ's sake,* he was saying. Why didn't he understand? Why didn't he recognize the object? Why was he trying to haul her away? But she had it in her fingers and was clutching it tightly even as Eric dragged her back toward the steps. Breathless, she sat on the top step. The thin material, stained and waterlogged, lay between her hands. She looked at it, tried to spread it flat on her lap, tried not to hear Eric asking his mundane questions: *What is it? Why the hell did you go in the water?* She kept trying to flatten it out, but the dampness made the thing stick to her legs. She closed her eyes. She wanted to weep. How could anybody do a thing like this? A thing so meaningless, so vicious? Speechlessly, she stared at her husband now. He was trying to take the thing away from her but she held on tightly.

Don't you know what this is, Eric?

Don't you remember being with me the night I wore it?
Don't you don't you don't you?

She turned and, her hands trembling, laid the object on the poolside, smoothed out what was left of it. Eric, standing above her, dripping, looking down at her, gasped.

Remember now, Eric? Remember?

She looked at the relic, at the pale blue material stained by water, bleached by chlorine, slashed to ribbons by something sharp—a razor, a carving knife, something deadly sharp—she looked at what remained of the maternity shirt. Then she shut her eyes and lowered her face.

Blue.
Pale blue.
The blue of a baby's eye.

You sit very still in a dark room with the scissors in your hand and for a frightening moment you can't remember why you are holding them and then it comes back to you, comes flashing back, and you rise and walk to the dressing table. You see your white face a moment in the mirror. You put the scissors down. You lay them alongside the buttons.
Blue.
See the scissors go through the blue.
See the scissors slash slash slash through the blue.

Six   *July 13*

●●

She couldn't stop shaking. Even with the hot coffee Eric had pressed into her hand, even with the dry clothes he'd made her wear, she couldn't stop the ridiculous feverlike spasms running through her body. She sat at the kitchen table, her hands clasped around the coffee mug, and stared at the steam rising from the dark surface, remembering the shirt—*her* shirt—and how it had floated, sliced and slashed, in the pool. When she shut her eyes all she could see were underwater lights and the sodden material of the garment, trailing its ribboned pieces like a dying octopus.

She looked at Eric. She shivered. He was standing against the refrigerator with a cigarette in his hand. She watched the

way he inhaled smoke quickly, expelling it in tiny dust-
colored clouds. He was tense: there was something furious in
the way he smoked, as if he were attacking the cigarette. The
clock above the stove registered the time in digital numerals:
12:23. After midnight. A new day. She raised a hand to her
mouth and held it clenched against her lips.

*The shirt, somebody had come in here, come into the
apartment, gone inside the bedroom, taken the shirt, hacked
it in a frenzy and thrown it into the pool—somebody, oh
Christ. Why? Why? What sense did that make?*

She looked once more at Eric. Why was he so silent? What
was he thinking? Why hadn't he done something positive,
something *active*, like maybe calling the cops? She got up
from the table and walked past Eric to the sink: The shirt lay
wrinkled and discolored against the porcelain. She put out
her hand to touch it, then drew her fingers away. She tried to
imagine a blade slashing through the material, she tried to
envisage the energy needed for such a thing—but she couldn't
get it straight in her mind, couldn't grasp it. Then she
imagined herself being inside the shirt when the attack
happened, the blade puncturing her skin, slashing through
her veins. She closed her eyes, shuddered, listening to the
sound of Eric exhaling smoke. *What is he thinking? What the
hell is going through his mind right now?* Senseless, the
whole thing was pointless. She put her hands over her
stomach and she thought about the baby: this delicate creature perched so precariously inside her, bound to her by the
frailty of a cord of flesh and blood. She thought how silent it
had become. Unmoving. A motionless object on a dead tide.
She glanced once at Eric and then walked through the living
room, down the corridor, into the bedroom. She lay down
and looked at the dark window. When she twisted her face a
little she could see the shadowy opening of the closet door.

The shirt.

She heard Eric clear his throat as he came into the
bedroom.

Explain it to me, Eric. Explain it to me in simple and clear
terms. Make me understand such a thing.

She looked at him. He approached the bed, lay down
alongside her, covered her hand with his own.

She licked her lips and said: "What happened? What does
it mean?"

He didn't answer her at once. Instead, he tightened his grip around her hand; it was almost as if the situation were reversed in some way, as if he were seeking some explanation from her.

"Tell me what's running through that brain of yours, Eric. Tell me that much."

She heard him sigh. "I'm trying to work it out," he said. "I'm trying to think."

"Don't you see it as some curious travesty of physics that enables a garment hanging in my closet to magic itself out through a closed window and into a swimming pool, while undergoing an apparent surgical operation at the same time? Don't you see it that way, Eric?" *That note in my voice,* she thought: the edge of panic, cold fear.

"Somebody must have been here," she said. Now her voice didn't seem like her own at all; it appeared to have no connection with her. She might have been a ventriloquist's doll. "Somebody must have come here and taken the damn thing and cut it to ribbons—"

"Like who?" he said. "Who would do such a thing? I mean, you've got to dream up a strange kind of burglar to answer that one. I've never heard of anybody entering an apartment just to steal a shirt. There's a whole bunch of stuff here worth hard cash—nobody in their right mind would go to all the trouble of getting in only to steal something worthless—"

"How did anybody get in, Eric?"

He sighed again. "I don't know. I looked. I checked the front door. I checked the balcony door. I couldn't find any signs of forced entry."

Forced entry, she thought. What would *he* know about signs of forced entry?

"You don't think *anybody* came here, Eric? Are you going to tell me that?"

He shook his head. He smiled in his quiet understanding way and stroked her brow with the palm of his hand. "I am just trying to find some other explanation, that was all. I was trying to think of something that didn't involve this weird burglar."

"Like what?" *Explain it to me, love. I'm scared and I'm waiting.*

"Okay. Maybe you accidentally threw the shirt out. You might have been taking it to the laundry and dropped it somewhere outside. Maybe some kids found it and just cut it for the hell of it. A prank. Mischief. You know what I mean. Then they threw it in the swimming pool."

"I didn't take it to the laundry, Eric. It's silk. And I don't remember throwing it out. It was almost brand new, for Christ's sake. Why would I throw it out?"

"I'm talking about a simple mistake, Ellen. It might have become mixed up with some garbage."

"And that's where the mischievous kids come in, right?"

"I'm not saying there *were* any mischievous kids, Ellen. I'm only offering you one kind of rational explanation, that's all."

Explanations.

Hypotheses.

Why was she having such a hard time getting a fix on some kids who found a good time in slicing a shirt to death?

"What's wrong with a burglar, Eric? A common burglar?"

"It wouldn't be a thief, love. It would be somebody else. A thief would have taken other kinds of things—"

Somebody else, she thought. Like who.

"We ought to call the cops," she said.

"You know what a cop would say? He'd want to know if your typewriter was still intact and if your stereo had been stolen or whether you were missing money, jewels, valuable possessions. That's all he'd want to know. You tell him about a shirt in a swimming pool and he's going to shut his notebook fast."

Okay, she thought. I should just confess it, I should own up to it, come right out and say I threw the thing in the trash by mistake along with all the other detritus of our lives and some crazed kid found it and went to work on it with his flick-knife. I should nod my head and smile and agree—because anything would be better than imagining somebody coming here in my absence and deliberately stealing a specific shirt, deliberately destroying it, deliberately dropping it in a swimming pool. Anything would be better than trying to imagine the face of this anonymous . . . joker. Joker, she thought. A very bad practical joke. A mean act.

I saw that shirt only a day or so ago.

I touched it. I touched it when Vicky was here.

I was thinking of wearing it.

Vicky.

I'll use your bathroom a moment before we leave—

Vicky.

That was so stupid as to be obscene. True, Vicky had gone through the bedroom, used the bathroom. True, she'd been alone for a couple of minutes at most. But why would Vicky, of all people, want to steal a shirt? Why would she hack the shape out of it? Senseless. The more you keep formulating ideas the more senseless they get. Go with Eric's mischievous kids. Go with the idea that you accidentally threw the shirt out. Go with all that. *I don't remember throwing it anywhere . . .*

Vicky.

You're pregnant, Ellen.

You're preoccupied.

You can't be expected to notice every little thing. You can't hope for that. Your mind is elsewhere, distracted. Maybe amnesia and forgetfulness and a certain amount of oversight is just part of the whole package of pregnancy.

She heard Eric move his head on the pillow. "Are you *sure* it was your shirt?"

"I'm sure."

"I know—but how can you be absolutely sure. The chlorine's bleached it. It's totally misshapen. How can you be sure beyond a doubt?"

She shrugged. He is only trying to be calm, only trying to make me feel calm too. I understand that. "I *can't* be sure beyond a doubt, Eric. But when I find a shirt that looks like mine and when I also see that my shirt isn't hanging on its hanger, then I'm no slouch in putting two and two together."

She wanted to think: He's right. It isn't mine at all. I was mistaken. Mine is just hiding someplace. One day it'll turn up and then I'll wonder why I made all this hysterical fuss. Right?

Right, Ellen. Whatever you need to believe.

She got out of bed. Inside the kitchen she stood by the sink and looked down at the wreck of the garment. Slowly, she put out her hand and picked the thing up and spread it out. The label was still intact. It had the Saks name stitched to it. Saks. The place where I bought the shirt. The same store. The same shirt. She flattened it out and looked at the torn streamers, the jagged ribbons. No doubt whatsoever.

She stared at it.

Even in its ruined state, even slashed and filled with holes, she realized something else was wrong.

The buttons. The blue buttons.

She crumpled the garment between her fingers, reached beneath the sink to the trash can, and dropped the thing inside.

The blue buttons, she thought.

It wasn't enough to hack and butcher the thing—but whoever had done that had also gone to the trouble of slicing each button out. Slicing—that wasn't the word: the rest of the shirt had been *sliced*, but the buttons appeared to have been removed systematically and with more care, almost as if they had been snipped off, quite deliberately, with scissors. *Somebody removes the buttons carefully and then some frenzy begins, maybe in a slow way at first, then growing, growing and growing to a screaming pitch.*

She slammed the cabinet door shut and stayed in the kitchen for a few moments, deliberately looking around—looking for signs of other small vandalisms, for the telltale marks left in passing by an intruder. She didn't see anything out of the ordinary.

There was nothing unusual.

Nothing at all.

In the bedroom, she heard Eric raise his head and saw his shadow against the window.

"I threw the shirt out," she said. *For the second time,* she thought—*except I don't remember the first.*

Seven   July 16

Ellen stared at the ceiling of the waiting-room for a while. Then she heard her name being called.

Irene Grabowski, Phelps's assistant, was looking at her. She was a tall woman of about thirty-three with a short tattered hairstyle that might have been created by a hairdresser working with his eyes closed. The chopped look. Her uniform was the cold white of a frosty morning and the matching shoes threw back reflections of light.

"Ready, Ellen?"

Ellen nodded and followed the nurse along the corridor to Phelps's office. The walls were covered with pictures and charts—fetal development stages, helpful hints during pregnancy, a compendium of vitamins, drug warnings. Each time she came here these diagrams and lists made her feel a little guilty—she tried to follow Phelps's prescriptions for expectant mothers, but invariably she skipped this or that, forgot to do her exercises, couldn't remember her vitamin intake.

"How are you feeling?" Grabowski asked.

"Heavy."

"You're going to feel even heavier before this is through." She had an authoritarian tone in her voice, a manner that was professionally aloof at times. I could wish for a little more warmth, Ellen thought. A few more smiles of sympathy now and then. She glanced at the nurse, the lean face, the gaunt jaw. Actually, Grabowski was more than just a nurse; she was a midwife Phelps had recently hired to help him with his growing caseload. A midwife who would be in the delivery room at the time of birth; presumably the first person to see *my* baby, Ellen thought. Even before me. It was an odd thought.

The nurse scribbled something on a chart attached to her clipboard and looked at Ellen. "It's all a question of patience, Ellen. You've got the patience, haven't you?"

It struck Ellen as a strange question in some way. Maybe it was just Irene Grabowski's manner of speaking, which was clipped, brisk; she sometimes seemed to be concealing herself behind a professional glaze, almost as though the real person were an entity trapped in a white uniform. Maybe Grabowski would be more sympathetic when the time came.

Phelps was in an inner office. He rose from behind his desk as Ellen entered. He frowned—a frown, Ellen had come to realize, which he wore perpetually the way some people grin all the time.

"Ellen. You look good. I must say you look good. Any plumbing complaints? Anything wrong with the pipes?"

It was how Phelps always began. She understood these references to plumbing to indicate humor: a conspiratorial kind of humor too—*I may be a man but we're all in this together, girls*. His bald head shone under the light, as though the skin were buffed with lemon Pledge. He wore thick sideburns that ran untidily across his cheeks and jaws.

"Nothing serious," Ellen said. "The usual stuff. I get tired easily. Sometimes I'm constipated. Also, I guess I must be a mess inside from all the baby's movements."

Phelps laughed, a deep throaty sound. "It's a good sign

when the child is active. You ought to feel good about it."

"I do—I just wish he were wearing slippers, that's all."

Phelps laughed again. She was aware of Grabowski moving around her, various instruments attached to her hands. Why did she always feel as if she were a slice of beef being examined by an inspector from the FDA? You should get a blue stamp slapped on the back of your hand, Grade A maybe. She took off her blouse and pants and sat with a white smock draped around her. Blood pressure was taken. Her temperature was recorded. She had to stand on scales and her weight was measured.

"Still doing the exercises?" Phelps asked.

"Most of the time."

"Wouldn't want any stretch marks to show, would we?"

Phelps leaned over, pressing on her abdomen, stethoscope dangling from his neck the way a rosary of garlic might hang from someone afraid of vampires. "I hope you're still taking the vitamins, Ellen. The body is under considerable duress during pregnancy. Depletion is high. Are you sleeping well?"

"I guess. I sleep odd hours, though. Sometimes I drop off in the afternoon. Sometimes I wake before dawn."

"Did you try the chamomile tea I suggested?"

"I didn't like the taste." Chamomile tea. The mere recollection of it caused her to feel a terrible disgust. She loathed the stuff.

"It's good for you." He was looking at her breasts now; gently he touched her nipples. They might have been fragile glass. Suddenly she wondered what he was like as a lover—whether he would be as gentle as he was now or whether, given his encyclopedic knowledge of the female body, he would simply be a technician of the clitoris, a manipulator of orgasms. She'd read somewhere that some women fell insanely in love with their obstetricians. He stood upright, smiled at her; then he went out of the room. This was characteristic of him—he had a warren of rooms where other women waited for his attention: it was the conveyor-belt principle of medicine. The door was closed behind him. Ellen looked at Nurse Grabowski.

"Doppler time," Grabowski said.

Ellen dreaded this moment. The Doppler, the fetoscope, was supposed to amplify the heartbeat of the child, but she always had the unsettling feeling that it might do just the opposite, it might inform her that the child's heart had stopped. Good news, bad news—the machine had no feelings.

She lay back, the smock swept upward, and she watched as Grabowski began to smear electroconductor jelly on her stomach. The stuff was cold and slimy and the nurse's touch was less than gentle. She might have been spreading glaze on a large ham. Ellen stared down at the woman's pale fingers—round and round, fingertips kneading, palms of the hands massaging the surface of the skin. She didn't have to be this rough, did she? Surely there were gentler ways of applying the jelly, softer ways.

"Lie perfectly still now, Ellen."

Ellen gazed at the woman. She had a small smile on her face: it wasn't an altogether pleasant expression somehow—it was as if Grabowski enjoyed the position of authority she occupied—enjoyed the awkward vulnerability, the nakedness, of the pregnant women who spread themselves openly before her. Ellen wanted to draw a sheet over herself, wishing she could feel less exposed.

She closed her eyes and tried to breathe in a relaxed way. Grabowski switched on the amplifier and then held the tiny microphone against Ellen's belly. There was no sound. Ellen shifted slightly. It wasn't unusual at first; sometimes it took several moments before the baby's heartbeat was found. She felt the microphone move over her skin. Still no sound.

"Hard to find the little varmint today," Grabowski˙ said. "Turn toward me, Ellen."

Ellen moved her body. She opened her eyes and stared at Grabowski's face: a look of intense concentration, the mouth slightly open. The microphone in Grabowski's hand moved slowly from spot to spot. Nothing. Still nothing.

"Lie on your side," the nurse said.

Awkwardly, Ellen twisted. She could feel the baby move even as she moved—so why couldn't Grabowski find the heartbeat? She gazed at the microphone. *What if the heart had stopped, what if the fetus had died and was beginning to shrivel up inside and she didn't know about it?*

"Is something wrong?"

Grabowski appeared not to hear the question. Head inclined, she was still concentrating on the movement of the microphone. Silence, silence.

"Is something wrong?" Ellen asked again.

Grabowski looked at her. "Nothing. Absolutely nothing. The child is being elusive, that's all. Relax. You don't help me by not relaxing, Ellen."

Ellen took a deep breath. Worry was such a dark thing, a long bleak shadow falling in your mind. Please find the heartbeat, please find it. Grabowski moved the microphone again. The quietness in the room was suffocating. The amplifier might have been dead, shorted out. Maybe it was something that simple. A faulty connection. Something technical. She stared again at the nurse: she wondered if Grabowski, given the same situation, would worry too—perhaps she wouldn't, perhaps she'd be in complete control, totally in charge of the stresses and changes in her body.

"What's wrong?" Ellen asked. "Why can't you find it?"

"Mmmm," Grabowski said.

Meaningless. The professional *Mmmm*. It was a neutral sound. She felt the microphone press against the jelly.

"Why can't you find it?" she asked again.

"Sometimes it's difficult, Ellen. You should know that by now."

"It isn't usually this difficult—"

"Try to relax." The nurse smiled at her, a quick expression, a flash of teeth; but it didn't reassure Ellen. It didn't console her at all. She felt an unbearable tension now, as if all her nerves were knotted, welded together like melted metal. The microphone moved again and still the amplifier was silent. Find it, for Christ's sake, find the heartbeat.

Nothing. Like the sound of death. Absolute silence.

Ellen turned over on her back and raised her face to watch the nurse.

"I didn't ask you to move, Ellen—"

"Why can't you find it?"

"Please, Ellen. You're not making this easy for me."

"It isn't exactly easy for me either—"

Grabowski was staring at the microphone.

"Is there something wrong with the machine?" Ellen asked.

"The machine is working perfectly."

"Why don't you check it to be sure?"

"I checked it," Grabowski said.

"Why don't you check it again?" That sound in her voice: it was the edge of panic. She tried to fight the feeling. "Please, why don't you check the amplifier again?"

Grabowski looked at her in a patronizing way. She didn't

make any move to touch the amplifier; instead, she continued to search with the microphone. Dear Christ, Ellen thought. What in the name of God is wrong? Struggling, she sat upright. Grabowski raised the microphone from her body.

"If you don't lie still, Ellen, I'll never be able to find the sound."

The door opened and Phelps returned and Ellen swung her face around to look at him. She heard Grabowski say, "We're having a little difficulty in locating the fetal heartbeat, doctor," and then Phelps had the microphone in his hand and was bending over Ellen with his eyes half-shut in concentration. He was saying, "Relax, relax, Ellen, just try to calm down." Take a deep breath, she told herself, take a deep breath, the baby is fine, the baby is doing okay, the baby is alive and well and moving inside you.

And then suddenly the room was filled with the amplified sound of the baby's heartbeat. Baby, she thought. Oh baby— and she wanted to weep with relief and happiness. It was a certain fragile happiness dependent on something as vulnerable as the fast regularity of a child's heart. A delicate joy. Phelps stood upright. "Fine, just fine," he said. He glanced at the nurse and then smiled at Ellen. "Feel better now, Ellen?"

Ellen sighed, nodded. "I was worried—"

"Of course you were worried. But the Doppler isn't exactly infallible. Sometimes it takes a while to find the heartbeat, Ellen. You can't just zoom in on it without fail every single time."

Ellen listened to the sound of her baby. She felt leaden and drained all at once.

Grabowski said, "She was being very naughty, doctor. She just wouldn't relax, that was all."

Phelps reached over and switched off the machine and the room was silent. He scribbled something on his clipboard, then he looked at Ellen. His manner was calm, soothing. "Are you worried about anything other than the baby?"

"Nothing," she said. *The shirt in the pool, the hacked blue shirt in the swimming pool*—she hadn't meant to flash on that so abruptly, to let it intrude on her mind again and distress her. She shoved the memory aside; she couldn't afford to worry about anything other than the child.

Phelps patted the back of her hand. "You sure?"

"I'm positive."

The physician was silent for a moment. "You can get dressed, Ellen. If it's any consolation, everything's coming along nicely on schedule."

She got down from the examining table and found her clothes. She dressed coyly behind the screen in the room. She heard Phelps say something to the nurse, something she couldn't quite catch. Maybe he was scolding her for not finding the heartbeat. Maybe it was something like that. She thought: It was my own fault, it was my own fault because I was nervous, because I wasn't at ease. She'd have to try to relax more in future, that was all. But she couldn't relax, couldn't still her nerves. When she emerged from behind the screen Phelps had already gone.

Grabowski said, "He's right, Ellen. The Doppler isn't an infallible device. You should know that. It really doesn't help when you panic."

"I know," Ellen said. "I'm sorry."

Grabowski smiled now, her expression suddenly easy, less stern. "The first baby always brings out the worst feelings, Ellen. It's perfectly natural. Perfectly natural."

"I guess so."

They walked together out of the room. They moved along the corridor. "Just don't give in to your fears," the nurse said.

"I'll try," Ellen answered.

"See you next week." Grabowski smiled once more, then turned and went back.

Outside, in the sunlight, Ellen looked across the parking lot in the direction of her car. I'm still afraid, she thought. I'm still worried. The absence of the baby's heartbeat—that panic, that sense of being suddenly and horrifyingly alone, beyond the help of physicians and nurses, locked in a place of the most frightening solitude. It was a feeling she couldn't shake as she drove home.

Back in the apartment, she went quickly to the bedroom. As soon as she opened the door she had to lie down. She made it to the bed and dropped onto the mattress, lying with her arms spread and her legs parted. A baby's heartbeat—like the pounding of a scared rabbit. She placed the palm of her hand over her belly and shut her eyes.

When the telephone rang in the kitchen, she had to struggle out of her numbness to realize what it was. She staggered toward the kitchen and picked up the receiver.

It was Eric.

"You sound cranky," he said. "One of those days?"

"I've been running around. I'm just tired." Tired: no, more than that. Fear created something more than just plain old weariness. It left you in a bleak place.

"You went to see Phelps?" he asked.

She was silent a moment. "They couldn't find the heartbeat on the Doppler machine," she said, realizing there was an edge in her voice, a connection to hysteria.

"What do you mean they couldn't find the heartbeat?"

"At first, Grabowski couldn't get it, I don't know why—"

"But it's okay?"

"It's okay now," she said.

She heard another telephone ringing somewhere in the background and Eric mumbled something about having to answer it, leaving her stranded for a few moments on a silent line. A silent line, she thought. They couldn't find the heartbeat and *he* has to answer another call. There was a weird sense of priorities there. She shut her eyes. Why was she thinking about the pool again, thinking about the shirt in the pool, when she'd promised herself she'd try to let that go forever, stuff the memory away in whatever attic room of the brain was reserved for unwanted images? Don't, she told herself. Don't slip back there. Try for control and calm now. Breathe deeply. Deeper still.

When Eric came back on the line, he said, "I'm sorry about that. We've got a hectic situation down here right now. It's been one of those days."

A hectic situation. What about my situation? she thought. Is your work more important than my situation? She tried to imagine him in his office, a place she'd visited only once, but the picture had the consistency of spilled quicksilver. He shared his office with a character called Wayne Downer, but she couldn't even remember what he looked like.

"Are you all right?" Eric asked.

What kind of question was that? *Are you all right?* Didn't I just tell you about the shock of the heartbeat? Didn't I just tell you how that made me feel? Eric, why are you being so distant, dammit?

"Yeah," she said. "I guess I'm fine."

He didn't even seem to catch the remote quality in her voice, the flatness in her tone. Ah, but he was having *one of those days* after all, don't forget that, don't forget he had a *hectic situation* going on. There was the sound of a telephone ringing again.

"Look, I better hang up now," he said. "I'll see you when I get home, Ellen."

"Okay," she said.

A flat okay. A cold sound.

She put the telephone down and walked through to the living room. Cut him a little slack, Ellen, she told herself, don't be so ludicrously hard on him. He's distracted, bothered, a busy man. She pressed her face against the glass of the balcony door and wondered why she was suddenly thinking about what to cook for supper. Supper—maybe it's the domestic stuff that provides the glue, the little adhesives that hold you together and make you finally relax. Maybe. *Trout and green beans and baked potatoes*. She opened her eyes and looked out at the parking lot.

A dark car, a familiar black car, was pulling out of the parking space Eric usually occupied. She watched it, wondering where she'd seen it before, wondering why it had gone into Eric's space. A black car of some anonymous breed— where? Where had she seen a car similar to that before?

When she remembered she stepped back from the door as if the glass had suddenly burned her. Her mother's, her mother's house in Paradise Valley, the car that had been idling in the driveway, blocking her. Now she watched it grind over a speedbreak, then disappear in the direction of the exit. The lot was silent, motionless: all that moved were the blue reflections of lights from the pool against the wire fence. A black car, the same car that—

Coincidence, she told herself.

Simple coincidence.

Better still, a mistake of her memory: it wasn't the same goddam car at all, it wasn't the car she'd seen in Paradise Valley, what did *she* know about car makes anyhow? She couldn't tell the difference between a Dodge and a Chevy and a Ford. One car looked the same as any other—only their colors were different.

She turned away from the door, rubbing her hands together. I'm nervous again, she thought. All of a sudden I'm nervous again. The shirt business. The car outside. The Doppler. Little conspiracies.

She moved into the kitchen now and sat down at the table to wait for Eric.

She began to think of the baby. She imagined the moment of birth, the moment of first holding the child in her arms, feeling it drink from her breasts, the soft touch of its small hands against her own; and she tried to see the world through the child's eyes, a huge place of bizarre shapes, unexpected encounters, obstacles, strange sounds and weird smells. A whole world unexplored—a world through which she'd have to help steer the child and keep it safe from harm. I can't afford this nervousness, she told herself: this child needs a mother who is well adjusted, balanced, trustworthy. *The kind of mother I need to be*.

The telephone was ringing again. For a moment she didn't want to answer it. She got up and lifted the receiver: persistent bell, persistent caller. Maybe it was Eric, maybe his hectic situation had passed.

She was surprised to hear the voice of Ralph Houseman. In the background somewhere was the sound of a piano being played—a cocktail bar, maybe. Houseman's voice was a little slurred, as if during the whole afternoon he'd been raising glasses rather than funds for charitable purposes.

"I hope you don't mind my calling, Ellen," he said. "I don't want you to think I'm interfering. That's not my style. I don't go in for that."

"Interfering in what, Ralph?"

"I'm Eric's boss, I mean I have to have some say in his life. Right?"

"I'm sure, Ralph. But I don't understand what you're trying to say about Eric." She was puzzled. What was Houseman going on about?

"I can't convince him he's working too hard. I want him to take a vacation. I don't want to see him burn himself out, Ellen. Everybody needs a little R and R sometimes, right?"

"I didn't know he was working *that* hard," she said.

"My opinion, Ellen. Speak to him. Make him take a week off. I've already offered my cabin in the White Mountains. Be good for both of you."

"Is he doing something wrong? Is his work suffering?"

"No, not so you'd notice. It's just my feeling. I see some kind of strain on his face. I've got good intuitions, Ellen. I go with my nose. I follow my instincts. You never noticed any strain, stress?"

"Not really," she said. That damned piano; it was drowning

out his voice. She couldn't think. "Have you discussed it with
him?"

"Sure I have. Once or twice. Hell, I kept him late a few
days ago just to air this whole thing."

"You kept him late for *that?*" Something spinning, lurching:
the cabin in the mountains—he'd never mentioned such a
thing. Never.

"Didn't he say we'd talked?" Houseman said.

*He mentioned something, sure, sure he did, but he wasn't
telling me the truth, he was lying to me.* Not Eric. Eric
doesn't lie, does he? She saw her hand tremble slightly. Why
hadn't he said something about this? It would have been so
easy to tell the truth: *Look, Houseman thinks I work too
hard, wants me to take time out.* It would have been the
easiest thing in the whole world for Christ's sake.

Such a casual pointless lie. Such a stupid lie. So utterly
futile.

Maybe he didn't want to worry you, maybe he didn't want
to cause you any concern, maybe maybe—but it didn't change
the fact that he'd lied.

Trust is the only true currency of a relationship . . .

"Well?" Houseman asked. "Didn't he say we'd talked?"

"Yes, he mentioned something—"

"Bet he just tossed it aside, right? That's like him, Ellen.
He wouldn't want you to worry about anything like this right
now—but I think he needs a break. I wouldn't be saying this
otherwise."

"Right," she said. "He just tossed it aside."

It's a pain. It's a pain you don't need.

"Look. Talk to him. You don't need to tell him I called. Just
say you'd like to get away for a week. Get out of this heat. You
know what I'm saying."

"I know—"

"And don't take me wrong, Ellen. Okay? I'm not a
buttinsky."

"I know that, Ralph." And she had a sudden picture of
him—a fat man in a pastel-colored, doubleknit leisure suit,
turquoise jewelry hanging around wrists and neck, plump
fingers shining with Indian rings.

"Give it a shot, Ellen. And call me. Let me know. I don't
want to see a good man blow his fuses."

"Thanks, Ralph."

She closed her eyes.

A small lie. A nothing lie. Fabricated out of zero—so meaningless.

He wanted to discuss a whole new strategy of fund raising. Why, Eric?

It wasn't the lie in itself—it was the realization that he was *capable* of lying.

Stress and strain. She hadn't noticed anything like that about Eric.

There was only the nightmare. And he didn't have it that often.

Only the nightmare.

Why did such a tiny lie cut with the ferocity of a serrated blade? Why did she feel she was bleeding somewhere? A tiny lie—but underneath it lay a complicated reassembling of facts.

It was only one lie, but what if there were others? Others she hadn't found out about?

She drummed her fingers on the kitchen table and wondered why she felt something more than disappointment.

She felt hurt as well.

You only had to tell me the truth, Eric.

And nothing but the truth.

She watched him read his newspaper in the living room, feeling as if she'd swallowed a fine bone, something that had become lodged at the back of her throat. The lie, the lie, all she had to do was bring it up, a small matter, all she had to do was come out and mention it—lightly, not with any gravity, lightly slide her way around it somehow. But she couldn't, she didn't have the heart. She just kept watching him. *You said you'd never lie, not even in something trivial. You said you'd always be truthful.* Ellen, Ellen, you're making mountains out of molehills. You're building this up and up and up, turning it into a balloon stretched to bursting point.

But a lie—

He folded his paper, set it down on the coffee table and sat back with his eyes closed. She wondered if what Houseman had said were true. Sure, he looked tired, the lids of his eyes seemed to have the wearied luminosity of pale glass. And sure, he worked hard because that was in his nature. But *too* hard? She studied his handsome face. When he suddenly opened his eyes she looked away a moment and when she gazed at him again he was smiling.

"I owe you an apology," he said.

She was suddenly tense. Maybe he knew she'd found out about the lie, maybe he was going to say something about it, explain himself, justify everything. She waited.

Then he said, "I was abrupt on the telephone today. I'm sorry about that. Really. Sometimes that job has pressures... I knew you wanted more consolation from me. But the time just wasn't right." And he rose and came across the room, kneeling at her feet, his hands grasping her wrists. Abrupt, she thought—she'd already forgotten that, released it from her mind. The lie, what about the lie?

"It won't happen again," he said.

Then he strained forward and he kissed her and when he pulled his face away he was looking at her with what she could only describe as a warmth of love in his eyes.

"I promise it won't happen again," he said.

She didn't say anything. How could she have?

She ran her hand through his black hair and, leaning back in her seat, closed her eyes.

Eight   *July 17*

❈❈❈❈❈❈❈❈❈❈❈❈❈❈❈❈❈❈❈❈❈❈❈❈❈❈❈❈❈

The midday heat had the force of a million falling bricks newly baked; inside her womb the child twisted and cavorted like a trapeze artist or a high diver breaking a surface of water. She walked quickly across the parking lot to the Opel and as she did, saw Anna Rosenberg moving along the poolside fence. The blonde girl wore a one-piece bathing suit of a shimmery red material. She had a bright smile beneath the shadow of her sun hat.

"Hey," the girl said. "How are you? How's the kid?"

Ellen shielded her eyes from the glare of white concrete and blue water. Why didn't the heat seem to affect this girl? Beyond the fence there were several young bodies glittering in the pool. Chlorine-blue splashes rose, seeming to hang in sunlight, where they were burnished gold.

"Everything seems fine," Ellen said. The association of blue water and girl—why was she remembering the shirt again when she'd vowed to herself that she wouldn't? Simple connections, that was all. There couldn't be anything sinister in the clean white smile, the healthy body; there couldn't be anything dark about this child of the sun.

"You swim?" Anna Rosenberg came closer.

"I used to. Now I can't get into a swimsuit." It wasn't true exactly: she didn't want to know how she would look in one. A hot dog that has burst through its papery skin in the middle—red, misshapen.

"It's good exercise," the girl said and touched the hood of the Opel. She pulled her hand away. "Maybe when you've had the baby we can go swimming together."

"Sure," Ellen said. She found herself staring at the girl's mouth: a perfect mouth, like something that might have been drawn in a child's storybook. A mouth designed for kissing. (Why the hell did I think that?)

Anna Rosenberg stared for a time, as if she were reluctant to leave. There was a vague smile on her face. Ellen wondered if the expression might be described as secretive, but she dismissed the notion. The girl might have been just a little stoned, a little spacey. Ellen felt an irritating trickle of sweat slide across her forehead and dabbed at it with her fingers. Anna Rosenberg would *never* sweat, Anna Rosenberg would keep *her* cool at all times. Miss Desert Perfect. Ellen looked away from the girl's infuriatingly attractive face and glanced at the pool. It was tempting, so tempting just to step out on the diving board and fall until you smacked the water. The baby moved inside her again, as if it had read her thought and disapproved of it.

"We ought to get to know each other better," the girl said. "Living in the same complex and everything."

"That would be nice," Ellen said.

"Does your husband swim? I've never seen him around the pool."

"Sure he swims. I guess he doesn't have time." She suddenly realized she didn't know if he was a swimmer or not. She couldn't remember ever having seen him in a pool. You can't know *everything* about another person, she thought, not even your spouse. You can't fill in all the blanks. (The lie came back to her. I have to deal with it. I can't just let it slide. How, though? How do you deal with the thing?) Beyond Anna Rosenberg's face, through the wire fence, she could see a group of girls lining up one behind the other on the diving board: they were laughing, pushing one another into the pool. Eight or nine bikinis falling through the sunlit air, like a troupe of amateur circus performers. They fell awkwardly, limbs ungainly, they fell surrounded by their own screaming laughter. Bikinis, she thought. I'd look like an idiot in a bikini right now. She turned her gaze on Anna Rosenberg. At least *she* wasn't wearing a bikini—just the simple one-piece outfit. Was this some new fashion in outdoor wear? The death of the bikini? Maybe Anna saw herself as a trend-setter around here, eschewing bikinis in favor of a one-piece. Perhaps she had some minor flaw she needed to conceal—the cicatrix of an old appendectomy or something like that. Ellen watched the last girl drop from the board: an outrageous orange color flashed in the light, then was consumed by water.

I've never seen him around the pool, Anna had said. Well, where had she seen him? And why was she looking?

Stop it, Ellen said to herself. She opened the door of the Opel.

"Well," Anna Rosenberg said. "See you around, okay?"

Ellen pulled the door shut, raised her hand in a brief gesture. She saw the girl framed in the rearview mirror, like some gold icon, as she drove out of the lot.

Why does that kid bother me anyhow?

Why do I let her get under my skin, dammit?

Does your husband swim?

Was it the question itself? Maybe it was a sense of casual familiarity in the way it was asked. Maybe it was because I didn't know the goddam answer.

She drove along Scottsdale Road, past the shimmering used-car lots, the souvenir and novelty shops, the sunlit riot of western commerce and its ongoing struggle with desert vegetation. Slamming the car into third gear she thought: I hope the desert wins. I hope it wins in the end. And she had a postholocaust picture of a solitary unharmed cactus rising proudly above the rubble of a bombed-out Cadillac dealership. Inside the restaurant, an Italian place with red-checkered tablecloths and artfully melted candles in chianti bottles—the kind of place where you expected to hear a bearded guy strum a guitar and sing *Little Boxes*—she said to Vicky: "When you were pregnant, did you ever forget things?"

"Like what?" Vicky asked.

"What I mean is . . . did things ever slip your mind?"

Vicky lit a cigarette and forced it inside her filter with a slight expression of distaste. "I guess so. It slipped my mind to have sex with Stan, for one thing."

"I don't mean that kind of thing, Vicky."

"Forgive me for saying so, but you're being a little obtuse here. I'm not exactly following you."

Ellen looked down at the table a moment. The remains of a pasta lunch lay on her plate—cold strands of fettucine lying in curdled cream. "It's hard to explain."

"I guess it must be," Vicky said.

"I mean, did you ever do something and forget you'd done it?"

"Give me an example."

Ellen paused for a time. The blue shirt: she'd been determined not to bring the matter up, but now she'd blundered into it. "Well, did you ever misplace clothing, for example? I mean, did you ever take stuff to the laundromat and forget you'd done it?"

"Stan had the decency to provide me with a matching set of Whirlpools. Washer and dryer in coppertone. I wasn't subjected to the donkey work of laundromats."

"Vicky, be serious."

"Only if you stop fudging around."

"Okay. I lost my best blouse. I remember seeing it, then it just wasn't there." How did that sound? Pretty silly? Ellen looked down at her plate again; she wouldn't take it any further, wouldn't bring up the savaged shirt in the pool, she'd stop just before that point. She guessed she was searching for some reinforcement here, an acknowledgment of prenatal amnesia. She thought she might be looking for some hook on which to hang Eric's version of the incident.

"Is *that* all?" Vicky asked. She blew out smoke, watched it spiral away. "I was forever forgetting things, Ellen. If I hadn't had the energy to make up little lists of things, I think I'd have forgotten Stan's name, for Christ's sake. And you're talking about a *blouse*?"

"It's no big deal," Ellen said and shrugged. *You were in the bedroom alone for a few minutes. You could have taken the shirt.* What a thought—bite your tongue, Ellen. She gazed at Vicky's hat, the brim of which was pulled down slightly over the forehead. The cowgirl look. The western conceit.

"Pregnancy does weird things," Vicky said.

"I guess so." But I'm not a forgetful person. I remember birthdays. Anniversaries. I even remember telephone numbers long disconnected. Christ, let it go. Let it pass. Why worry it now? She raised her coffee and sipped: it was cold and bitter in her mouth. Vicky stubbed out her cigarette, carefully took off her hat, ran one hand through her thick hair. Ellen thought, She looks unusually spectacular today, even for her.

"Is your affair with the weight lifter going on?"

"It's kaput," Vicky said. "It was either me or his biceps. The biceps won. I've moved on to other things."

"*Another* married man?"

Vicky fidgeted with the ashtray. "He's married but I think I've got the beginnings of something special going on..."

"Really?"

"I'm keeping my fingers crossed. I'd tell you more, kid, but in my experience it's just bad luck to talk about bridges you ain't crossed, you know what I mean?"

"I think I do." But she wasn't sure she did at all—it wasn't like Vicky to be mysterious about her relationships, it just wasn't characteristic. She added: "I don't like being kept in the dark, though."

"I don't mean to. Call me superstitious this time." A small enigmatic smile, the motion of a hand through hair: Ellen imagined she saw something nervous in both the expression and the gesture. "If it works out this time, you'll be the first to know all about it. Believe me."

Despite herself, despite her hopes for her friend, Ellen found herself sympathizing more than a little with the faceless wife of Vicky's new conquest. Maybe the poor woman waited up nights for her husband to return, sitting in the dark of some tract house, some spotless homestead, entertaining the suspicion that her husband was doing something more than merely staying late at the office. Still, she couldn't bring herself to think of Vicky as a home wrecker, she couldn't quite make that condemnation.

"I wish you all the luck in the world," she said, trying not to sound feeble about it.

"You don't exactly sound convincing," Vicky said. Still the same mysterious little smile. "Sometimes I get the feeling, Ellen, that you don't entirely approve of me. Maybe you don't like my morals."

"I didn't say that."

"Sometimes you don't have to say things out loud to make yourself heard," Vicky said. Suddenly the smile was gone and she had tilted her head back, laughing. "It's too hot for such a heavy conversation. In this kind of weather, you don't have the energy for philosophical chitchat, do you?"

Ellen smiled. *Maybe you don't like my morals.* She wondered how true that might or might not be; it was probably less connected to Vicky's sexual behavior than it was to sympathy for betrayed wives.

A waiter was hovering nearby with a check in his hand. Ellen brushed aside Vicky's attempt to pay and got up from the table. She went to the door and stared miserably out into the sunlight. (Let it rain. Please let it rain.) Vicky stood at her side. "You need a ride home?"

"I came in my own car. Remember?" Ellen said.

"And *you* talk about amnesia?"

They walked together across the parking lot. Then Vicky paused beside a car. It wasn't the Mustang she normally drove. Something else. Ellen stared at the paintwork of the vehicle—it trapped light with the tenacity of a miser. It trapped and held light with dulled determination.

"Where's your car?" Ellen asked.

"In the shop. Something too complicated to ask about. This little dog is a company loaner." Vicky kicked lazily at a tire.

A dog.

A black dog. Ellen felt heat press down upon her eyelids.

"It doesn't run well," Vicky was saying. "I don't know why the company invested in such things. German *and* black. I mean, who needs a black car in this weather? It looks like it might be the hearse of some goddam dwarf."

A black car. The hearse of some dwarf.

Idling. Backing out of the parking lot. A black car.

Ellen opened her eyes. Vicky was smiling.

"Look, I'm going to be busy the next few days. I'll give you a call when I see a light at the end of the tunnel. Okay?"

"Sure. Fine."

The baby twisted. She imagined she could hear an echo, a muffled echo, of its motion: *slap* against the bruised walls of the womb. Vicky kissed her lightly on the cheek. Ellen watched her get inside her car and reverse it so quickly the tires screamed. And then Vicky was waving, looking lovely and aloof behind bright glass.

Ellen moved towards the Opel. A black car. A small black car. A prune, she thought. You could become a prune in this scandalous climate. Then, wrinkled, dried up, you could sit

up nights with other women of your same dehydrated type
and sluggishly play round after round of whist while dark
desert creatures slinked and crawled outside your window.
Your black window.

The rim of the steering wheel scalded her fingertips.

I don't know anything about cars, she thought. I don't know
one from another. *Nothing*. I know *nothing* about cars of any
color.

She realized why she'd been avoiding the subject of the lie
with Eric. On the one hand, it seemed at times so trivial as to
be unworthy of her attention; then on the other she encountered
a principle, the matter of truth—something of value, something worth discussion. But what she also understood was
that she disliked any kind of confrontation, however mild and
innocent. And beneath this realization there lay, like a dark
weed billowing in an undercurrent of water, the possibility
that he might cover the fiction with yet another untruth—and
then where would she be? Confusion and mistrust—they
were outcomes she hated.

She sat with him in the Arizona Room after supper. Night
pressed against the glass walls. The realtor had been proud
of this small room for some reason; she seemed to have
regarded it as the centerpiece of the entire apartment. At first
Ellen and Eric had found it mildly amusing. *Hey, our own
Arizona Room! What do we keep in here? Gila monsters?
Vultures? Roadrunners?* In the end they had filled the room
with cool green plants and simple wicker furniture. During
the day, when the sun was at its most vindictive, the room
baked.

He'd been watching *Star Trek* again—an episode entitled
"Space Seed" in which Ricardo Montalban looked appropri-
ately superhuman and cool—and then he'd come into the
atrium with his newspaper under his arm. He smoked his
solitary cigarette while she watched him, realizing she was
scrutinizing him for some sign of uneasiness, nerves, anything which might link him to what Ralph Houseman had
said. *Overworked. I don't want to see a good man blow his
fuse.* I watch him, she thought, the way the visitor might
watch the patient in the terminal ward: I watch him and I
hate doing it.

He flicked the pages of the newspaper, then reached
toward the coffee table and stubbed out his cigarette. Framed

by plants, by leaves and stalks pushing upward against the windows, he looked oddly ethereal and almost too handsome, as if he'd stepped out of a romantic painting. She tilted her head to one side and tried to catch his eye, but he seemed lost. She put down the book she'd been reading—an overdue library book, a bad novel about some upstate New York town taken over by an unknown force—and closed the covers noisily. Eric looked up, smiled, and started to rise. She shut her eyes a moment. Why in the name of God was it really so difficult to bring up the lie? What was a marriage anyway but some form of bonding, of mutual trust, lives shared and open and easy to read?

"What's on your mind?" he asked.

"Do I look so obvious?"

"Ever since supper. Unless you get it out, you're going to suffer a mild apoplexy."

"Well..." She still couldn't bring herself to the point.

He was waiting for her. He was leaning against one of the glass walls, waiting, with the look of a man about to drum his fingers impatiently.

"Eric," she said.

"You've got the name right."

That tone in his voice: what was it? Cutting, sharp, a severe edge of frost. How could she match that tone?

"Eric..." She looked down at the cover of the book: dark blues and electric yellows shone. "Why did you lie to me?"

"Lie?" He smiled faintly. "When did I lie?"

"The night you were late, Eric. You lied to me then."

The smile left his face; it might have been wiped off with the rapidity of a conjurer's hand. "I don't remember—"

"You said you were discussing office strategies with Houseman—"

"That's right—"

I hate myself for doing this, she thought.

"Houseman told me you were talking about something else. Something to do with you overworking yourself."

Eric laughed. "You mean he bothered you with that old stuff?"

"He said he's worried."

"Worried? Look, ever since I started there he's been worried about my overworking. He thinks I do too much. He thinks I'm going to just fall apart. For Christ's sake, I don't know why he bothered you with that rubbish."

She put her book aside. "Is it rubbish, Eric?"

"Goddam right it is." He approached her chair, lowered himself to a squatting position, touched the back of her hand with fingertips that were cold. "It's out and out baloney, Ellen. Can't you tell that? I mean, do I look like somebody who's working himself to death? Huh? Do I remind you of that kind of person? Show me—where's the tremor in the hands and the sickly pallor and the bloodshot eyes? You see anything like that?"

"No," she said. He was trying to make it light, turn it into a joke of sorts.

"Houseman worries like an old woman, Ellen. I'm just surprised he took it into his head to lay this crap on you at a time like this. No, dammit. I'm more than surprised. I'm *pissed.*"

She looked into his eyes. It was hard to tell what he was thinking; it was hard to locate him somehow, to discover where he was—and she experienced a sense of loss, a sharp little jab in her heart. He'd never seemed quite so distant, aloof, cold. The chill descends, she thought. How can you just blow that coldness off? I want him to be like he always was—Eric, my husband, my love.

"So why did you lie?"

"A white lie—"

"A lie doesn't have any color, Eric—"

"It was harmless. It was harmless and thoughtless. I was trying to spare you any worry. What am I supposed to say— *my boss thinks I'm having a mental breakdown?* Is that it? How the hell would you have reacted if I'd told you the truth? You'd have worried yourself sick, right?"

"Maybe—"

"Maybe *nothing*. I know you, Ellen. I know how you would've reacted to a tidbit like that."

"It doesn't make it any easier to find out the truth from somebody else, does it?"

Eric laughed again. "I was trying to spare you. I was trying to shield you from Himself's crazy obsession about me. Take a vacation, he says. You need a rest, Eric. Why don't you and the little woman borrow my cabin in the White Mountains for a week? I get this from him all the time, Ellen. He's wrong. He's off the wall."

"You could have explained it. You didn't have to lie, did you?" She watched him. He had shut his eyes and was swaying almost imperceptibly from side to side, as if the faint rocking motion might waft the lie away. The lie—it was a hammer, the claw of some awful hammer, shattering through a dainty surface.

"Okay. I lied. I had the best intentions. I lied anyway. I can't change that." He got to his feet. She heard him move in the direction of the kitchen, the sound of running water. A glass broke in the sink. She didn't move. You're overreacting, Ellen. You're making an issue out of nothing. You're behaving as if this lie were a stick of dynamite burning away at the foundations of your marriage. *He was trying to spare you worry. That's what he was doing. You have to love him for that consideration at least.*

He came back with a glass of water in one hand, a piece of blood-stained tissue wrapped around the other.

"I cut my hand," he said.

"Let me look."

"It's okay. I stopped the bleeding. It's nothing."

She stared at the blood in the fibers of the paper. "I should take a look anyway—"

"It's all right. I checked. There's no glass in the cut."

She sat in silence for a moment, then: "I'm sorry, Eric."

"Yeah. Me too."

"I didn't mean to sound like I was accusing you," she said.

"I probably deserved it." He drank noisily from his glass. Water slicked across his chin.

"You've always made a point of . . . truth."

"I always will." He sat down facing her. The plants appeared to envelop him again. His face vanished in shadow, the shadow of leaf, stem, stalk.

"Let's drop it," she said. "You agree to drop it?"

"I agree."

She sighed. Eric rose from his chair and moved slowly across the floor, then he kneeled alongside her and put his hands on her shoulders. He looked unbearably solemn all at once: "It won't happen again. I promise you that. I'm not cut out to lie. I don't do it very well anyhow. You can take my word for it—I'm not overworked no matter what Houseman says. If anything, it's quite the opposite."

"Truthfully?"

"Truthfully," he said. He rose, kissed her, walked toward one of the glass walls. He stuck his hands in his pockets and stared out for a time. Then he laughed and turned around to face her: "You know what we haven't done in a long time? We haven't been to a movie. You feel up to one?"

"Sure." She shrugged. She didn't want to go out. She didn't want the hot night clamping down on her.

"What takes your fancy?"

"Anything escapist," she said.

"It's all escapist," Eric answered, rattling the newspaper.

Inside the bedroom she sat for a time in front of the dressing-table mirror. That wretched lie—why couldn't it simply be swept aside like a mound of ash, a cobweb? It has to be: it simply has to be, because if it isn't it's going to fester away in silence and emerge in some other guise, some monstrous way.

She brushed her hair languidly.

You watch the dark light of a tinted window.

Behind glass you see shapes move. You see the shadows of plants.

And then the light dies. The windows are black now.

Movement, a sudden movement.

You catch your breath and your heart knocks hard and you step back beneath the broad leaves of a palm, where you wait in silence and the night crawls around you.

You see them come out of the building. Shadows.

How beautiful he looks. How beautiful. And the woman walking alongside him, her arm linked through his—how fat and loathsome. You wonder how he can bear to touch her. And something shifts inside you—

Dark and deep and fiery, your whole being involved, swept away, you realize you want to stamp her out of existence, demolish her, you understand the ice of rage as it shivers through you, cold cold cold, colder than cold. The picture is wrong, all wrong, she doesn't belong with him, doesn't belong like that walking alongside him arm in arm, carrying his child.

You understand that he hasn't forgotten. You grasp this in a moment of clarity. You understand that he could never forget you. Time, you think. Only a matter of time.

And you put your hand in your pocket.

What you feel is a key and a knife.

The dark of the cinema was cool. She sat and watched a series of unbelievable events occur on the screen and thought: A piece of nonsense. Eric seemed to enjoy it—at least he sat with a glazed look on his face and his palm sweated when he held her hand. When it was over she rose from her seat and followed him outside; even the heat of the dark seemed preferable to the movie's boredom.

"I thought it was okay," Eric said.

She suddenly didn't want to contradict him. What if he needed the rest? What if they argued and he got upset? Jesus, she couldn't even behave naturally with her own husband anymore.

Eric's Datsun was parked some way across the lot. As they moved toward it, Eric paused and turned to look at her. "You look cranky. Is that how you feel?"

She shrugged and stifled a yawn. "I guess I'm a little tired, that's all. I didn't like the movie, but I didn't mean to be difficult."

He opened the passenger door for her. She sat back in her seat and watched the lights of Scottsdale slide past. Through the open window came the smell of food weaving out of restaurants. For a moment she felt hungry but the pang passed. She turned to look at Eric, who had been driving in silence.

"What's on your mind?" she asked.

"I was thinking about our baby," he said. "I was beginning to feel a real sense of anticipation."

She leaned her face against his shoulder. Warm, comfortable, a safe place—the uneasiness of the lie didn't belong between them, didn't have any room in their lives. Anticipation, she thought. There was something delicious in that word. There was a quality of ease she felt existed between them right now—love and security and ease, a thing shared, halved: *our baby.* Two simple words could erase a million doubts. She closed her eyes; the fabric of his jacket touched her face. It was a good moment, a good time. When she opened her eyes again he was sliding the Datsun into its parking slot in the complex. He helped her out of the car: she glanced a moment in the direction of the pool—but she didn't linger. She just wanted to go upstairs to their home.

Inside, except for the light burning over the stove, the apartment was in darkness. She moved ahead of Eric, stepped into the living room, turned on the lamp.

Then, as if she'd been struck low in the stomach, the air violently expelled from her, she gasped.

She lurched toward the sofa, lowered herself, eyes darting round the room.

Eric moved quickly to her side. "What's wrong?"

She opened her mouth to speak. Nothing came out.

"Ellen, what the hell is wrong?"

"The room..." She couldn't finish the sentence, wasn't sure what she was going to say anyhow, wasn't certain how she could say what she wanted and not sound insane, crazy. She stared at her husband: there was a look of alarm in his eyes. *The baby, he imagines I'm having the baby right now.*

"What about the room?"

"Don't you..." She closed her eyes. She laid her head against the back of the sofa. Don't you see anything, Eric? Can't you tell? The palms of her hands were sticky and her armpits were wet and she was shaking.

"Don't I what, Ellen? For Christ's sake—"

Lips dry as chalk, old desert flint.

She struggled with memory. Tried to step back a few hours in time. Tried to taste the immediate past. It wouldn't come. Recollection just wouldn't come. A blank, terrible as a human face without features.

"This room," she said.

"Tell me."

"Look at it, Eric. Look at this room." She rose from the sofa and went quickly into the kitchen. The same, exactly the same. Somebody, she thought.

Somebody has been here.

Somebody has come here.

And then she was thinking of the blue shirt hanging in the bedroom closet and how somebody must have come here and taken it and how the same person had come back here in their absence and done this, done all this.

She caught the edge of the sink and gasped. Her eyes watered.

Clean. The dirty dishes from supper had been stacked in the dishwasher. The skins of baked potatoes had gone. The porcelain surface of the sink was clean. The kitchen table had been wiped. She covered her face with her hands and thought: I don't remember doing all this. I don't remember any of this.

She went back into the living room, where Eric was watching her in a puzzled way.

Ashtrays emptied, cleaned.

Books on shelves rearranged neatly.

Coffee table freshly polished.

Magazines and newspapers placed in a tidy stack the way you saw them when you were the first patient of the day in a doctor's office.

Carpet looked as if it had been vacuumed.

The smell of furniture polish in the air.

I don't remember, don't remember, don't remember doing these things.

"What the hell is wrong, Ellen?"

"Don't you see?" Her voice sounded broken.

"I don't see anything," he said.

Then you're blind, you are blind.

She turned away from him and moved as quickly as she could toward the bedroom.

The bed had been made.

The various bottles of pills on the bedside table were standing in an immaculate line—as if they were awaiting an examination.

In the bathroom, the washbasin was spotless, shining porcelain.

She sat on the bed. Eric stood in the doorway.

"Are you going to tell me?" he said.

"Answer me one question. When you came home from work tonight, what was I doing?"

"You were getting dressed, I think . . ."

"And this apartment—how untidy did it strike you?"

Eric shrugged. "I don't really remember, Ellen."

"Did you look in the kitchen sink?"

He laughed. "I don't exactly make a habit—"

"I'm serious, Eric. Was this goddam place *untidy*? Was it?"

"I didn't notice, love—"

She closed her eyes. "It's tidy now, isn't it?"

"I guess."

"It's tidy now. And I don't *remember* cleaning it up, Eric."

He was silent. Then he said, "You can't be expected to remember everything, Ellen. I mean, housework is kind of automatic. You don't exactly go around thinking about it, do you?"

She opened her eyes. She stared at him.

"I would remember, Eric. I would *remember* something like that."

He crossed the floor to the bed. "Hey, relax. Relax. It's no big deal, Ellen. You forgot. You went through the hausfrau motions, then you forgot. That's all."

It wasn't me, she thought.

I didn't do all this. *Somebody else made this bed.*

I don't have the energy for it all.

Somebody else—

She turned her face away from Eric, feeling suddenly strange, violated. "Somebody came here when we were out," she said. She tried to keep her voice flat and rational. Somebody. Who? She searched her mind desperately, fighting a feeling of fear, rising panic.

Vicky. Why would that name pop into her mind out of nowhere? Vicky, why would Vicky do such a thing? What possible reason could she have? None. None at all. Vicky was her friend. Her best friend. Who else would come here— Anna, Anna Rosenberg? Where in hell was there a reason? Think think think. Maybe Anna Rosenberg was in love with Eric, maybe she was insane with jealousy, maybe she'd come here out of some maniacal spite to destroy—there were all kinds of maybes, whole chains of them.

"If somebody went to all the trouble of breaking in, you've got to admit it's a weird kind of burglary, Ellen. Look around. You notice anything missing? I mean, what kind of housebreaker forces entry just because he wants to do some cleaning up?" Eric put his arms around her shoulders and hugged her. She was thankful for the touch. Then he said, "I'll just check, make sure nothing's missing."

"Please—" Somebody touched my bed, she thought. *Who's been eating my porridge?* She sat down in an armchair and tried to relax. She let her arms go limp. Her fingertips trailed in the pile of the rug. Try to remember. *Try!* Why doesn't anything come? Why is the brain so empty, so unhelpful?

Eric returned. He stood in the middle of the room, working one foot back and forth in the rug. "I gave the living room a quick check. I can't see anything *obvious* missing, Ellen. Everything looks like usual. I'm sorry."

Sorry? Why was he sorry?

"I'll check this room as well."

"Don't bother," and her voice was hoarse, cracking. "I

doesn't matter. I probably did it myself, then it slipped my mind."

Eric said, "I told you."

"I know, I know. Chalk it up to my condition."

She looked at him. He'd moved to the window, a silhouette pressed against the pale drapes. She wished she could see his face, his real expression. Maybe he looked concerned, worried—how could she know? Maybe he had the expression of a man who suddenly realizes he's alone with a maniac.

I just forgot I did it.

My memory broke down.

No, she thought. Impossible.

She gazed slowly around the bedroom. *I know. I just know.* The bedroom was strange. She hated that sense of well-known objects sloughing off their quiet familiarity. The lamps. The bedside table. The mirror. The hand-painted flowerpot. They were strange to her now. Touched. Touched and altered.

And it wasn't me. I didn't do these things.

I know it.

She looked at the glass cabinet that contained the antique dolls. Something else was wrong there but for a moment she couldn't quite think straight. Count them, make a count of the dolls, but this had slipped her mind too—how many dolls were there supposed to be?

Eleven, twelve—she couldn't remember now.

Ellen, try to get it right.

She glanced at Eric: He was standing in the middle of the floor and rubbing his chin in the manner of a detective.

She moved toward the glass cabinet. But she couldn't remember the exact number, the count. She stepped backward in the direction of the bed.

How many goddam dolls?

She lay across the bed, staring at the glass, the tiny porcelain faces, the cherubic lips. If you could talk, if someone could come along and breathe life into you, what could you tell me?

We saw somebody here. We saw somebody in your bedroom.

She moved her body over the mattress.

Something hard. Something sharp pressed against the base of her spine. Something that lay under the covers. Don't look, she said to herself. Don't pull back the covers and look. Try to pretend this is just a bad dream. You'll wake. Everything will be normal again. Open your eyes, Ellen.

My eyes *are* open.

She reached out a hand and slowly began to pull the
bedcovers back.

Slowly. Slowly. Somehow knowing there was a horror yet to
find. *What kind of horror?*

She drew the sheets back and Eric's shadow fell across the
bed so that at first she couldn't see; all she knew was that she
heard Eric make a funny little sound, air rushing from his
open lips.

The doll lay there against the mattress.

No—part of the doll.

"Jesus, Jesus, Jesus," Eric was saying.

Part of the doll. Something missing.

And something very wrong with the mattress.

It had been slit crudely, slit with one violent unerring
stroke. And into the slit someone had placed a doll.

Someone had stuffed one of the antique dolls into the
gash—only the thing had no head, the head and neck had
been twisted off so it lay there like a guillotined torso, legs
twisted, arms pinned to the sides.

The head missing.

She stared a moment, then she closed her eyes.

Darkness.

Nine   *July 18*

She could barely hear their voices in the living room. She sat
at the kitchen table and the world around her was a thing she
drifted in and out of, as if none of the objects she saw had any
permanence whatsoever. Sometimes she felt herself float to
the edge of a numbing sleep; sometimes she thought she was
going to yield to the chaos of hysteria; at other times she
realized she wasn't a part of herself, that if she dared to look
she would be floating in a high place peering down on a tiny
figure huddled in a white kitchen. *The doll. Somebody had
cut the head from the doll. Slashed the mattress open, placed
the doll in the slit in a way that was obscene. And this same
person—whoever, whoever it might be—this same person,
this crazed person, had also cleaned the apartment. You*

could look and look and you wouldn't ever see any connections between those acts. You could probe, search your brain, and you wouldn't come up with a single link. Clean, then cut. Cut, then clean. She opened her mouth and put a hand against her teeth to bite hard on the knuckles.

When Eric came inside the kitchen, he was followed by the cop, a thin and mournful man called Patrick McDonald, who was holding his notebook open. He put one hand in a pocket of his cream-colored lightweight jacket. She had time to notice that it hung badly on him—a size too big, and looking as if it had been slept in. Beyond him, beyond the slats of the blind on the kitchen window, she was aware of darkness dissolving and the first light of day rising. Where had the time gone between discovering the doll and the cop's arrival? She just didn't know. Couldn't tell. She glanced at McDonald, saw how he sometimes exchanged looks with Eric, and she wondered what might be passing between them—concern for her in her condition? Some kind of pity? She wasn't sure if she imagined the looks or whether they meant anything anyhow. McDonald cleared his throat but his voice was hoarse when he spoke.

"You got home from the movies around eleven," he was saying.

Gibberish, she thought. He was regurgitating old gibberish.

"We've been through that," she said.

"For the record, Mrs. Campbell. I know you're upset." He paused and looked at his notebook. "Eleven. You found the apartment had been cleaned up. Then you found the doll in the mattress."

She nodded her head and looked at him. He had an accent of some kind—it might have been British, something in the way he exaggerated his *r* sounds. His eyes: she saw a hooded kind of sympathy in his eyes. A weary kindness.

"Somebody came here when we were out," she said. Did she sound hysterical? Deranged?

Eric flipped a cigarette into the sink, where it sizzled.

Then McDonald was sitting at the table facing her. She looked at him again and she wondered if Eric had told him about the shirt, because now she saw that the two were connected, even if the thread linking them was obscure. They *had* to be related; it couldn't have been otherwise. She glanced at Eric, who was massaging his eyelids in a tired fashion.

McDonald closed his notebook, tilted his chair back. "It's weird. I run into some pretty funny things, you know, but this one's weird. The more I think about it, the more it has the ring of some sick joke. Some people have a slightly bizarre sense of humor, Mrs. Campbell. Do you know anybody...anybody like that?"

She shook her head. Who did she know that would do such a thing? She found herself staring at Eric now. He was standing silently by the sink. The shirt—had he mentioned the shirt? Her lips were dry and she needed water but she didn't have the energy to ask for it. And the baby was kicking in a repetitive way, monotonously knocking against the womb.

"Try to think, Mrs. Campbell. Anybody—somebody who might bear you a grudge. Anybody who might be hostile toward you. Try to think."

She shook her head again. Nobody. She didn't have enemies. She'd never had enemies—any that she knew of anyhow. But how could you possibly tell what might lurk out there? She remembered the night she thought she saw someone watching her from the palm tree below, but how could she know? The imagination tricks. You stumble into coincidences involving black cars. You couldn't add up those things and come out with something sensible.

"I'm sorry," she said. Whispering.

"Somebody breaks in here—although 'breaks' is probably a strong word since I can't find a sign of anything being forced—somebody comes in here, takes the time to clean the place up, then cuts your bed open, steals the head of a doll, stuffs the doll inside a mattress—" He stopped now, as if he were exasperated. As he lit a cigarette, she looked beyond him a moment, and saw the headless doll lying there with its legs dangling over the side. Why did dolls seem so nightmarish? she wondered. Why did broken dolls seem so perfectly a part of some bad dream?

McDonald said, "How do I figure those events?"

It's your goddam job, she thought. It's what you're supposed to do for a living. She was looking at the slats of the blind again, glad to see daylight coming, pleased that the night was yielding—darkness wasn't what she needed now. She wanted light to flood everything even if it meant the draining force of heat. She could stand anything now but dark.

"Your husband says he can't see anything else missing. He made a quick check around. Nothing. So somebody goes to all this trouble to steal the head of an antique doll. It doesn't feel like theft to me, Mrs. Campbell. It doesn't feel like that at all. I put myself in the burglar's shoes—it's obvious what I'd take. Nice stereo. Prints. Jewels. I wouldn't waste my damn time cleaning and cutting and twisting a head off a doll. So where does that leave us?" He brought his chair forward and he smiled, a small sorrowful smile. "You know, if we were characters in some crime story, I'd say there was something inside the doll's head. Narcotics. Microdots. Who knows?"

She stared at him. She saw it was a weak joke, something to alleviate her tensions. Eric shifted slightly at the sink. Silent Eric. What was he brooding about?

McDonald was still smiling.

You're trying, she thought. I like you for at least trying to put me at ease. I'm sorry I can't respond. He finished his cigarette and fumbled around for an ashtray.

She said, "Did my husband tell you about the shirt?"

"Shirt?" The cop looked surprised.

Eric, why didn't you tell him?

Eric said, "I guess it slipped my mind with all this going on."

"So tell me about this shirt," McDonald said and folded his arms.

She told him.

When she was through he asked, "You still have the garment?"

"I threw it out."

He didn't say anything. He took a rubber band from a pocket and twisted it between thumb and finger like a slingshot. He might have been testing it for tension, elasticity. Finally he got up and moved toward the stove, looked at his watch, checked the time on the stove clock. He sighed in a weary way. "Unless we've got an impossible coincidence going on here, you've got to assume it's the same person. And this idiot is fond of coming into your apartment for the sole purpose, it seems, of bloody bad jokes."

He sounded angry all at once. *This idiot.* She liked his anger because it implied a lack of detachment, it meant he responded like a person who can't quite slip easily into his official role. A real person, she thought.

"Sick sick sick," he was saying. "Why didn't you tell me about the shirt, Mr. Campbell?"

"It slipped my mind in all the confusion—" Eric looked defensive, like a boy caught cheating during an exam.

"It would probably slip mine as well," the cop said.

He walked up and down. For a moment she felt he was on the edge of a revelation, one of those striking insights of detection in which all the clues fall tidily into place—but that belonged in books, for heaven's sake. It belonged in a world of master sleuths who spend most of their time cultivating orchids.

He looked at her for a time. "I want you to check your personal belongings carefully. Check your jewels. I want to know if anything of substance has been stolen. Then I want you to call me. I'm going to leave you my card, okay?" He turned to Eric and said, "As soon as the stores open I want you to go out and change the locks on the front door." Then his manner changed; he suddenly looked almost tender as he gazed at Ellen. "You should try and get some rest, Mrs. Campbell. I've got four of my own at home, so I've been through it. I know what it's like."

She watched him walk toward the hallway followed by Eric and realized she felt a sense of disappointment, anticlimax— was this all? Was there nothing more to it than this flimsy questioning, a couple of scratched notes, a card with a telephone number? What did you expect, Ellen? Immediate apprehension of the culprit?

He stopped at the front door and turned with a smile and said, "I shouldn't really be helping anybody by the name of Campbell, you know. I have this race memory of what happened in 1692."

"1692?" Eric asked.

"The Glencoe Massacre. Never heard of it? You don't know your ethnic history, Mr. Campbell. The Campbells slaughtered the McDonalds while they were sleeping. Your clan ancestors were a bloodthirsty lot. A systematic slaughter. Men. Women. Kids. It didn't matter to the Campbells."

"I never knew that," Eric said.

McDonald opened the door, still smiling. "You've got a lot to answer for," he said. "But don't worry about it now. Don't worry about anything now. Your wife needs some rest. I'll be in touch."

And then he was gone.

*   *   *

She went out to the balcony and watched McDonald walk across the parking lot; then she looked up at the sky—half dark, half light, the stars fading into a rust-colored dawn. There was no air; the morning was already lifeless, inert. When she went back indoors, she locked the balcony door. Eric was sitting on the sofa, hunched forward slightly, hands dangling between his legs. She looked at him: he was pale, drained. She sat down beside him and took his hand and he turned his face to look at her.

"He laid a little guilt on me, didn't he?" he said.

"McDonald?"

"When I forgot to mention the shirt business, I mean."

"You just overlooked it," she said. Why was she so suddenly calm? It might never have happened—the intruder, the violation of private space, the insane destruction of things. *Shirt buttons. The head of a doll.* What did these things mean? She might have been looking at an impossible crossword in which all the clues were in a language foreign to her. She stroked Eric's wrist.

"I shouldn't have overlooked it," he said.

Ellen rose from the sofa and walked across the room. It seemed to her she'd gone beyond fatigue, she'd reached the point people strangely called the second wind, a place where fatigue meets fatigue and weariness is somehow canceled out. At the bookshelf she stopped, about to raise her hand to touch the spines of volumes—she couldn't, she couldn't do it. That sense of violation assailed her again. *Somebody.* Somebody had touched these books, rearranged them. Straightened them up. She let her hand fall to her side and wondered if she would ever overcome the sense of having been raped, plundered, if the apartment would ever feel like home again.

She turned to look at Eric: "What makes somebody do...?" She let the question fall away helplessly.

Eric shrugged and stood up. She suddenly remembered something her mother had said: *Out there*... silently implying the monsters of the dark places. *Out there.* She watched the sun slide up, slicing the last remnants of night. She'd never been so glad to see the day start.

"I can't understand it," Eric said. "It's beyond me. It doesn't make sense. I think about it and it's so far outside the range of my experience I don't get any pictures."

She yawned. All at once the second wind was gone and what she felt now was a deep tiredness. She needed to sleep—but she knew she couldn't go back inside the bedroom, encounter the mattress. She didn't want to step back in that particular room. Eric had picked up the torso of the doll from the counter and was holding it in his hands. Twisted thing, a travesty, limp in his fingers. She closed her eyes—you get pictures behind your lids, you see a shadow closing a door, stepping inside your home, touching things, changing things, interfering in the private parts of your life, you get pictures that melt one into another and what they amount to is a wild and inexplicable series of superimposed snapshots.

She lay across the sofa, trying to force the images out of her mind. Eric went out of the room and after a few minutes came back with a sheet, which he draped over her.

"Where will you sleep?" she asked.

"The armchair," he said. "It's as good a place as any right now."

He kissed her lightly on the cheek.

She looked at him and tried to smile.

She realized they were trying to comfort each other, trying to find some mutual strength, a unified front, against whatever had so crudely entered their lives.

It was the first time in weeks and it was the worst she'd ever witnessed. She woke in bright daylight, abruptly, raising her face to see Eric twisting and turning in the armchair. His mouth was open, a dark oval, and his forehead was covered with the sweat of a fever. His damp hair stuck to his scalp, and his hands, hanging over the sides of the chair, were clenched tightly. He might have been holding something precious in those locked fists. She rose and crossed the floor to bend over him. The sounds he was making—a low kind of moaning you might associate with grief, the noise of a terrible loss.

She put her hand on his forehead. His sweat was chilly.

That noise. That sound.

Where was he, where might he be traveling, what was he observing across the landscape of his brain? Clouds, storms, eruptions—what awful things were going on inside? What awful things to which only he had access?

She tried to put her arms around him and somehow stop the twisting motions, but he was tense, muscled and hard.

Please, Eric. Come out of that place.

Come back from that nightmare.

She placed a hand over his open mouth. But she succeeded only in muffling the noise, not in silencing it.

He dragged his face away from beneath her hand, the edge of his teeth catching the padded flesh under her thumb—a slight pain, a faint line of blood rising out of the grids of her palm.

She placed both hands against the sides of his face and began to slap gently.

Unexpectedly, his eyes opened.

She saw only the blank whites. The whites, nothing else. Blank eyes. What are you looking at, Eric? Where are you?

Then the lids fell again.

She moved a few steps away from him.

Suddenly he was very still. His face looked peaceful. His hands became slack. For a moment she felt relieved, but then she realized his lips were moving, moving in a curiously stiff way, as if the mouth might have been attached to the face by hinges. He said something, something broken, spaced by pauses but audible nevertheless. Something in a voice barely his own, only vaguely recognizable.

He said: *The baby should live.*

He said.

He said.

She shut her eyes. The baby should live.

She opened her eyes when she felt his hand settle against her shoulder. He was staring at her wide-eyed, awake, looking for all the world like a man emerging from a normal refreshing sleep.

"It happened again," he said.

She nodded.

"Was it bad?"

"Yes."

"The strange thing is that I don't remember anything. I don't remember it at all."

He kissed her on the side of the mouth. His lips were as cold as the core of an ice cube.

The baby should live, she thought.

Was that the heart of his nightmare? Did it lie in some concealed anxiety about the birth of the child? Fear of death—a wild paternal concern over the vulnerability of the unborn infant. Was that what came in the darkness of his sleeping brain and haunted him so much? A dead baby.

She put her hand over her forehead. A dull pain raked her

skull. Was it something else, something other than a deep-
rooted concern? But what? You can think until your brain's
burned out. You can turn a thing over and over until you're
stuck in a maze of your own creation. Guilt, she thought
suddenly. Maybe there was some old guilt burning away
inside him somewhere—something he tried and tried to keep
hidden, a thing that rebelled against him through the sickness of a recurring dream. She didn't like this train of
thought, didn't want to entertain it. A dream comes back,
comes back again—did it boil down to some unanswerable
question of conscience?

Don't, Ellen. Don't do this to yourself. He's only concerned
with the unborn baby. It's perfectly natural. Perfectly in
order. Any father might feel the same, the same anxieties, the
same repressed fears.

And she laid her hands across her stomach and stroked
herself gently and thought: You'll live, darling. You'll live.
And all your father's bad dreams will fade forever.

She felt the child move inside her, an agreeable motion,
almost as if it were emphasizing its existence.

All the bad dreams will fade for good.

Ten   *July 22*

●●

She'd gone to answer the doorbell, imagining some ersatz
student peddling subscriptions or a pale young man with an
encyclopedia sample—instead, framed by the peephole, she
found the cop, looking as weary, as harried, as he'd been a
few nights ago.

A few nights ago, she thought.

How had she managed to deal with that episode? How had
she contrived to free her memory of it all?

*I haven't been able to set it aside, put it away in some
secure box of recollection, defuse it—it keeps coming back
like a bad taste in the throat—*

She saw the cop turn around and face her. He was working
the end of his thin tie between his fingers, rolling it up and
then releasing it, repeating the performance in a nervous
manner.

"I was in the neighborhood, Mrs. Campbell. I thought I'd drop in and see how you're getting along," he said. "I didn't want you to think I'd somehow overlooked you." He smiled in a shy way. "When are you due?"

"Early September. It's a rough estimate," she said. It was a comfort, she thought, to have the cop here.

He said, "I was a wee bit worried after the other night. I kept thinking about the things that happened."

She gazed at his hands. The fingers were stained with nicotine. What have you solved? she wondered. Found some vital clue? Discovered the body in the trunk? She watched McDonald move to the sofa: he didn't sit down.

"The plain truth is, Mrs. Campbell, the whole thing's got me puzzled. I've turned it this way. I've twisted it that way. And I can't come up with a damn thing." For a moment he looked despairing. "Did you check to see if anything else might be missing?"

"There's nothing," she said. "Nothing we've noticed anyhow."

"Did you think about your friends—I mean, did you think of anybody who might be playing some kind of joke on you?"

A joke? Why the hell wasn't it funny then? She shook her head. "I don't have many friends, Mr. McDonald. And the few I do have don't strike me as practical jokers."

McDonald sighed and took a draw on his cigarette. Ash spilled down the front of his jacket. He ignored it. She imagined him creating stains wherever he went, spilling coffee, beer, overturning bottles of ink. Somehow this ignorance of self, this clumsiness, was endearing: he reminded her in certain ways of an awkward adolescent. She couldn't imagine him dancing with his wife without stepping on the woman's toes.

"Your husband changed the lock?" he asked.

She nodded. "The morning after you were here."

"Good. Good." He appeared to withdraw inside himself for a time, shrinking into his own silence. "Have you always locked up this place before you went out?"

"I think so," she said.

"The reason I ask is I couldn't find any sign of forced entry the other night. Whoever did come here must have used a key. Either that or the door was left unlocked."

"How could anybody get a key? There are only two—"

A look of mild irritation crossed his face. "Why does everybody always assume that a specific number of keys exist to their home? It bewilders me. In my experience I've found that there's usually another key nobody ever thought about. The key everybody forgot. For instance, what about the custodian of these apartments? He would have a passkey, right? And what if an apartment came up for sale or rent, a realtor would have a key, right?"

"I guess—"

"Somebody could have stolen the key, made a copy of it, and replaced it before it was missed. I'm not saying that's what happened, you understand. I'm only pointing out the possibility of extra keys. You lock yourself up at night and you think you're safe and secure and snug as a bug in a rug—but you overlook the accessibility of keys, Mrs. Campbell. Everybody does. You're no exception."

She suddenly imagined him standing in front of a group of housewives, delivering a lecture on home security. She saw him gesticulating, growing serious, pointing out the menace of The Hidden Key. Prowlers in the shrubbery, shadows under palms—nobody was ever safe, ladies, *nobody*. Custodians and realtors. *Vicky*, she thought. But Vicky hadn't been the agent on this apartment. Vicky hadn't been involved in this particular sale.

McDonald said, "I don't like mysteries. I don't like slashed shirts and sliced mattresses and broken dolls. Sometimes I have to remind myself we live in a world filled with mysteries that haven't ever been solved. Nobody ever found Judge Crater, did they? Nobody's ever been able to explain why frogs and crabs can fall out of the sky, have they? We peel away as much as we can but there's still a core of mystery."

Frogs and crabs and Judge Crater, she thought. She looked at the cop and she asked: "Is that how you categorize my affair? Along with Judge Crater and crabs and things that go bump in the night?"

He made a quirky little gesture with his hand: he might have been directing traffic through an intersection with a broken signal. "I didn't say that, did I? People always think that a cop's work involves mysteries, Mrs. Campbell. Mysteries and solutions. That's only sometimes. Usually I find myself buried in reports. Suffocated in paperwork. The more paperwork there is, the less likely the solution." He paused, smiled: "Sorry. I get off on tangents."

She sat down on the sofa.

McDonald said, "Has anything else unusual happened since I saw you last?"

She shook her head. "Unless it's something I haven't noticed."

He looked at his watch, an old-fashioned thing on a chain he took from the pocket of his pants. "I've got a meeting to attend," he said. "I just wanted you to know you haven't been forgotten, if that's worth anything. I'll keep in touch. Remember to call me if. . ." He stopped, his face brightening, and he reached inside the pocket of his jacket. He took something out and held it toward her. It was a small packet. A little puzzled, she took it.

"I was telling my wife about you," he said. "She asked me to drop this off when I came around. She recommends it highly for relaxation."

"It's very kind of you. And her."

"She says it saved her life when she was pregnant. Helped her unwind."

Ellen looked at the package. *Chamomile tea*. "I'll certainly try it," she said.

"She said to brew yourself a good strong cup if you can't sleep."

"Will you thank her for me?"

"I'll do that."

Now he moved toward the hallway. At the front door he turned around and said, "Call me if you need to."

"I will," she said. Chamomile tea: it was the thought that counted.

He smiled and then he was gone, leaving behind a scent of old tobacco smoke and the whisper of his crumpled jacket as it touched the wall.

Late in the afternoon she went reluctantly for her monthly afternoon tea with her mother—a ritual tea, a habit her mother had apparently picked up during a trip to London long ago. The location never varied: it was always in the restaurant of a hyperexpensive department store in Scottsdale, an ambience of white latticework and ferns that seemed to invigorate Ellen's mother. Ellen parked the Opel and hurried toward the squat gray building through the permanent barrage of sunshine. Her mother was already in place and looking like some frail ornament, her iron-gray walker parked next to the table.

As soon as Ellen slid into her seat her mother said, "You look awful, dear."

Ellen didn't answer at once. She watched her mother pour tea—she watched the marvelous flick of the wrist to which the teapot was attached, the fluid gesture of those accustomed to the act of pouring. No splashes, leaks, spills. All the social graces were intact.

"Have you been eating and sleeping properly, Ellen?"

"It's hard to sleep sometimes," Ellen said. "Dragging this body around through the heat isn't exactly a barrel of laughs either."

"I can understand that. Is anything else troubling you?"

The question was asked almost hopefully. Ellen looked at her mother's face: *she's waiting for me to say, Everything's wrong, I need your help, Mother . . .* I might never have grown up. I might never have grown up and married and conceived this child. She reached for her tea and sipped it. A swirl of pale cream floated on the surface. She looked around the restaurant. All the women at other tables—most of them with their pinkies upraised in the act of drinking—looked alike, pressed out of the same mold: older versions, she thought, of Eric's desert clones.

"There are circles under your eyes. Your hair's dull. You look ragged, Ellen."

"I'm *pregnant*, Mother. I'm not exactly on display, you know. I'm not a mannequin for maternity wear."

"I'm only concerned about you, Ellen dear. Mothers have their concerns, you know." She reached out and lightly tapped the back of Ellen's hand. Her fingertips were cold. "Mothers see more than people suppose. Are you sure there isn't something you want to tell me?"

Shirts and dolls and a clean apartment, she thought. You open that particular box in front of your mother—and—presto— she'd have the Federal Bureau of Investigation camping on your balcony. She'd interfere, all in the name of maternal concern. She stared at some dainty cookies on a tray: they looked like ethereal flowers. She was tempted to try one, certain that if she did it would crumble between her fingers. They were the kind of cookies that might be lifted only if you were wearing surgical gloves.

The older woman said, "Mothers and children must maintain a certain closeness, Ellen. You'll find out soon enough."

Pause. The deceptively frail jaws munched a cookie. "Have you tried hot milk at bedtime? It would relax you, dear."

"I hate hot milk—"

"We frequently hate the things that are good for us."

I daresay, Ellen thought. She wondered if her mother were a movable compendium of pithy utterances.

"You always *did* hate hot milk, Ellen. But then you had a stubborn streak in you even as a child. You liked to go your own way regardless. A certain headstrong quality."

Please, Ellen thought. Not some nostalgic narrative which would invariably turn out to be a mixture of half-remembered facts and fabricated fancies. A memory of taffeta dresses and dance classes and piano lessons and Things That Might Have Been. She felt the child press against her, the sudden sharpness of what might have been a knee. *The baby should live,* she thought. And it crossed her mind all over again: Somebody moving around the empty apartment, prying, probing violently, perhaps even now as she sat here pointlessly with her mother. But the lock had been changed and there were only two keys and Eric had the other. Two keys.

"You do seem nervous, dear. Don't take that as a criticism. You seem upset. Your hand's shaking."

"I don't feel nervous, Mother," Ellen said.

Ellen's mother sighed. "I'll ask you directly. I am not prying—but is everything well in the state of your marriage?"

"What do you mean?"

"When I see my daughter look so... *shopworn*... I wonder if things are well back at the hearth, so to speak."

The hearth? It was quaint and certain to become quainter.

"There's *nothing* wrong. I think you look for things that don't exist, Mother." *Sometimes I think you'd like to see this marriage fall apart, dammit.* Then you could mother me and console me and say *I told you so*.

"Even if there were, Ellen, I doubt if you'd tell me."

Ellen stared at her mother. That look of pain: it was so melodramatic it was almost funny. That feigned look of hurt that implied: *That's right, leave me out of your life, it's none of my business anyhow, I'm only your mother, I only happened to carry you for nine long painful months.* She felt suddenly exhausted, wearied by weather, by pregnancy, by the imposing company of her mother. She watched the older woman's hand cover her wrist.

"I love you, dear," she said. "I'm sorry if I show it in all the wrong ways."

A front-running candidate for martyrdom: *I'm sorry if I show it in all the wrong ways.*

"It isn't that, Mother. It's just sometimes..."

"Sometimes what?" The arched eyebrows, the waiting expression on the face.

"Sometimes I think you'd like it if I hadn't ever left home. If I hadn't ever married. Sometimes I think you dwell too much on what I used to be and don't think enough about what I am now."

"Did I ever say such things?"

"Not in so many words, Mother—"

"Then you're reading between lines which most certainly do not exist, Ellen. I happen to think you might have married better—but that isn't my business. My business is your happiness. That's all I'm interested in."

It was odd, Ellen thought: Martyrdom had the effect of a strong downer. Her eyelids were becoming heavy.

"And if Eric makes you happy, then that's fine with me."

"He does, Mother. Honestly. He makes me happy." What am I doing? she wondered. I might be standing in front of a judge and pleading my emotional case. I don't *need* to do this.

"I hardly know him—"

"You should get to know him better," Ellen said.

"I suppose I should." Her mother seemed to drift away now, seemed to be recalling something. Then her lips became tight, drawn into one distended line as if they had been stitched together. "On the other hand, he might make an attempt to get to know *me* better."

But you shut him out, she thought. You haven't exactly welcomed him with open arms, have you? You haven't gone out of your way to make him feel good. Instead, you've looked down at him. You've disapproved of him. All because he wasn't born into what passes, in your own quaint way, as a certain social class.

Suddenly her mother said, "When you first announced your intended marriage, my first impulse... my first impulse was to hire a private detective to check his background."

"A what?"

"I didn't go ahead with it, of course. One does not want outsiders involved in family affairs, after all."

A *private detective*. It was squalid and disgusting. A private eye legging his way through Eric's life, sifting the actions, sorting out the events. How could her mother have ever considered such a thing? How? She felt angry all at once: this sordid little confession of her mother's—was this her mother's notion of love, of concern?

"I find it disgusting," Ellen said. "I can't believe you."

"My dear, I didn't go ahead with it."

"You thought about it, though—"

"Not for long—"

"How long is long, Mother? It's the thought, goddammit."

"Don't swear, Ellen. And please keep your voice down."

"Afraid I'll upset the matrons in here? Worried I'll cause anxiety attacks to the dowagers?"

"You're overwrought, dear—"

"A private detective, Christ! I find it hard to believe you even considered such a thing."

"I was trying to be honest, Ellen."

Honest, sure. Coming clean. Easing your conscience. *If this is mother love, it provides good groundwork for arguments in favor of matricide*. She pushed her chair away from the table.

"I think I'll go home, Mother."

"Ellen, dear, you shouldn't be disappointed in me. After all, I only considered such a possibility. The fact that I didn't put it into effect is surely something in my favor?"

"Yes," Ellen said. "It's something in your favor. I just wish I knew what."

"At least I told you the truth."

"For which I thank you."

Ellen turned away. She heard the heels of her sandals scuffling across the thick rug. A private eye, she thought. It was awful, it was dreadful to realize that her own mother had contemplated such a step.

But she didn't actually *do* it, Ellen.

She only thought it.

And you'd crucify her for her thoughts?

Don't be so hard on her. Don't ride her so roughly.

Outside, the sun scorched the day, laid it to waste.

She crossed the parking lot and saw her mother's maroon Bentley slide alongside her, Hattie Dalrymple at the wheel. What did Hattie do? Did she just cruise around in the heat, waiting for her employer to return? It didn't seem like much of a life to Ellen and, for a moment, she felt sorry for the woman. Hattie braked and rolled the window down. I can't stop and talk, Ellen thought. It's too hot, too stifling.

"You need a ride anywhere?" Hattie asked.

"I'm just walking to my car—"

"Walking? You looked like you were about to break into a sprint, Ellen."

"The heat. I can't stand it."

"The heat from your mother, you mean?"

Ellen smiled half-heartedly. She wondered how much Hattie understood about the lack of a relationship between her mother and Eric, how much had been explained to her. There was a knowing look on Hattie's face, an expression that made Ellen feel uncomfortable. She shifted her weight from foot to foot. In the distance she could see the Opel.

"One day," Hattie said. "One day, who knows?"

The enigmatic comment seemed to hang in the air.

"One day they might get used to each other."

"And cows might fly, Hattie."

Hattie looked away for a moment, apparently locked into a thought. When she turned once more to face Ellen she was smiling. "You should drag your husband around to the house sometime, Ellen. You should have them confront each other. Sometimes you need to let a little daylight in, you know?"

Ellen shrugged. She felt like a plump, wilted plant in the heat. The Opel seemed to recede in the distance. Another illusion of light.

"What do you think your husband would say to that idea?" Hattie asked—asked in such a way it was obvious she didn't expect an answer.

"I hate to think," Ellen said.

Hattie gazed at her for a while: "I better let you get to your car before you melt, Ellen."

Ellen raised a hand in a tired way as Hattie rolled up the window. The Bentley slipped away. She hurried as fast as she might across the lot, reached the Opel, and got inside. The interior of the car was like a blacksmith's forge. This hell, she thought. This heat, this hell.

You think: They changed the lock. They changed the lock on the door. It was probably her suggestion. He wouldn't ever want to shut you out. Not him, not ever. You laugh. The idea

*of it. Something as simple as a lock could never keep you out
of his heart. Bars and bolts and padlocks could never keep
you from where you really belonged.*

Not even straitjackets.

*Suddenly an old memory turns inside you, makes you
squirm. Your arms grow stiff. Your hands feel paralyzed.*

Straitjackets.

But nothing can keep you away from him.

*You don't need to dwell on the past. You realize this. You
bring his face back into your mind and you understand there
is a future ahead, a future for both of you.*

*You hardly feel the heat of the day now. The sun might not
exist. It might have exploded. And everything in the parking
lot around you might have evaporated. All you are conscious
of is the singular, wrenching feeling of hatred as you watch
her drag her fat self toward her car.*

Suffer, bitch.

But she hasn't really suffered yet, has she?

Ellen lay on the bed and felt the stream of the air conditioner.
She needed to calm down. She needed routine, ordinariness,
She'd taken off her dress and parted her legs so that the cool
draft moved directly across her belly. She wanted to sleep
and yet at the same time find enough energy to get up and
make it to the kitchen, prepare something for Eric's supper.
Eventually, she forced herself to rise and go look inside the
refrigerator where she found some hamburger meat which
she molded lazily in the vague shape of a meatloaf. As she
stuck it in the oven, she heard the front doorbell ringing.

Her eye to the peephole, careful now, she saw the face of
Anna Rosenberg faintly distorted by the lens. Puzzled, she
opened the door. The girl, her yellow hair held back by black
clips which gave her the look of a 1940s singer—one of a trio,
Ellen thought—was wearing a swimsuit and faded sneakers.
She looked older somehow than Ellen had seen her before.
The Andrews Sisters hairstyle maybe; whatever, she appeared
to be in her middle twenties rather than her late teens.

"Hi, Ellen." Chewing gum: a faint flash of pink in the open
mouth. Ellen was suddenly conscious of the fact that she was
wearing only a slip, a flimsy silken thing that did nothing to
disguise her shape.

"This is a surprise," Ellen said. She held the door wider,

tried the impossible task of tightening her stomach muscles, hauling her belly in. This girl is affecting me again, getting to me.

"You don't mind, do you? I mean, I guess I thought I'd just kinda look in on you, see how you're doing."

"It's nice of you," Ellen said as the girl passed her, stepped into the hallway, and moved toward the living room as if she knew where to go. But of course she'd *know* where the living room was—her own apartment was probably a duplicate of this one. Ellen followed her slowly. The slip, goddam—why hadn't she thought to pull on a robe or some clothing?

Anna Rosenberg was standing in the middle of the living-room floor. For a moment, as if she were absentmindedly doing a ballet exercise, she stood poised on one leg. Then she looked around the room almost in the manner of a person seeking something in particular. She stared at the rows of books and then moved toward the stereo system.

"Hey, this is good stuff." She stroked the black plastic lid of the phonograph.

"Eric chose it. He's the one who goes for all that kind of thing," Ellen said.

"He's got great taste. This is a fine sound system." The girl turned a knob and after a moment there was the sound of classical music coming from an FM channel. Ellen thought she recognized it as something modern, maybe by Bartok, maybe Schoenberg. She wasn't sure. She watched the girl flick the off switch. "Real nice. Does he listen to classical music much?"

"Eric? Sometimes. It depends on his mood." Why do you want to know about my husband? Why do you have to ask questions about him? Ellen stared at the flashing color of the girl's hair, the whiteness of the smile. She realized now that it was almost impossible to guess the girl's age—she might have been between seventeen and twenty-seven. Maybe the sun had begun to eat away at her skin, dry her out.

"I'm mostly into rock, I guess," the girl said. "I figure the classical bit is out of my range." She shrugged and looked at Ellen a moment, eyes seeming to drop to the swollen stomach: that expression, Ellen wondered—what was it precisely? A vague look of triumph? Was this desert queen mentally contrasting her own slim shape with Ellen's fatness?

"I see your husband now and again," the girl said. "He's pretty friendly."

"I'm glad," Ellen said. *Pretty friendly.* How could she interpret that one?

"He always says hi when I 'see him," Anna Rosenberg said. "Nice."

The girl was silent for a time, looking at the books on the shelves. If any of the titles meant anything to her, if they had any significance, she didn't say so. Instead, she reached up and took the clips from her hair and tossed her head so that the fullness of her hair spread across her shoulders. Ellen watched with some dismay: she had magnificent hair. It was almost the color of the sun itself.

"What kind of work does he do?"

"He helps raise money for charities," Ellen said.

"Yeah? Like he works for some kind of foundation?"

"Something like that."

"Downtown?"

"Downtown, right," Ellen said. Question and answer time. This kid, she thought—this girl appears to have a crush on Eric. It was obvious now that she hadn't come to the apartment to see how Ellen was doing—rather, she was here to steal some insights into Eric's life.

"I never go downtown," the girl said. "It's a drag. Traffic. Weather. Everybody moves like the world's going to end the next minute, you know? Hurry here, hurry there. I kinda like to sit back and take my time."

And smell the flowers, Ellen thought.

Anna Rosenberg moved around the room. "I like the way you've got this place done up. It feels good. Warm, hospitable. I enjoy that I get feelings about places as soon as I enter them. That happen to you?"

"Oh, all the time," Ellen said.

The girl stopped by the balcony door. She looked out, apparently in the direction of the swimming pool. Maybe she's looking for Eric, Ellen thought; maybe she's going to hang out here long enough until Eric gets back.

"Does he raise a lot of money?"

"I think he's pretty good at what he does," Ellen said.

"I figured he would be," the girl said and turned her face and smiled—an ambiguous smile, Ellen thought, the kind of look that might easily hide some thin double-entendre.

Ellen was quiet for a time. Suddenly the other presence in the apartment was stifling to her; suddenly she wanted to be on her own. An excuse, make an excuse. For a moment she couldn't think of anything except for the single notion that spun round and round in her head like a gerbil trapped in a wheel. *This girl is interested in your husband. This girl is openly and blatantly interested in your husband.* She also felt defenseless, stripped of emotional weapons, devoid of sexual attractiveness—in her slip she perceived herself as drab. The portcullis is up, the enemy is crossing the drawbridge, the guards have abandoned the turrets—and the falling castle is my marriage. Good Christ, Ellen, what are you thinking? Eric has no interest in this mindless little thing. Eric couldn't *possibly* have any interest. She rubbed her stomach.

"Anna—would you think me rude if I went for my afternoon nap? Doctor's orders." Ellen felt herself smile. "You know what physicians are like."

For a second, the girl appeared disappointed. Then she brightened and moved toward the hallway—a light-footed movement, almost a skip. "Say, if you need anything, if there's anything I can do for you, I live in C-sixteen. Drop in sometime. I'm usually home."

Ellen followed her toward the front door. "That's very kind of you, Anna. I'll remember that."

The girl opened the front door, stepped out, looked back with a white smile. (She polishes those teeth, Ellen thought. Or she must paint them with a glossy white. You don't come by that kind of shine naturally, do you?)

"See you around," she said.

"See you," Ellen answered. She closed the front door and leaned against it a moment, wondering why the presence of the girl had been such a strain.

Suddenly she resented herself, her own wild thoughts, suddenly she resented her puffed-up appearance. Soon, Ellen, soon. Then you can go flaunt your slim new shape around the pool and show Anna Rosenberg something she doesn't even suspect exists—to wit, an attractive woman underneath this bulging slip, beneath all this unruly hair and drained appearance. Soon now.

When the telephone rang, she reached for it awkwardly, cradling it against her ear as she twisted to the side to peer at the meatloaf. (A private detective, she thought. The memory still galled her, needled her.)

For a moment she didn't understand the voice at the other end. It was a woman's voice, light and pleasant, a voice

accustomed to clipped economy of speech, efficient and yet
melodic. The woman asked to speak with Mr. Campbell.

"He isn't home yet," Ellen said.

"Oh." The woman seemed surprised.

"I can take a message for him."

There was a silence. Ellen imagined she'd said something
wrong, transgressed in some way. She wasn't sure how.

"Are you his wife?"

"Yes." Why was that important? Why did she have to be
Eric's wife to be capable of taking a simple message?

"Can you tell him that Dr. Ely won't be able to meet with
him tomorrow afternoon? Can you tell him that?"

"Dr. who?"

"Ely. *E, l, y* as in young. Can you give him that message,
Mrs. Campbell?"

"Of course."

"Dr. Ely would like him to call and make another
appointment."

"I'll tell him."

"Thank you." And then the line was cut abruptly, as if what
had been transacted were of national importance, a matter of
top-level security. Ellen put the telephone down, opened the
oven door, stared at the sorry meatloaf. Dr. Ely, she thought.
She hadn't heard Eric ever mention that name before; she
hadn't even heard him say anything about an appointment
with a physician. What was wrong with him? She wondered if
perhaps it had something to do with the strain Ralph Houseman had spoken about—but Eric had talked all that away as
being Houseman's own anxieties. What then? Irritated for
some reason, she slammed the oven door shut and experienced a strange sense of dread all at once, as if she'd
stumbled across a secret fact of Eric's life, a feeling as intense
and as unsettling as the one that had accompanied his tiny
lie. It was like pulling the petals of a daisy—*you know this
man, you don't know this man, you know this man, you don't
know him*. It was like pulling the pieces of the plant away and
allowing the randomness of the wind to provide you with an
answer.

She sat down at the kitchen table.

Dr. Ely.

Who the hell was Dr. *E, l, y* as in young anyhow?

Ely. Ely. Ely.

Eric was home. She heard him whistle monotonously, and

then he was in the kitchen, dropping his briefcase at the entrance. She looked at him, pleased to see him and yet troubled by his appearance in a way she didn't like. He undid the knot of his tie and leaned down to kiss her on the cheek.

"What's up?" he asked.

"Why do you ask that?"

"I don't know. You look. . ." He shrugged, opened the oven door, glanced inside. She watched the light bulb go on and off automatically.

"How do I look?"

"Like you always do when it's tea-with-Mama day. She give you the usual hard time, huh?"

"More than usual." She rose from the table and awkwardly opened the refrigerator and looked inside. She had a sense of things moldering unseen, penicillin taking shape beneath the vegetable crispers. What am I doing looking inside this thing anyhow? What do I expect to find? She felt Eric touch her shoulders and then gently message the muscles.

"You're uptight. You're tense," he said.

"*I'm* tense?"

"You feel that way. Your body betrays you, babe. Maybe you should quit those monthly monstrosities for a while?"

"Maybe I should." I'm being foolish and sullen, she thought. I'm acting like a brat, a spoiled housewife. I'm allowing the possibility of a secret to tear away at myself. She swung around and faced him. His hands fell to his sides.

"Are you sick, Eric?"

He laughed. "Not that I know about—"

"Then why are you seeing a doctor?"

"What doctor?"

"*E, l, y* as in young. Ely. El*ee*. However you say it. Why are you seeing a doctor?"

He touched the bridge of his nose in a nervous way. Then he went to the sink and filled a glass with water. "It's nothing. In fact, I almost forgot about it." He gulped the water quickly at the sink. "My eyes," he said. "It's an appointment about my eyes. I've been having trouble lately with my vision, so I figured I needed glasses. I almost forgot."

"What's *wrong* with your eyes?"

"When I read I sometimes get headaches. Sometimes my eyesight seems to blur. I thought I'd get it checked out. Did Ely's office call or something?"

"A canceled appointment. They want you to get in touch."

"Okay." He sat at the kitchen table. He looked so handsome to her suddenly that he appeared almost pretty, a description she'd never associated with him before. She realized she was filled with an abrupt desire, something that fired her mind, made her wish her body could find a way to satisfy.

He reached for her hand and held it, fingertips rubbing the spaces between her knuckles. She raised her free hand and laid that palm flat against the side of his face.

She said, "I was surprised you didn't mention this doctor before. I don't know what I imagined. Maybe I thought you were ill and you weren't telling me."

He laughed and drained his water glass, then set it down on the table. "What you need to do, my love, is pin up a memo pad on the wall. Then I can write down everything that crops up before I forget to tell you."

Was he being facetious? She stared at him, decided he wasn't. "I like to know things, Eric. I like to be kept in touch."

"I'll make sure in the future," he answered.

"I hate to feel excluded. Worse than that, I hate to *admit* I feel excluded. Does that make sense?"

"Somehow." he said.

"It's just one more of the general inconveniences of being in my condition. I'm beat and I whine and I'm up to here with insecurities—and I'm not even talking about our insane intruder, Eric." Could you make light of that one? she wondered. Could you look forward to a day when you'd sit down together and laugh at the intrusions, the trespasses, the violence? "How can you put up with me?"

"I love you. It's easy."

"You're sure?"

"Actually, I'm sitting here making it all up."

She smiled and checked the meatloaf, which had assumed the shape and appearance of a muddy football. "Another thing. I can't cook worth a damn these days."

"Some things don't change."

He was standing by the table with his empty glass in his hand. He was watching her, a light in his eyes that was unmistakable, one of deep affection, of love. I could glow and explode in that light, she thought. I could glow and swell and take form like malleable glass.

He loves me.

No mistake.

Eleven   *July 26*

Someone held her hand. She felt her knuckles become tight. The bones might break through the thin flesh. She dug with her fingernails into the skin of the other's hand. Overhead, some kind of light glared, the kind of light you saw in movies where somebody was interrogated by unscrupulous forces. The heat from this light was concentrated, burning on her skin. And between her legs—

Between her legs there was the most awful sensation she'd ever felt, the sensation of a hot needle piercing the fragile skin over the pubic bone and somehow she knew she was bleeding, she had to be bleeding, otherwise why would something wet and sticky be sliding down the insides of her legs? She screwed her eyes up against the light. She wanted to say: *Please turn the light away from me, it's hurting my eyes*—but then she realized the salty dryness of her mouth made speech impossible. Her gums were numb. Her teeth seemed not to exist. She tried to move her tongue around the inside of her mouth but it was inflexible, stiff, as if anesthetized.

The room was tiled in white. She could see that much beyond the blaze of the overhead lamp. Then something was clamped hard across her face. Oxygen—was that it? *Breathe, Ellen. Breathe deeply.* For a time she relaxed, felt good, floating away from the table upon which she lay.

Push, Ellen, push push push harder give it all you've got, dear. The voice was Nurse Grabowski's.

And then she heard Phelps talking in the background someplace. There was the sound of rubber gloves being pulled tight over skin, a rasping noise. And the nurse was smiling down at her: *Premature. It doesn't matter. We're old hands at this kind of thing, Ellen.*

Premature.

The pain was the pain of the baby emerging.

She could see Phelps working between her upraised legs. She could see shadows thrown on the ceiling by her knees, sharp shadows.

Premature and *push*.

It doesn't matter and *push*.

We're old hands and *push*.

The oxygen was taken away. And she was still gripping the hand of whoever it was that sat beside her. Gripping, digging. It was neither Phelps nor Grabowski. It wasn't Eric's hand either.

Who was sitting just behind her, where she couldn't see? Who was holding her hand?

She felt Grabowski mop her forehead with a damp cloth.

The masked face of the nurse. Phelps, too, wore a mask.

They looked different in masks, like fugitives from a fancy-dress ball. A suspicion crossed her mind that they weren't Phelps and Grabowski at all, but imposters come to steal her child away.

Where's Eric? Why isn't Eric here in the delivery room? Did she ask that aloud?

Grabowski said, *Your husband's coming, Ellen. He's on his way. Push harder and we'll have a little surprise for him when he gets here, huh?*

Push. Try to concentrate. Push downward as hard as you can. Why isn't Eric here to help me through this suffering, all this pain? Why is he late?

And who the hell is holding my hand?

She heard herself scream, imagined flesh tearing open, skin breaking away from muscle and bone and vein, imagined blood running between her legs and the pale white of bone protruding from a surface of red. An amputation, a limb lost, something cut forever from the body, a thing that couldn't be replaced even by the most advanced prosthesis. Baby baby baby—help me, come out of me, take this pain away.

I can see the head, Ellen. A few more pushes. A few more.

She forced her body in the air, hips lifted up as if for the act of sex, the exquisite anguish of the orgasm—and the pain scissored through her like metal slicing paper. How could that scream come from her, from any human being? They gave her oxygen again. Briefly, too briefly.

She closed her eyes. Her scalp sweated; hair stuck to her brow. The baby—why was there still this goddam pain?

Someone might have taken a blade and sliced her down
there: episiotomy, of course, that was the name of the operation. They slashed a line under your body so the baby's head
wouldn't rip you open. Blood—she'd been right, then. A lot
of blood. Distantly she thought she heard a baby cry.

And then she knew the room was empty, as empty as her
body. Whoever had been holding her hand was gone. Phelps
and Grabowski had gone also. The light still blinded her.
Why in the name of Christ was the room empty? Where was
the baby?

A door opened.

Phelps stood there. He was holding a child in his arms.

Something is wrong. Something is horribly wrong, she
thought.

Phelps was frowning at her. The child he held was wrapped
in a shawl. A name tag dangled from under the shawl.

*I don't think you'd want to see the baby, Ellen. I really
don't think you'd want to hold it.*

Why did her heart stop, her pulses run down to silence?

Something shaped like a blood clot clung to the back of her
throat. Viscous, mucuslike.

Phelps said: *Sometimes these things happen, Ellen. We
don't know why.*

What things what things?

Swirling. Dust clouds. Falling through the vast vacancy of
space—

A genetic freak, Ellen.

She stared at the misshapen thing Phelps held. The eyes,
unseeing, seemed to look at her with the pity of a small
creature on the way to the abattoir. Its head was tilted to one
side, level with its small shoulders. The body was covered
with glistening blood and mucus. The arms hung uselessly
loose. The torso sagged forward without support. Implosion—it
was the only word that came to her mind. A terrible word,
implosion. The child was caving in, torso slack and loose and
floppy, skin sagging and spreading, ribcage falling forward
and pressing directly on the flesh so that it made it bulge.

Born without a spine, Phelps said.

Without a spine. Without. The head swung, dropped,
hung in a posture of death. But the eyes were still alive, still
watching her blindly, imploringly. Jesus, Jesus.

Needles. The acupuncture of grief.

Impossible. It doesn't happen like this.

My baby.

My *baby*.

She found herself fighting for air, struggling, trying to raise herself from the table. The world can't be so savage, so without mercy, kindness, so fucking *unjust*. How can it be like that?

She put a hand to her throat. Constriction. Can't swallow. Choking. Then panic becomes a whirlpool and you're drawn down into it and sucked toward some turbulent sea floor where the silt swirls endlessly. She kicked. She thrust the bedsheets aside with her foot.

Eric had his arms around her. He was saying something flip, something amusing.

Don't you think it's enough to have one bad dreamer in this family? You trying to steal my limelight?

The baby, she thought. What happened to the baby?

She sat up in the bed. The palms of her hands adhered to the bedsheets. *The baby died*.

She heard Eric move just behind her. His hands began to lightly massage her shoulders. She closed her eyes. Sunlight and confusion. What happened to the child?

She placed her hands over her stomach. There was a sudden rippling motion in her womb, like the lazy glide of a fish through clear water. Oh, baby, baby.

She lay down.

"You want to tell me about it?" Eric said.

A sick dream. A nightmare. A treacherous substance spun out by the sleeping mind—it envelops you, turns illusion to reality, perverts all the facts of the physical world. *Nightmare*. She looked at her husband. She had a feeling now of two flimsy realities on a collision course, two sets of laws governing worlds equally substantial.

"How bad was it?"

"Awful. The worst."

"I tried to wake you. You were shouting about something. You scared me for a moment, Ellen."

She looked into his concerned eyes. She felt his hand clasp hers. Without warning, you simply step across a line into terror manufactured by the wild chemicals of your brain. You create your own theater of violence. The sight of that wretched baby—

"I guess I'm scared," she said. "That's the bottom line. I'm plain scared. I'm scared about the baby. I'm scared of the other things that have been happening. Sometimes I can cope with it all, I can fight most of the anxieties... but when my defenses are down I don't have any control over them."

Like your own nightmares, Eric. Just like your own.

"Phelps said fears concerning the baby were perfectly natural, didn't he? Didn't he tell you that?"

"That doesn't altogether help."

She suddenly thought of the mattress on which they were lying, half-expecting to slide her hand down several inches and encounter the gash—but they'd bought a new one since then, they'd thrown the old one away. Why did she still expect to find her fingers touching the slit? An old memory that wouldn't go away, a stain across everything. Let it go, she thought, let the dream go, let the memory of violence go. Let it all slide away somewhere and be lost. Then she shivered. A spine. Without a spine. You don't know where the images come from or what inspires them or why the familiar faces of Phelps and Grabowski suddenly shift and change and everything becomes charged with the magnetism of menace. The baby rippled inside her. She thought: *You're* not the nightmare baby, kid. You're going to be born in first-class condition. They're going to give you a blue ribbon as the prettiest baby in the maternity ward. They're going to give you a prize. She rubbed her stomach with slow circular motions and she wondered if you could convey love to an unborn baby, if you could send vibrations of caring through the strata of skin and into the womb itself.

Eric placed an arm around her shoulder. "You sure you're okay?"

"You know what dreams are like, Eric. They fade. Then you begin to wonder why they terrified you so badly." She shrugged and smiled a weak smile. (The dream-child's pained eyes. How long before that faded?)

She rose from the bed and went to the window. It would be easier to forget the nightmare than the memory of someone entering this room; it would be far easier to forget that. And already, mercifully, the dream was beginning to fall apart, images becoming shredded.

She turned to look at Eric.

She said, "I love you."

He smiled at her: "I love you too."

*   *   *

You open the tiny metal box.

Inside you see nine round blue buttons.

Count them. Seven, eight, nine. Nine blue buttons.

You look at the face of the doll. Pretty. Pretty to look at.

The claw of your hammer goes down down and the pieces of shattered china skitter away from you and you gather them up. Gather them up neatly. Then you sit down, breathing hard.

You forget for a moment. A clean apartment. It wasn't clean before. Slut, slut. Don't forget. Don't forget the other things you still have to do. Don't let them slip your mind.

The other things.

The other things you have to do for Eric.

Part Two

The Eighth Month

Twelve   August 5

It was the call from the girl in Eric's office that made her rush
to the Opel and drive into downtown Phoenix through gas
fumes and paralyzing heat and maddeningly sluggish early-
evening traffic. Crawling along Camelback Mountain, tapping
her fingers on the rim of the wheel, feeling sweat streak her
face—it was dreadful to sit at the center of this urban insanity
and wonder about her husband and the call from the girl.

I don't want to worry you, Mrs. Campbell . . .

It was the kind of line she might have imagined hearing in
the dead of night, a call from some soft-voiced solicitous cop
with an awful duty to perform. (*He's dead. I don't know any
other way to tell you.*)

What? What is it? Is something wrong?

The girl had paused and the line seemed dead a moment,
and then when she spoke again her voice had a certain hush
to it—the lowering in tone that warns you something serious
is about to be said. Something that will change everything.

It's about your husband . . .

The telephone cord went slack and her hand lost its grip on
the plastic surface of the receiver.

She hadn't been able to speak then for several moments,
hearing the girl's voice at the other end as if she were talking
from the estuaries of deep space. My husband, my husband:
those words went in a crazed circle around her brain.

Suddenly the traffic started forward again. She let the
clutch out in the Opel, moved a couple of feet, then stopped
again. Maybe she could find some quiet back way and save
time, but then she realized she still didn't know her way
around very well, knew no short cuts, commuter tricks.
You're stuck here in this traffic that has all the urgency of a
funeral cortege.

She wiped her face with the sleeve of her shirt.

She fumbled black glasses from the dash and put them on,
then stared at the sliding-down sun. The girl's voice. The
girl's awful voice.

I don't think it's anything serious, Mrs. Campbell . . .
Can't you tell me what's wrong with him? *Please* tell me.
It seems he fainted in his office, Mrs. Campbell.
Fainted?
Fainted. Right. He just passed out, it seems.
Passed out? (Not Eric, no.)
He's feeling shook-up. We don't know what it is, Mrs.
Campbell.
Let me get this straight. Let me see if I can get this
straight. You mean my husband just . . . passed out?
Yes. He fainted at his desk. He feels really weak. He wants
to know if you'll come down and drive him home.
And you said: As fast as I can, of course. I'll get there just
as fast as I can.
You said.
Now you're bogged down in this grim procession of dead
traffic stuck in the violent heat of the late afternoon, the
commuter's nightmare, snails crawling, fumes thickening in
the still, still air.
She stopped at a red light. The traffic was a bewildering
maze of metal. She took off her dark glasses, wiped them,
replaced them. Eric—what in the name of God was wrong
with him anyhow? She tried to think back, find some signs of
stress—there was only the nightmare.
The light changed.
On an impulse she swung left into a narrow street of
houses, those quiet well-kept houses that suggest lives of
irreproachable order. She turned the car where the street
twisted and saw ahead another main thoroughfare clogged
with sullen traffic. Okay, you blundered: so you edge your
way out and try to make up for lost time. A kindly old man in
a dusty pickup let her slip out of the side street and back into
the mainstream. Eric. Please don't let it be anything serious.
Please please please.
Be calm, for God's sake. It isn't much farther. It isn't a long
way now to the left turn that will take you to Central and the
heart of the city. Even from where she sat she could see the
tall spires of commerce that rose from the core of downtown
with the smug certainty of religious edifices.
And then she was traveling south into the glare of thick
traffic. How many blocks? She couldn't remember, not the
appearance of the building where he worked, not the number—
the mind slides away, frayed at the edges by a sense of

impending panic. You'll be okay, love. You'll be all right. I'll
be with you soon.

Soon.

I don't want to worry you, Mrs. Campbell . . .

Why was it always a certain *kind* of voice that delivered
bad news? Why did it always sound like a schoolteacher
addressing kindergarten kids or a librarian showing six-year-
olds the complexities of the Dewey decimal system?

She glanced at the line of buildings just ahead. Was that
the one? Some sixteen stories of blank glass. Maybe. She'd
take a chance on it anyway, turn into the parking lot and run
into the lobby to look at the names on the board. She parked
the car badly in a lot that was almost empty and rushed as fast
as she could toward the entrance—the height of the building,
enlarged somehow by the quality of light, made her dizzy as
she looked up.

She pushed the doors open.

There was nobody at the reception desk. She hurried past
it to the list of those businesses whose offices were in this
building. Blank—for a bewildering moment, blankness. She
couldn't remember the name of Eric's company.

Fight the blankness, Ellen. Fight it.

She stared at the board again. Of course, of course, of
course—how could she have forgotten?

She reached out and ran her finger down the glass surface
of the board. There: Saffron Fund-Raising Enterprises, Inc.
Saffron—she'd thought it an odd name when she'd first heard
it and it seemed even stranger to her now.

A modern elevator: you might not have been moving at all.
She watched the floor numbers change above her, then the
door opened and she stepped out into the corridor of the
fourteenth floor. Quickly along the corridor, trying to remember the location of Eric's office, trying to remember if the
door had his name on it.

Every office was empty.

They've gone home.

Everybody's gone home.

Eric might have been driven home already because I was
held up in traffic. Damn. No, they'd wait for her, she was
sure they would.

Empty. The whole place had that strangely tense feeling of
emptiness. She was surrounded by absences, unringing telephones, silent typewriters. She was surrounded by the kind

of hollowness that is left behind in offices when everybody has gone—an absence that seems fraught with the whispered and dying echoes of frantic recent activity.

Spooky.

Quite spooky.

And then she found herself standing outside the door of Eric's office. She regarded the nameplates: *Eric Campbell. General Funds*. What the hell were General Funds? She put her hand out to touch the doorknob then she stopped and, turning her face, looked this way and that along the empty corridor.

Why did she feel she was doing something forbidden?

A moment of panic. A sense of fear—as if some invisible predatory bird were flapping around her, wanting to settle on her shoulders.

"Eric," she said. And she knocked on the door.

Nothing.

Nobody.

She could hear the distant thin sound of the elevator rising in the shaft. It lasted a moment, then there was silence.

Eric.

She turned the handle lightly, heard the metal click beneath the tips of her fingers. Now she could see half of the office—an empty desk, a window, a telephone, a pile of papers in a tray. She tapped the door again, and it swung wide and she stepped inside the room.

Empty.

Two empty desks. Chairs. Filing cabinets.

No Eric.

Her blood was rising, rushing to her head, a stifling sensation. Her legs were strangely weak. The room didn't seem solid to her—it might have been suspended on flimsy wires, a structure about to swing back and forth like a pendulum. She had to sit down and close her eyes. Pain behind the eyes. Deep shooting pain as if there were burning fibers connecting eyes to brain. Her throat was dry. A pulse in her neck beat in a way she imagined might have been audible to somebody else—

But there wasn't anybody else.

She was alone on this floor. Alone on the fourteenth floor.

Then where in the name of heaven was Eric? Where was her sick husband?

I don't want to worry you, Mrs. Campbell . . .

Intrusion, a sense of trespassing—why did she feel like that anyway? This was the place where her husband worked.

This was the place that took up so much of his time.

His place of business.

The other half of his life.

She stared from the window at the mountains to the south. The sun had completely gone now; the sky was streaked with pale flares of yellow that reminded her of the dying traces of fireworks. Eric—why couldn't you wait for me? Did you think I wouldn't come? Is that what you thought?

She moved to his desk, dialed her own number and let it ring. There was no answer. He hadn't made it home yet. That's all. Maybe he's stuck in the traffic somewhere. Maybe. Simple: he felt better, tried to call me, I'd already left . . . it wasn't that simple. *Why the hell didn't he wait if he knew I was coming?*

Why, Ellen?

She stared at the folders and the neat piles of paper on his desk. *It's wrong, it's all wrong, something is hideously wrong . . .*

The call. The girl. The idea of Eric's fainting.

It didn't add up. Make sense.

But if he hadn't been sick, if he hadn't fainted, then—

Then who had made the call? And why?

A hoax. A practical joke. Something simple and wicked and inconvenient. But who then? (Anna Rosenberg? Sweet doped-out Anna wanting to spend a few minutes alone with handsome Eric in the parking lot? Yes? Why did that seem so terribly preposterous?)

Who the hell would scare a pregnant woman and send her through the ravaging traffic and the penetrating heat—just for kicks? Just for a laugh?

She stared into his drawer and listened to the silence of the building. She realized she was too weary to feel as angry as she might have—she was too weary, too relieved by the idea that Eric wasn't, after all, sick.

But something was wrong.

Then she heard the silence of the building change: there was a sound, a faint humming, a vague vibration. Someone was riding the elevator. Someone was going down.

Or coming up.

She was about to close the drawer when she noticed a piece of paper tucked at the back, half-hidden by rubber bands. She pulled it out, made curious by the fact she could read the name *Dr. Ely* printed on it. In the fading light she spread the paper on the desk. It was a prescription. A prescription from Eric's eye doctor. It was covered with the kind of primitive scrawl to which physicians have the exclusive patent and she couldn't make it out. As she raised it from the desk, she heard the elevator stop. A door slid open in the corridor.

She got up from the chair, wandered toward the door and peered out. Under the fluorescent light the hall stretched away emptily. She saw the elevator slide shut, heard it hum as it began to descend. Somebody just got out, she thought. Somebody got out quickly and went inside one of the other offices.

The thought paralyzed her. It struck her and paralyzed.

Somebody gets me to come down here. Somebody goes to all that trouble. Somebody who thinks the offices will be empty. Who deliberately wants me to be alone and helpless.

Why?

She edged out of the doorway and looked along the empty corridor. Doors, doors, and more doors, some of them open, some closed. Who the hell had come out of the elevator?

The association was irresistible: the same person who made the telephone call. That's who. The same joker.

Joker—that wasn't the word.

She moved slowly toward the elevators. Four doors. Four shafts. She was conscious of the sound her sandals made on the carpet, a scuffling, an occasional flapping. Somebody could be waiting for me— waiting behind one of those office doors. Somebody. Anybody.

Don't go to the elevators.

Use the stairs.

Use the stairs if you can find them.

She turned around and walked back the way she had come, unable to avoid the feeling that she was being watched from behind—a feeling she couldn't dispel even when she turned to look and saw nobody.

Emergency Exit.

She moved the metal bar, found herself on the stairs, started to move down. And then she thought: You're being stupid. You're imagining things. A practical joke is one kettle of fish, kid, but malicious intent, the idea of physical harm, is quite another. Walk slow. Walk very slow.

The person who came up in the elevator—an office worker coming back to put in those few extra hours that prove his dedication and speed his early promotion. That's all.

Why keep to the stairs? She could feel the baby jiggle inside her as she went down.

On the tenth floor she paused, out of breath.

Go back inside, she thought. Walk along the corridor and ride the elevator the rest of the way down.

From overhead, echoing down the stairwell, she heard the clang of an emergency door swing shut.

Somebody coming down.

She pushed a door hard and found herself—even as she listened to the quickness of footsteps on the stairs above—walking the corridor of the tenth floor, moving toward the elevators. She stopped by the elevators and pressed all four buttons. Hurry, she thought. Hurry.

She looked back in the direction of the emergency exit, the door the color of ocher, its two small windows reinforced with wire mesh.

Fear becomes electricity; it becomes the dry fire of an electric shock. She stood close to the wall, trembling, tilting her head back so she could see the numbers change on the wall above. Five. Six. Seven. An elevator rising.

Seven. Seven. Seven.

Why had it stopped on seven?

Somebody getting in? Or getting out?

She glanced back at the emergency exit: there was a shadow against one of the windows.

But she wasn't sure.

She wasn't sure because of the grids of wire set in the glass.

Seven. Eight.

The emergency door opened a little way.

Eight, nine.

Nine.

The shadow spilled like some ugly stain into the corridor.

Hurry, hurry, for Christ's sake, hurry.

Nine. Ten.

Slowly—why did the elevator open so slowly?

She glanced once more at the emergency door. It was shut now. Quickly, she stepped inside the elevator and pressed the button for the ground floor and then she wondered, as the cage dropped in the darkness of the shaft, whether the shadow was rushing down the stairs, racing the elevator.

You're imagining things, Ellen. No, you saw that door open. You saw a shadow fall. Nine. Seven. Five.

When the elevator hit the ground floor she stepped out quickly into an empty hallway and turned toward the glass doors that led outside. She was breathing hard; her lungs felt tight, her body was wet. She reached the glass doors and shoved them open and the heat of the early darkness came in at her with the force of burning ashes. Once, before she ran to her car, she turned and stared back through the doors at the lobby.

It was empty, starkly lit, shadowless. There was nothing.

She paused by her car and tried to breathe the sullied air around her—and she realized she was still clutching Eric's prescription in her moist hand. Without thinking, she stuck it in the breast pocket of her denim shirt.

She scares. She scares like a trapped mouse. You watch her hurry across the parking lot to her car and you think: She is not for him. She never could be. And you close your eyes and press them to the window, no longer interested in the sight of her. Instead, you are thinking of him. You remember going inside his empty office and sitting behind his desk, you remember waiting until he'd gone home, waiting in the stairwell and holding your breath, you recall going into the room where he worked and touching the things on his desk, smelling the smell of him, reconstructing him in your mind. He works here. He sits here. His telephone. His papers. His desk. And it brings back all the sunlit depths of love. All the bright days of the heart. It brings back a moment of purity.

You press your face to the window. You notice the yellow car is gone from below. The parking lot is empty now. She has gone. You notice all this absently. Your eyes are suddenly wet and your sight fuzzy but your inner eye is clear and what you see there is the sight of your broken belly and a single misshapen life floating away from you through pain, through dark red water, a life attached to you by a slender thread.

Darling Eric, you think.

That lost life was ours.

That lost life was something we made together, out of love.

Eric was standing at the balcony door when she returned to the apartment. He had his hands in his pockets, his legs spread slightly apart. She could hear coins rattling in his pockets. Fatigued, her mouth parched, her muscles weary, she found she couldn't say anything to him at first, it wasn't possible to tell him what had happened. There was the aftermath of her fear to cope with—some internal collapse, nerves oscillating between numbness and vibrancy. He doesn't even look as if he might have been sick, she thought. But you'd already made up your mind that it was all some mad joke anyway—so what did you expect? Eric lying pale in bed with a thermometer in his mouth? His color that of a bedsheet drying in the wind?

He opened his mouth, as if he were about to speak, but said nothing. He walked to the armchair and, standing behind her, placed his hands on her shoulders and massaged them lightly. He isn't sick. He hasn't been sick. *Somebody out there somewhere wanted you to panic, to suffer, whatever.* She closed her eyes and could see, locked behind the lids, the numbers of an elevator panel, a shadow falling through a half-open door. Then her head became dark, unlit, a labyrinth of shuttered windows and sealed rooms. Somehow she knew she had to live in this darkness for a time, this place where she didn't have to think because thoughts became lost and confusing.

"I was worried about you," he said.

She felt her lips move in a smile. Worried about *me*?

"I didn't know where you might be."

She leaned forward. She opened her eyes and stared at the rug. The balcony door was black glass. It suggested that nothing lay beyond. No world out there.

She got up from the armchair and walked to the glass door. Blind night. Only a blue light from the pool indicated life, a shape passed in front of the light a moment.

"She said you were sick, Eric. She said you'd fainted. You wanted me to come down to the office and pick you up and I went down there—" She stopped. Her own voice—why was it rising like the notes on a musical scale?

"Wait. Hold it. Who called? Who said I was sick?"

"A girl in your office. She said you were ill. I drove down there to get you, only the place was empty," and she paused. She was clutching the drapes in a clenched fist. A phrase from a nursery rhyme went through her head without reason: *Here we go 'round the mulberry bush.* She turned and looked at his face.

"Are you serious?"

"No, Eric. I just made the whole thing up. I just invented a telephone call from a stranger. I wasn't at your office at all. I was trying to pick up strange men in a cocktail lounge. How can you *ask* if I'm serious? Can't you see what I look like?"

"Let me get this straight. Somebody called and said I was sick."

"Yes—that's what I said."

"Did she give you her name?"

Ellen shook her head.

"Why didn't you think to call the office? Why didn't you think to have the message confirmed?"

"A voice tells you your husband's sick and suddenly your heart is in your throat and all you can think of is getting down there to help. I didn't have the time to sit around and ponder the whole thing, Eric. I was worrying about you, dead scared."

Hold me, she thought. Cross the floor and put your arms round me and explain to me the troubled psychology of the practical joke. Tell me what makes a person do such a thing, Eric. Spell it out in simple sentences if you will. I'm a slow learner these days. Human nature is a puzzle to me. Won't you help?

The shadow, she thought. Darkness set in a tiny pane of glass, filling the space of a half-open door.

She couldn't bring herself to tell him about the shadow. A figment—could it have been only that?

No—it had happened. It had all happened—the shirt in the pool, the clean apartment, the mattress and the doll, the telephone call, the figure behind the emergency door. These things were real. They were *damn* real.

Somebody is doing things to me.

Somebody is stealing things from me.

You had the map of a country, only all the place names and all the rivers and all the mountains had been omitted and you were expected to recognize the country from its green and brown contours alone. It was a game like that. A killing game.

Somebody is trying to hurt me.

And the hell of it is, I can't think why.

She glanced at Eric and then she went toward the bedroom. When he called her name a couple of times, she couldn't answer. The weariness was heavy now. It lay across the surface of her body like layers of old grime. She sprawled across the bed and stared at the ceiling.

He should be calling the police, she thought. Right now, he should be dialing McDonald's number and relating this latest episode: *The joker struck again, McDonald, what are you going to do about it? We're going mad with fear. Aren't you people paid to protect us?*

She listened, concentrated, hoping to hear the sound of his voice on the telephone.

There was silence.

She sat upright. She put her hands to her breasts, and heard the crackle of paper. Eric's prescription in her breast pocket. She took out the crumpled slip—wondering, half-wondering, what kind of prescription an eye doctor might give to a patient. The writing was awful. She held the paper under the bedside lamp.

Why am I so curious anyhow?

What is this compulsive nosiness?

Curiosity kills. Ask too many questions and you end up being guillotined by your own inquiries. A prescription from an eye doctor, that was all. Why had he thrown it into his desk without having it filled?

Dr. Ely, whoever you are, you don't know how to write.

She screwed up her eyes and gazed at the backward-slanting writing, done in dense black ink. Maybe it was for one of those medications eye doctors used before examinations, the kind that blurred your eyesight and made your pupils grow enlarged. Why should she care?

HOWARD G. ELY
3000 Millar Road
Scottsdale, Arizona
Tel: 947-1767

She stared at the handwriting.

30 300mg tabs

Tabs of what? What else was written there?

And why would an eye doctor prescribe thirty of anything? Glaucoma? Cataracts? What else?

Her hand was trembling. She shut her eyes and tried not to remember the phone call, the girl's voice, the figure behind the door, tried not to think that somebody was—what

other word could she come up with?—*conspiring* against her.
A conspiracy.

The paper was rattling in her trembling fingers. Shaking
like this: it was the consequence of fear, the sharp arrowhead
of terror. Somebody.

Eric's medication: she tried to read.

The first word looked like *Lithium*.

Lithium—what could that be?

The second word apparently began with the letter C.

Car.

In the hallway beyond the closed door she heard Eric
move. There was the sound of running water from the
kitchen.

Carbon?

She realized she was feeling suddenly furtive, criminal,
like a burglar with expectations of an impending arrest. I'm
spying, she thought. I'm opening one of the closed boxes of
my husband's life.

Why? Why do I feel there *are* any closed boxes?

Carbon something.

She heard Eric approach the bedroom door.

Carbonate. Lithium carbonate.

She stuffed the prescription under the pillow just as he
stepped into the room. He stood in the doorway with a glass
of iced water in one hand, a cigarette in the other. She looked
at him and the thought came back with all the frenzy of a
whirlpool's heart: *Somebody is trying to harm me*.

He smiled and approached the bed and momentarily touched
her on the back of her hand. The smile, the smile is concealing
something, she thought, behind the smile there's a quality
hidden, locked away, a secret thing I can't get at. She wanted
to evacuate the perception, rid her mind of such an intrusion—
but it returned, vengefully persistent, again and again.

"How are you feeling now?" he asked.

She said nothing, nodded her head in an indeterminate
way. She rose after a moment and walked through to the
kitchen, picked up the Yellow Pages, flicking through it.
Stopped at the letter P.

Physicians, physicians, so many physicians in Phoenix. (So
why did northern doctors recommend the desert for so many
patients?) Physicians. What was the word for an eye doctor?

Opthalmologist.

She ran down the list of names.

There was a Dulany and then a Falkenstein.

There was no doctor between those two, no doctor whose name began with the letter E. Unlisted? Whoever heard of an unlisted physician? She flicked the pages again. Ely Ely Ely.

She found Howard G. Ely under the general listings for *Physicians & Surgeons*. She had to work her way through several more pages, reading rapidly, scanning quickly, until she located the name under the specialty listings.

Howard G. Ely was a psychiatrist.

Thirteen   *August 9*

A virus? A sickness?

She wasn't sure, knew only that an affliction weakened her and induced the worst lethargy she'd ever felt. She lay in bed for three days and drifted in and out of deep sleeps; there were dreams she couldn't remember on waking—she recalled only that the dreams were in some way troubled ones. Names and faces came and went, each in a fashion familiar to her.

Flu. She told Eric it was mild flu. He bought Tylenol and some kind of sinus capsules from the drugstore but she didn't take them. She knew it had nothing to do with flu, that if there were any basic cause for what she felt it belonged in the vague category of existential malaise, whatever such a phrase might mean.

Why couldn't she talk to him about it?

There were pains in her womb as well, pains of a kind she hadn't felt before. For hours she worried about the well-being of the baby, but at other times—when the pain would vanish—she couldn't even think about the child. She lay alone in the bedroom trying to follow the wispy, evaporating trails of her own thoughts.

Trails. There weren't any trails. There were no signposts. The world had assumed the unfamiliarity of the dark side of the moon. She wanted sleep more than she wanted thought, rest more than conjecture.

Who could you talk to when you'd lost your main resource? She found it hard to look at Eric when he came inside the bedroom. Howard G. Ely—the man's name came between her and her husband with the certainty of a scaffold's shadow. She wished she'd never opened the drawer of that desk and taken out the prescription, never read it, checked the Yellow Pages. She wished she had the impossible gift of stepping back in time, changing the clocks, pasting back discarded sheets from the calendar of her life. Eric even looked different— thinner, grayer, there were lines on his face she'd never noticed before, and she wondered: *Have I married a stranger?* (Maybe that was a perception that came to every married person with the cold smack of a tide, maybe that happened to everyone at some time or other in a relationship.) He seemed also . . . furtive, but then why shouldn't he? He was hiding behind a lie, a big lie. And if there was one lie, why shouldn't there be others? Whole stacks of lies, whole tarnished piles of falsehood smelling like rust in the rain.

Eric. Who are you? Why didn't you tell me about your sickness?

Ah, the sickness. Now there was a puzzle.

She played games with herself. *Let's Put a Name to Eric's Malady.* It began, on square one, with the general harmlessness called "a nervous condition"—and it rose to schizophrenia, delusions of grandeur, a total breakdown. *Dementia praecox.* Hallucinations. The whole screwed-up cerebral breakdown.

What is it called, Eric?

Why are you seeing a shrink?

Why did you say he was an eye doctor?

Why did you *lie*?

The lie was a stain; it might have been spilled blood spreading over the pillow beneath her skull. When he entered the room she felt a slight shiver—as of fear, but not quite. It seemed a stranger was stepping inside, the stranger whose wedding band she wore, a man to whom she was bound by heart and by law and about whose history she knew apparently nothing. She could have drawn up a questionnaire.

Where did you go to school?

Why did you disappear for three days after your proposal and why didn't your parents come to our wedding?

What axlike stroke of fate was it that engineered our first encounter, Eric? Why did you just happen to talk to me in a public library because I was carrying a copy of a book called *A Death in Canaan?* (*Interesting. You'll like it. Just finished it.*)

Why did we drag ourselves and our love three thousand miles?

Questions and questions and questions until they became utterly tiresome. They circled one another as warring foxes might.

A shrink, for heaven's sake. Sometimes when she looked at her husband she wondered how long it had been going on, this medicinal infidelity, this betrayal of nerves. She knew now that she wouldn't ask him, without quite understanding why: in part it would have been an admission of her minor act of espionage, but more than that it was because, in some deep place, she didn't want to know the answers, not any of them. He's the father of my child; so what if he's a mystery, a psychiatric patient, a liar? He's still the father of my child.

The biological father of my unborn baby.

And I love him. Even if I don't know where trust begins and ends, I love him—and that was something all the fabrication in the world would never demolish.

I love him.

On the second day of her sickness he called Dr. Phelps. She heard him through the open bedroom door. When he came inside the bedroom afterward he didn't say anything. He sat on the edge of the mattress and clasped his hands together and, with his head bowed, gazed at the rug. Eventually he said: *I'll call Phelps tomorrow if you don't feel better. He told me to do that.* She heard the words without feeling anything because for a time it seemed to her that her womb was empty and shriveled and barren—and the child had been little more than a phantom of her fevered brain.

On the night of the second day, when she lay awake beside her sleeping husband and watched the moon glaze the window, she felt a sense of danger all around her.

Danger.

Darkness, menace.

It was the shadow in the doorway again. The girl on the telephone, the thefts. There might have been spidery cracks in the fabric of the night and something poisonous lying in wait in each fissure. Danger. Was she alone in recognizing it? Had it come down to that? Why hadn't Eric called the police after the telephone call? And what terrible apathy had her in its grip so that she could do nothing, nothing at all to save herself?

The answer didn't matter finally; what mattered was that

she shake the sickness and the lethargy of her life and get the hell out of bed and do something to ward off the menace—she couldn't just lie around and wait for it to get her.

On the morning of the third day, although she was still weak, she got up to answer the front doorbell and found her mother standing outside.

"Your husband tells me you've been sick, Ellen."

"I didn't know he'd called."

"I was the one who *called*, dear. I hadn't heard from you. I was a little concerned after our last meeting, so I called."

"I'm not exactly sick anymore. I'm feeling better." I must feel better.

Ellen went inside the kitchen, put a kettle on the stove, watched how the red coils began to glow. And then she was thinking suddenly of McDonald: I ought to call him, I *have* to call him, I have to tell him about the most recent incident. This weakness, this illness, this retreat to bed—you've got all kinds of excuses. What they came down to in the end was the terror of Eric's lie—your little world disturbed from the outside by an insane joker, a dangerous joker—but in some way more distressing still, violated from the inside by your husband's lack of truth.

She carried the tea tray into the living room. Her mother was sitting on the sofa, assessing the drapes over the balcony door. Ellen set the tray down on the coffee table and, for one long moment of weakness, longed to blurt it out, tell her mother everything. Instead she poured two cups of tea and sat down, watching her mother drink hers.

"I expected to find you at death's door, dear. So I had Hattie drive me over."

"Where is Hattie?"

"Waiting in the car."

"In this heat?"

"Hattie is used to the heat."

Again Ellen wondered at Hattie's life. Maybe she was hoping to be named in the will, a substantial legacy of some sort. More likely she'd inherit a velvet armchair with matching antimacassars in return for years of loyalty.

"What *was* wrong with you, dear?"

"A virus, I guess."

"You're so pale. I've never seen you look so pale."

Ellen sipped her tea. The weakness was debilitating. She felt sleepy, longing to lie down on the sofa and close her eyes.

"The baby?" Ellen's mother asked. "How is my first grandchild?"

"Kicking well."

"You had a fine old time inside me, dear, when I was carrying you. I imagined you were wearing boots."

I can't imagine being inside my mother's body, Ellen thought. She drained her cup and set it down and looked at the older woman, who asked: "How is your husband? He seemed somewhat reticent when I called."

"He's fine," Ellen said. What am I supposed to say—*he's seeing a shrink and hasn't said a word to me about it?* She looked away from her mother, quite unable to meet the rather penetrating stare of the older woman; she still had the same pent-up feelings of needing to confide in her and tell her about Eric—echoes of pressure being released, steam hissing.

"You know, Ellen, you get a slight quiver in your voice when you lie."

"A quiver?"

"Even when you were a child, dear."

"I'm not lying."

"Well, it's none of my business anyhow."

Ellen glanced at her mother, then away. She felt tense inside, a tension more coiled, tighter than anything she'd felt before. It was like a single scream rising in her stomach and seeking the opening of the throat, like a column of errant blood sucked suddenly into a scarlet hurricane.

Don't let me fall apart in front of her, she thought.

Don't let her see me weak like this. I don't need to be smothered, not now.

She twisted her head to one side, realized her eyesight was blurry suddenly. *Goddammit, no.* Not in front of my mother, not like this. She raised her hand to her face, closed her eyes, tried to hide. And then, to her horror, she heard herself sob—one low moaning sound that seemed to fill the room, after which there was a silence riddled with awkwardness and embarrassment. She got to her feet and went inside the kitchen and blew her nose into a paper towel, flushing water into the sink to cover the sound. Suddenly it all swells up inside you and the tensions break through to the surface and the only course of action you can take is to let it go, no matter what, no matter the consequences, the embarrassment, you just let it slip out of you and you're caught with all your weaknesses flapping in the air like an illusionist's doves. Oh, why, for Christ's sake, why did it have to be in front of my own mother?

She pressed her body against the edge of the sink, felt warm tears slip across her cheeks and touch the corners of her lips. Who do I turn to? who do I go to for help in all this mess? She heard the sound of the walker tap-tapping across the tiled floor of the kitchen. I will not turn around, she thought. I will not turn around and give her the satisfaction of seeing my red eyes. My anxieties. Or whatever else she chooses to see in her daughter's face.

"Ellen."

A pause. She couldn't look. She hated herself for having acted with such abrupt stupidity.

"Ellen. Let me say something. I understand that we have our disagreements. I further understand I haven't always been the most... shall we say, warm and affectionate of mothers? But I want you to understand one thing. If you are in any kind of trouble, if—as it seems—something is unsettling you, I want you to know you can rely on my help. You can turn to me."

She felt her mother's hand on her elbow.

"You can call me, Ellen. Any time of night or day. I will not ask any questions until you're prepared to tell me. Do you understand?"

Ellen nodded.

She heard the sound of the walker recede. She heard the outer door close. Then she pulled another towel from the kitchen roll and soaked it under the faucet and clamped the sodden sheet over her face.

I will be *strong*, she thought—a thought that, in itself, seemed to require a sudden outburst of energy, of resolve. I will not have a husband who lies to me. And I will not let anyone out there mess around with *my* life.

From this point on, strong and alone.

All at once she saw herself from a point overhead, as if through the eyes of some indolent fly hanging to the lightshade—fat with child, disheveled robe, uncombed hair, pale face. And solitary in her terrifying white kitchen.

Don't perceive yourself like that, she thought.

Don't start coming down on yourself. Somebody along the way taught you about logical thinking, some decrepit old math teacher explained the nature of problem solving. Separate the strands: never confuse them. Divide and conquer.

You have two problems.

You have Eric. One.

And out there somewhere in all this gloriously agonizing sunlight you have a joker playing malicious games. Two.

Ellen, take action.

Suddenly, the first step was perfectly clear. She didn't need Eric do to it, she could do it herself. But when she called the number McDonald had given her, she learned he'd been home sick for the last four days—*a bad cold*, she was informed. *Could somebody else help her? Would she like to leave a name?* No, she couldn't do that—she didn't dare trust another. How many cops would believe that these things added up. Even her own husband didn't believe. Now she realized that she'd come to see McDonald as a friend, a sympathetic albeit objective friend, as something more than a policeman performing his duties. And now he wasn't there for her. Then she called the number of Vicky's office, thinking it might help to unload some of the weight if she could sit down with Vicky and relate the sequence of events—after all, what did she have to lose by confiding in Vicky? But she wasn't in her office and she wasn't at home, so Ellen left a message with a secretary whose voice suggested she might be sucking on a cough drop.

Time to act. Time to do one small thing.

She dressed quickly, sloppily, pulling on jeans and a smock, sandals, and going out into the dead heat of the desperate afternoon, it was a day for dropping in the streets, a day for seizures and strokes, a day in which even the palms seemed to wilt and the scavenging birds, in their quest for shade, had given up any notion of singing. She braved the baking Opel and as she drove she thought: I'm doing something, I'm doing something about events, I'm eight months pregnant and melting in the goddam sun and I'm more uncomfortable now than ever before in my life but I'm *doing something*.

It wasn't a bad feeling. It was good to act, even if the action were instinctive and not at all calculated. It was good to do something. Just good.

I'm returning borrowed books to the public library, she told herself, glancing at the pile of novels stacked in the passenger seat. An impenetrable Le Carré. Something inconclusive by Diane Johnson. A thriller she hadn't been able to finish despite the extravagant claim of the blurb that *it couldn't be put down*. A nonfiction work on the life of Albert Schweitzer. I'm returning these books, she thought.

But that isn't what I'm really doing.

And she slipped the prescription of Dr. Ely's from her smock pocket, checked the name of the drug, stuck it back. Lithium carbonate. She would find out exactly what it was that Eric was getting from a shrink. She would find out why he'd been prescribed lithium whatever. A small thing, a step—but a step forward, a move in the direction of controlling things. Life didn't always have to seem like a pack of wild horses you couldn't manage, did it?

She was already out of the garage and walking across the plaza in the direction of the library when she stopped—she stopped in the downpour of sunlight and thought: Damn, I left the books on the passenger seat. It didn't matter in any case; they hadn't been her main reason in wanting to visit the library; she'd brought them along because they were overdue, because she'd had some notion of killing two birds, of saving energy, sparing herself a return trip. So much for reasonable considerations. They could wait.

Under a sign that said REFERENCE sat a young woman. Ellen waited for her to raise her face from a stack of computer printouts. When she did so she stared unsmilingly at Ellen: it was a face without soul.

"Can I help you," and it wasn't put as a question.

"I want to find out about a certain drug," Ellen said.

"A drug?"

"I found some drugs in my house inside a prescription bottle and I can't remember what they were for so I'd like to find out." Why the lie? She didn't have to explain her whole life story to this woman.

"Safer to throw the stuff away," the librarian said.

"I know, I'm just curious," Ellen said.

"Go over to the reference shelf." The librarian pointed somewhere in the distance. "You'll find the *Physician's Desk Reference*. That should help if you know the name of the drug."

Ellen looked along the various rows until she found the volume, a fat red thing. She hauled it to a nearby table and sat down. I don't want to open this, she thought.

I don't want to look inside.

What will you learn?

The function of the drug, perhaps. Would that explain Eric for you? Would you learn something about Eric's life from some technical data concerning the chemical makeup of a drug?

She stared back in the direction of the reference desk. The woman was surrounded by printouts, stack after stack. Don't stall, Ellen. Don't procrastinate.

Open the damn thing.

Find out.

She felt a peculiar buzzing, a humming, in her ears. There was a quickening of blood, a rush of warmth to her face. *You're spying on Eric.*

Only because he lied.

Suddenly she was very cold. She stared across the room, possessed by the curious sensation that she was about to see somebody she knew, somebody familiar. A man was idly leafing through the pages of a large book, maybe an atlas. I don't know him, she thought. I've never seen him before in my life—so why the feeling, the odd presentiment? She shook her head, opened the *PDR*, turned the pages.

She couldn't shake the feeling.

It was strange; it was as if while she spied on Eric, somebody else, somebody out of her range of vision, was spying on her.

Guilt.

Nothing but guilt. You hate yourself for doing this. She turned more pages. There were several kinds of indexes, designed to confuse the nonspecialist. *Alphabetical Index by Manufacturer.* Useless to her. *Generic and Chemical Name Index.* She couldn't make that one work. *Alphabetical Index by Brand Name.* Fine. She took the prescription from her pocket and opened it up. Lithium Carbonate. Page 1232.

Don't, she thought.

Don't go on.

Why don't you just ask Eric flat out?

Because

Because

Because you're afraid you don't really know him anymore.

The thought stung her. It might have been a trespassing insect burrowing through the structure of her brain. The thought hurt. It hurt more than she needed to admit.

She found the page she wanted.

Silly not to look.
She flattened her hands on the page just over the words

LITHIUM CARBONATE
CAPSULES AND TABLETS, USP, 300 mg

Beneath, there was small writing. There were several columns of smaller print. I can't. I just can't. It was a form of betrayal—and she wondered how you could find any justice, any equality, in answering one betrayal with another.

She raised her face and saw that the librarian wasn't at her desk. Only the great pile of printouts; no librarian. The noise she was making as she tore the page out of the reference book, paper ripping away from its binding, was enormous. It seemed impossible that they would not come running over: What are you doing?

But there was only silence.

The page was torn free from the book and she was folding it over furtively, slipping it inside her pocket with the prescription. Later. If ever.

You'll read it later, won't you?

Yes, Ellen. Of course you will.

And she rose from the table and walked out of the library into a sunlight she no longer found so completely intolerable. Anything but the darkness of snooping, cheating, sneaking around.

The sun burned her face, the back of her neck, but she barely felt it now. She reached the garage and stepped into the shade and began the slow climb to the third floor.

She made it to where the Opel was parked.

She opened the door and lowered herself slowly into the seat: Do it. Just unfold the piece of paper and read the goddam thing.

She took it from her pocket and smoothed it out against her knee.

LITHIUM CARBONATE
CAPSULES AND TABLETS, USP, 300 mg

Maybe it's something simple. Some primitive salve for migraine, something like that.

You're kidding yourself, Ellen.

Read.

LITHIUM CARBONATE.

When she read the smaller print underneath she had a sensation of being suddenly immersed in the same gold fire that lit the day. Cindered responses. An incineration of the brain.

Read. Read again. Read again, Ellen.

What was this wild thing burning in her mind?

Her eyesight darkened.

For Control of Manic Episodes
in Manic-Depressive Psychotics

Manic, Psychotic. The words were like alarm bells going off in such a way that they might never be stopped again. Manic-Depressive Psychotics. She let the page slip from her knee and she thought, *Eric, oh Eric, Eric, is that why you are in a place I can't reach.*

She tried to bring his features to mind, but there was nothing. I don't remember, she thought. I don't even remember now what my husband looks like. I see only the black words printed on the clinical page, nothing more.

Love, oh love.

She wanted to weep.

She put a hand over her face, the moisture of the palm adhering to the sweat on her forehead. Dear love. With her eyes shut she was conscious of a sound from outside, the terrible rasping revving of a car gathering speed in a low gear. The noise pierced her. She massaged her eyelids: at the back of her head was a dull ache she knew would grow and grow if she let it. She wanted to weep but she didn't want to let herself go. Be strong. Be strong and just face things. And still the noise of the car grew louder, wilder, the roar of the motor rising until you would think the engine might explode. She dropped her hand from her face and stared through the window into the direct line of sunlight just in time to see a small black car go storming past, just in time to see a shadow as black as the car itself behind the wheel. She swung her head round, thinking she might get the license-plate number, but the car had already vanished. She felt tight in her chest, almost as if the fractured tip of a rib were pressing against a lung. Her eyes watered.

Be strong, for God's sake be strong. Promise yourself.

She looked down at the crumpled piece of paper in her hand.

And then she was conscious of something else.

The passenger seat was empty.
There was no sign of her library books.

*Even now you sometimes feel the pain of the old scar. Even
now it aches, hurts you. You double over in your parked car
and let your head hang from the rolled-down window. Why
does it hurt you now? A time will come, very soon, when it
won't hurt you at all, when all the pains of the past will have
gone and you will be well again, well and complete. This
thought reassures you, the pain diminishes. You open your
eyes and look across a stretch of desert waste. A large bird, a
vulture, makes circles in the blue sky.*

*Then you turn the pages of the books but the cold print
doesn't mean anything. She touched these books, turned the
pages, devoured these words. She.*

Her.

Even now it's hard for you to admit she has a name.

*Say it. Say it aloud. Go on. Get it over with. Just say the
name.*

Say, Ellen.

But you still can't, can you?

*You're afraid to admit she exists. But she does. She exists
and she's in the way.*

Time. In Time, you think, everything will be good again.

*A wispy cloud passes the sun. The vulture goes out of
sight. The day seems empty.*

You think: She won't always be in the way.

Fourteen   *August 12*

For three days she felt she was always watching him. Watching
him and waiting for something to show, a crack in his facade,
an opening into which she might peer and say to herself: Yes,
this is the sign, this is the madness I've been waiting for. At
night she listened for his nightmare, which didn't happen.
She listened to the droning regularity of his breathing and
waited for his dream to take shape and fill the bedroom with
its panic and fear. The dream didn't come. For two days she
watched a man who seemed perfectly normal in all respects—

except for the fact he'd been prescribed tablets for the control of manic-depressive psychosis. For two days she went through sporadic conversations with him and answered his apparently solicitous questions in such a way that if their dialogues had been taped they would have sounded commonplace to any listener. It was like living alongside a silent bomb, a bomb that has stopped ticking but it's still active nevertheless. She wondered how long the fuse might be and how much of it had already burned away.

Once or twice she picked up the telephone to call Dr. Ely, but she knew she couldn't; even if she did, she wouldn't get any information. Confidentiality. Professional ethics. She knew she wouldn't learn anything there. When Eric went to work she would read and read again the pilfered page and each time she did so she would experience a sense of horror. Sometimes the words would rise aggressively from the page as if to seize her around the throat; at other times they shed all meaning they might have had.

Lithium is an element of the alkali-metal group with atomic number 3, atomic weight 6.94, and an emission line at 671 nm on the flame photometer.

Meaningless. What did all this jargon have to do with the flesh-and-blood creature that was her husband? What did she care about atomic weight?

Typical symptoms of mania include pressure of speech (What was that? What did "pressure of speech" mean?) *motor hyperactivity, reduced need for sleep, flight of ideas, grandiosity, elation, poor judgment, aggressiveness, and possibly hostility* ...

Sometimes she wanted to take the sheet of paper and flush it away or burn it and forget everything she'd learned and go back to a life of normality and leave Eric alone with his secret, his private medication, his shrink; but then it seemed more important somehow to understand why Eric had become this way, why some shrink sitting in his Naugahyde office would prescribe such a potent drug. And she would throw her mind back, searching for tiny clues, sifting elements of his behavior, looking for the essence of all this—only to reach the same conclusion: *Something in Eric's life is closed to me. Something in his world happened before me.*

She looked up words in the dictionary.

Psychosis was its own horror show—*fundamental mental*

derangement characterized by defective or lost contact with reality.

It was like looking through tiny fissures in the structures of words for a sight of her own husband, almost as if she'd let him slip away somewhere and lost him in the middle of a technical sentence.

Possibly hostility. Lost contact with reality. Why did she sometimes think *she* was the one who'd let reality go? Digging into Eric's life, doing her own amateur archaeology in his heart—she was learning nothing, losing everything. She felt she wanted to hibernate, give birth somewhere in the deep-sleep cycle, and wake next spring a new woman, refreshed and revitalized and mercifully forgetful. But this kind of self-imposed amnesia wasn't a gift she possessed. She couldn't let a thing go until she'd found out all she needed to know.

And then there was the obstacle course involved in Lithium carbonate. *Fine hand tremor, polyuria, mild thirst may occur during initial therapy for the acute manic phase. . . . Diarrhea, vomiting, drowsiness, muscular weakness and lack of coordination . . .*

Relate these things to Eric.

And these—*blackout spells, slurred speech, restlessness, confusion, stupor, coma.*

Blurred vision. Dry mouth.

Fatigue, lethargy, tendency to sleep.

There were wild contradictions amongst the *Adverse Reactions.* If you added them up, if you lumped them all together, they would give you a sorry picture of a very confused individual. Jesus, what was this drug supposed to cure? It seemed to her, the more she read, that it produced side effects almost as troublesome as the psychosis it was supposed to combat.

Poor Eric. What had brought him to all this?

Something she didn't know about.

So she watched him and hoped he didn't know she was watching; she caught herself observing him, noticing the number of glasses of water he drank, waiting for his hand to shake, waiting for anything that would have the words *manic-depressive* stamped all over it. And she hated herself for doing so; she started to feel like a visitor passing time with an incarcerated man, wondering whether she might smuggle him the iron file with which to escape his cell. She thought: Maybe Ralph Houseman was right, more perceptive than she'd given him credit for, seeing signs freely inscribed on Eric's personality. She became almost addicted to observing him, craving the sight of a symptom, anything at all that would prove or disprove the clinical facts she read on her sheet of paper. *Tremor, twitching.*

Hyperactive deep tendon reflexes, whatever that might mean.

Anything at all.

It was late in the afternoon when McDonald came to the apartment. She was surprised to see him; it was suddenly as if another world, a forgotten series of events, had resuscitated itself to appear on her doorstep. The thefts, the odd occurrences—they had almost begun to slip from her mind because of Eric, because of Eric's lie. She looked at the policeman and thought: Today must be a special day, a birthday or an anniversary, because he has a good suit on—dark blue with a thin red stripe, neatly cut, white shirt and dark tie. Only the tie, badly knotted, was a sign of the crumpled cop she'd seen before.

"I just came from a funeral," he said. "I thought I'd look in on you. You don't mind?"

Ellen shook her head; she was glad for the company. Any company she didn't have to watch and watch in the manner of a border guard staring into a darkened horizon for a sign of life. (She vaguely remembered now having left a message for Vicky a couple of days ago; the call hadn't been returned. Some secretaries existed to obstruct, she thought. They found an odd triumph in failing to convey information.)

"I don't mind funerals. Something mournful in the Celtic blood," McDonald said. "I don't exactly get my kicks, but I don't have that Anglo-Saxon distaste for the things. Keep death in the spare back-room, if you know what I mean. I just hate having to get dressed up."

"Was it somebody close?"

McDonald lit a cigarette. He picked a flake of tobacco from his lower teeth and examined it a moment on the tip of his finger. A nice man, she suddenly thought. For a cop, he's a nice man.

"A young cop," he said. "You might have seen it in the papers. He was shot during a holdup at one of those convenience stores. A Circle K, I think. Damned thing is, they got away with eighteen bucks and change. It makes you stop dead in your tracks, Mrs. Campbell. You start to take stock."

"Do you want some tea?" Ellen asked.

McDonald shook his head. "I was passing. Thought I'd check you out. Actually, my wife keeps asking about you. How's that young woman with the baby, that's what she wants to know. Did you like the tea?"

Ellen smiled. "I have to confess. I didn't touch it. I hate the stuff."

McDonald laughed. It was a good open laugh. "To tell you the truth, my wife couldn't stand it either. It was left over from the last dose of pregnancy."

"I was beginning to feel guilty about it."

"No need. I'm sure she'll think it's funny."

"Is she from the same country as you?" Young love. Innocence. These are what normal people remembered when they cast their minds back into the past. Light, not darkness.

McDonald glanced a moment at the balcony door: he might have been absent-mindedly checking the lock. "Same city. Same country. I knew her since she was this high. If you want a real romantic story, it's the old childhood sweetheart thing. I had to drag her away from rainy old Scotland, though. Didn't want to leave her mother. But this isn't the time for stories."

McDonald stubbed his cigarette. "So," he said in a flat way. "What's new?"

What could she tell him? How much of the recent past could she ransack? Eric—well, she could put that to one side, she could safely deposit that in a box marked *personal*. The other things—the other things were what would interest McDonald. She watched him light another cigarette and go through the business of picking tobacco from his teeth. It was interesting how the nervous habit of smoking had produced still the other nervous habit of pulling strands from his lower teeth.

She said, "I had a crank call."

"Crank like how? Sexy crank? Deranged?"

"A woman's voice said my husband was sick. I went downtown. His office was empty. He wasn't sick. But there was somebody in the building. Somebody following me around."

"What happened?"

"I ran out of the building. That's what happened."

"You didn't recognize the voice?"

She shook her head. "No, I didn't."

"And you're sure somebody was in the building?"

"Sure?" How could she say? Shadows. Sounds. What point could you reach when you knew you were utterly sure? *For God's sake, of course I'm sure.* Don't go on splitting hairs. "I'm sure."

"Did you see somebody?"

"Only in shadow."

McDonald's jacket swung open. There was a gun in a shoulder holster. He buttoned the jacket and looked almost ashamed at the need to carry a weapon.

"No face? No features? Nothing you'd recognize again?"

"I'm sorry. No. I didn't get a good look." *I only got a good look inside Eric's desk—but you wouldn't want to know about that.* "I've also noticed this black car sometimes. Once I saw it at my mother's house in Paradise Valley. Then I saw it another time in the parking lot here. Then when I had my library books stolen, I saw it again."

"Somebody stole your library books?"

She nodded. "It could have been anybody. A kid could have done it. I left the books in my car. They weren't there when I got back. There was a black car hurrying past me, though."

"Is it always the same car?"

She shrugged. "I can't really say for sure."

"Do you know anybody who has a black car?"

"Not really," and she thought about Vicky, but that car belonged to her company, it had only been lent to her. And besides, it was preposterous to link Vicky with any of this.

"Why wasn't I told about all this?" McDonald asked. He looked suddenly annoyed with things, with the lack of communication.

"I guess we meant to tell you. Then I got sick. It kind of slipped my mind. When I finally *did* call, I found out *you* were sick."

"Sickness," he said: it might have been a curse word. "I should have been told one way or another, Mrs. Campbell. I can put the thefts down to silly jokes, vindictive things, but when you get a threatening crank call and you find yourself in a menacing situation, it's quite another matter."

"The call wasn't threatening—"

"Not in itself. But it turned out that way. You reach a point where you've gone beyond mischief, you know. You reach a point where a situation changes. It turns from one thing into another. Do you see what I mean? I don't know why I wasn't informed. I mean, why didn't your husband bother to call me?"

"I don't know," she said. But then she was thinking about the drug he'd been prescribed: she was thinking about his state of mind. What state might he have been in at the time? The origins of *grandiosity*? Nascent *elation*? Caught in that twilight between *lethargy* and *restlessness*? She didn't know. (Why are you assuming he took the drug anyhow? You've got only one unfilled prescription to go on. You never even saw him take any. How can you be positive?)

McDonald spread his legs, sprawled. "The stolen objects," he said, changing the subject—as if he were afraid to stumble across a territory of some marital discord. "There's something weird about the stolen objects. A shirt."

"It wasn't the shirt," she said. "I fished the shirt out of the pool, remember? All the buttons were missing."

"Buttons, shirt, I don't see the difference. The fact is, the shirt was stolen. An antique doll's head. A couple of library books. I don't see the relationship between these things. The shirt, for example, what was so special about the shirt?"

"It was expensive."

"Expensive enough to steal and then destroy? Throw away? That doesn't grab me, Mrs. Campbell. What about the books?"

"There was a Le Carré and a life of Albert Schweitzer."

"I'd have to be a genius to figure out the connection there," McDonald said. "And the doll, Christ. Why steal the head of a doll, then put the torso in a ripped mattress?"

She felt the baby move inside her. The ripple effect, a chain of little shudders. She changed the position of her body slightly.

He was silent a moment, then he said: "We have to assume that there's a connection between the person who called you and had you drive all the way to Phoenix, and the person who stole all the stuff. We have to assume it's the same person. And that's troublesome."

"Troublesome?"

"It's obvious, if you think about it. Somebody is watching you. Somebody is following you. Somebody knows when you've gone out and where you've gone. That somebody knows, for instance, that you've gone to the library. They've followed you there."

She shivered. I know, she thought. I know he's right. Watched. Followed. I know he's right and I don't want to think about it.

"This same somebody also knows your husband's place of business. It's troublesome, Mrs. Campbell. They know the hours when the office is closed. When nobody is likely to be there. If you add all this up, this person knows a helluva lot about your life."

She looked at him. His face was grim. Chamomile tea and exercises and the fear of the delivery room—Jesus, these things were more than enough. What the hell did she need all the rest of it for? She was afraid again.

"I wish I had a theory, Mrs. Campbell. I wish I knew what was going on. I won't lie to you. I haven't got a clue."

"A candid admission from a cop," she said.

He wrote something on a scrap of paper. "Here. This is my home phone. You already know the office number. If you need me, day or bloody night, you dial either of those numbers."

She followed him along the hallway, watched him open the front door. He studied the new lock for a moment, approving. "Day or night. Promise."

"I promise," she answered.

And then he was gone.

She went inside the living room and walked to the balcony door and looked out. *I am being watched.* Out there. Out there in the Great Sunshine, someone is watching me.

Whoever you are, I'm fighting back—and she pulled the drapes across the door.

But she didn't know how she would.

The sun had gone when she stepped onto the balcony and waited for the sight of Eric's car. What remained of the day was little more than a sequence of streaks in the darkening sky: with a little rain, a drop of moisture, there would have been a glorious rainbow. She looked in the direction of the pylon lights hanging over the tennis courts, the blue pool shimmering, the signs of someone falling toward the surface of water at the deep end. It might have been tranquil and ordinary, serene even—a summer's day winding down to the placid hot night.

But it wasn't.

She saw the Datsun slide into the parking lot, watched Eric park, get out—and then, out of nowhere, it seemed, there was a yellow-hatted girl standing at his side. Anna Rosenberg. Ellen watched, feeling nothing, numbness—no, not even numbness. Just nothing. The girl was saying something to Eric and he, being taller, inclined his head to listen. Whatever they discussed was brief. The girl pointed in the direction of the pool. Eric didn't move. Ellen thought: She's inviting him for a swim. That's what she's doing. Teasing him toward the water. She doesn't know what I know about him. *What would she think then?* Eric walked toward the building with his characteristically long strides, a man without time to waste, and the girl slid away, lost in palms and shrubbery. You're cute as a goddam button, Rosenberg. Cute as all hell.

Ellen went back inside the apartment, slid the door closed.

Dread: God, how she dreaded seeing Eric come into the apartment, dreaded the sight of her husband. It was the worst feeling she'd known. She felt a little dizzy, swayed, wondering what had passed between Eric and the girl, what kind of conversation. She entered the kitchen and sat down at the table and waited.

Anna Rosenberg—had it been Anna Rosenberg who'd made the telephone call? Had she been the one who'd slipped inside the apartment, stolen things, razored the shirt and tossed it into the pool?

There was a line of speculation here she didn't want to follow. A line that led directly through a maze to the heart of madness. Down and down and down. This is not your direction, Ellen. This isn't how you want to go.

She heard him close the door, whistle a moment, say something. She felt him come up behind and kiss her on the side of the face and ask, *How was your day?*, and she stifled the urge to look at him and say, *I had this great day, I got a call from the Queen of England, something to do with my uncollected honors, I had a letter from Ronnie Reagan and an invitation to cut the ribbon of some new hydroelectric power plant in New Mexico, busy busy busy.* But she didn't speak. Suspicion was sharp when you touched it, sharp-edged and hard and clean. Then you lost sight of it and it changed, it turned to certainty. Dear God, what am I thinking?

What in the sweet suffering name of Christ am I playing around with here?

Your husband is crazy.

Anna Rosenberg is.

Is.

She shut her eyes. That's right, Eric, go to the sink and drink your water. Gulp it down. Just don't ask me to talk as if nothing's happened.

Anna Rosenberg is his woman.

Between the two of them, they have something going, something of which I am not a part.

I don't belong in their game plan. I am disposable.

Between the two of them they are planning to drive me insane.

She rose quickly from the table, twisted a muscle, moaned, went into the bedroom, then the bathroom, locked the door, and looked at her face in the mirror. A bottomless world, a shifting world, silt stirred 'round and 'round.

The two of them, they are doing this to me because they want me out of their way.

(He gives her the key, simple. She comes in here. She does this, she does that. He meets her during the day, some motel. They fall in love. Fat wife has to be got rid of, right? What better way than to induce a complete state of madness? And isn't little Miss Rosenberg well placed to observe my comings and goings?)

Ellen, stop. Why are you regurgitating the plot of some late-night movie? Why are you playing Ingrid Bergman to his Charles Boyer? It was sick, the reckonings, the bad reckonings and miscalculations of a pitiful mind. The state you're in, she thought: just look at what you've managed to drag up out of your sorry condition. There was nothing sinister in the fact that a young girl found your husband attractive.

Your manic-depressive husband.

She heard him knock on the door. She heard him say: "Are you coming out, Ellen? Or do I have to come in there and get you?"

Please. Please don't try to come in.

"A minute," she said.

"You okay?"

How could he make his voice sound so solicitous?

"Come on," he was saying. "I haven't told you today that I love you."

She wondered: Was this one of his periods of elation? One of those high times of motor hyperactivity?

She unlocked the door, looked at him. She said, "McDonald was here today."

"Really? What did he have to say?"

"Nothing much." She shrugged. Get to the failure of communication, she thought—ask him why he didn't call. Just ask him. "He was pretty pissed off at the fact that we didn't call him after I'd gone down to your office..."

"I don't understand that," Eric said.

"What don't you understand?"

"I *did* call. The very next day. Somebody in his office said he was sick. I left a message. He never called back."

Oh, she thought. You left a message. You left a message. Did you try again, did you keep trying? *He can't be lying if he already knew McDonald was sick, can he?* Do I find small consolation in that fact?

"Then *you* got sick," he said. "And I guess I was worried about you so I forgot about calling him back. Besides, it sounds like he never got my message."

You forgot to call him back?

You *forgot?*

I hate myself, this twisted thinking I'm getting into. The mind as corkscrew. He called—at least he tried to call. And the twisted logic of imagining him together with Rosenberg, inventing a whole mad plot, a convoluted fiction. Stop it, Ellen. Stop it now. But how can you stop when you keep running into lies, when you keep seeing lies all over the place?

She felt the palm of his hand against her cheek.

He said, "I don't know what's been bothering you lately. I just don't know what it is or why you won't tell me. You've seemed so...I don't know, so *withdrawn*, shut away inside yourself. Sometimes I can't seem to get through to you." He hesitated. "I know all the stuff that's been going on is affecting you, but—I just wish you'd talk with me, that's all."

Liar, she thought. How could you drag your own darkness all over our marriage like this? Confused, bewildered, she shut her eyes. She felt herself clutched against his chest.

She retreated into a safe place.

A deep place inside herself.

*   *   *

*Count the flowers. Violets and carnations and roses. Count
them stem by stem. You try to remember the flowers from
long ago. Sometimes it's a hard memory to lock on to,
sometimes it comes in clear as water. You remember—yes,
there were violets, carnations, roses, all the flowers woven
together into a delightful pattern, a thing of beauty. Now, out
of nowhere, you find yourself thinking about her again. The
image is a rage inside you. How could he have entered her
body and left his seed there, how could he have done something so treacherous?*

*He was misled, that was all. He was confused. He never
really understood, poor darling, what he was doing. That
was all.*

*You stare at the pages torn from the binders of books and
some of the pages are blackened from the flames of matches.*

He lost his way. He forgot his heart.

Yes.

Torn pages, blue buttons, the smashed china of a doll's head.

Black and white and blue and pink.

Then the flowers.

*But that's not all. There's still something you have to do
after the flowers.*

Try not to forget.

*After the flowers you still have to do the most important
thing of all.*

Fifteen   August 15

==

At first Ellen didn't recognize her voice. "Dr. Phelps wanted
to know how you've been feeling, Ellen. Your husband called.
We were a little worried about you. You missed your last
appointment."

"It was a touch of cold," Ellen said. "Everything's fine."
(The dream came back to her—Phelps and Grabowski and
the dead baby. She thought she'd forgotten it, but it came
back with the sudden force of a fist.)

"Are you *sure* everything is fine?" the nurse asked.

"I'm sure."

"It's important at this point in the pregnancy that you not miss too many appointments, Ellen. You've reached a critical stage now. We've got to keep an eye on you, you know."

"I know," Ellen said. "I'm feeling better now. It was just a slight touch of cold..."

"And that's all?"

God, Ellen thought, how many times do I have to say it? "That's all," she answered. "Cross my heart."

There was a pause here of an awkward kind. An opportunity, Ellen thought: all she had to do was to jump into the space. "Can I ask you something?"

"Sure. Go ahead."

"Have you ever heard of a drug called lithium carbonate?"

"I've heard of it. Why?"

"I came across it—"

"Do you know somebody who's taking it? Is that it?"

"No, I came across it when I was reading something and I was just curious, that's all."

The nurse was silent for a moment, then she said: "Well, I don't know a great deal about it. I know it's used to control wild swings in moods. It's supposed to help the patient maintain a balance between extremes. Some people call it surgery without the knife. I've even heard it called a poor man's lobotomy. It's a controversial drug."

A poor man's lobotomy, Ellen thought. Surgery without the knife. She had a picture of Eric flattened out and anesthetized on a table, surrounded by neurosurgeons, the top of his scalp cut open like the lid of a can.

Grabowski said, "You've got another appointment next week, Ellen. I really think you should try to make it this time."

"I will."

"Promise?"

"I promise."

Why can't I just bring the subject up with him anyway? she asked herself as she put down the phone. Get it out in the open, set it free, say something like, *Hey, guy, I know about your shrink, your drug*—but she knew she wouldn't because it had gone beyond that. It was worse. It was: How could she be certain he'd tell her the truth? How could she know he wouldn't drag out some wild lie? There was only one man she could ask to be absolutely sure: Howard G. Ely. But when she fantasized sitting in his office and asking, *What exactly is*

Eric's problem?, she couldn't imagine Howard G. giving anything away. He was sworn to the same secrecy as a priest.

She needed to talk with *somebody*. She needed to open herself up to *somebody*. Vicky, she thought. She couldn't think of anyone else. Maybe her doubts and faint suspicions of Vicky were groundless anyhow; maybe she had cause to feel a little foolish about them. When you got to the bottom line, she thought, she didn't *have* anybody else but Vicky. After a brief hesitation, she picked up the telephone and tried to call the other woman, both at her office and at home. She wasn't to be found. She left a message with the same secretary as before and wondered why Vicky hadn't been in touch with her. Busy, she supposed. Busy showing houses in distant places to prospective buyers.

No Vicky. A vacuum instead. An empty space.

Something, she thought. She had to do something. She couldn't simply stand by and watch her life slip away in fears and suspicions. She had to act. She had to get out of this apartment and *act*.

If she didn't, what was she going to be left with?

It wasn't the best idea in the world, but it was the only one she could entertain; it was the only thought that occurred to her. It wouldn't get her anywhere but at least it meant movement, it meant contact with a world outside, a sense of involvement. For a solitary detached moment she was a plump woman with a rather desperate expression traveling down a street of suburban houses in a mundane little car. What she saw was a small human speck made more insignificant by the violence of the awesome sunlight.

But you're doing *something*, she told herself.

At least you can say that much about yourself.

You're doing something.

She drove past some small office buildings, some ordinary middle-class houses, the usual palms with their fronds browning in the sun.

She slowed the Opel.

She found the place she was looking for, parked the car, got out.

It was one of those medical plazas that houses all sorts of physicians and dentists. A boxlike building with narrow slits for windows. She walked slowly past the various office doors, glancing at names, qualifications. So many people labored here over so many different breakdowns in the human animal. Cavities and cancers, gastro-intestinal diseases and dislocated bones.

When she found the door she was looking for, she paused. This won't bring you a victory, she thought. It won't get you anywhere. *You can't afford to think this way, Ellen Campbell. If you're not positive now, when will you ever be?*

The waiting room was empty. She imagined Eric sitting on one of the white leather armchairs, perhaps staring at the dwarf pomegranate she was looking at herself at that moment, perhaps idly scrutinizing the ceiling with its concealed lighting or picking up a copy of *Sports Illustrated* from a low-slung coffee table. It wasn't a room calculated to raise your spirits: it had a clinical facelessness about it, a lack of heart. She glanced in the direction of the reception window—a woman with long red hair was staring at her. Was this the one who had called such a long time ago?

She wanted to turn and leave. I've seen the place, she thought. I've seen enough. But you didn't come down here just to look, did you? Just to get some impression of where Eric had his mania treated? She moved toward the window. The woman behind the glass smiled, the kind of smile that always seems to accompany the phrase—*I think you've come to the wrong place.* Why? Weren't pregnant women allowed to have psychoses? Ellen placed her hands on her belly and waddled stiffly: I'm pregnant, don't you see, and I deserve some sympathy. One woman to another, members of the same sorority. She watched the window being slid open.

"Can I help you?" the woman asked.

Hesitation. Be firm, Ellen. Think of something to say.

"Can I help you?" Again: it was the same voice Ellen had heard on the telephone. The voice with a plum in its mouth.

"I want to see Dr. Ely," Ellen said. She moaned, a sound that wasn't strictly for effect. The baby had punched her.

"Do you have an appointment?" The woman looked down at her ledger.

"No," Ellen said.

"Oh, dear. I'm afraid you need one. Would you like to make one?"

Ellen leaned against the wall. "I want to see him now," she said.

"I'm afraid that won't be possible—"

"Why not?"

"Because he's busy—"

"Is he in his office?"

The red-haired woman rose. She had a scrawny neck which all the makeup in the world wouldn't conceal. "Now, look—"

"*Is* he in his office?"

"Please, don't make trouble for yourself—"

"I'm in enough trouble," Ellen said. "I'm a raving maniac and I need medical help."

A desperate farce, she thought. But once you've launched yourself on a course of theatrics, how do you pull yourself back?

The red-haired woman slid the window shut and Ellen rapped on the glass with her wedding ring. The woman glared at her, picked up a telephone, pressed a button. Maybe they had some system here of dealing with sudden emergencies—maybe they would have to, if patients were given to going totally berserk. A door beyond the reception area opened and a man came out—a man in a tweed jacket with leather elbow patches, a wild bunch of corn-colored hair, glasses, a dimple in his chin. Ellen watched him come through the reception room and into the waiting room.

"Are you Dr. Ely?"

The man didn't answer the question. He said, "Why don't you sit down? Why don't you sit down and rest and maybe we can discuss this."

Ellen moved to the nearest chair.

The man stood over her, hands tucked authoritatively in his pockets.

"Now what's the trouble?" he asked.

Ellen didn't answer him at once. She'd seen something, something just beyond the bewildered receptionist's head—a whole wall of files, initialed files, black folders. Eric's, she thought. How can I get my hands on Eric's?

"I need to see Dr. Ely," she said.

"I'm Howard Ely. But we normally use a system of appointments. It makes everything a little more orderly, you understand."

Patronizing fool. "I didn't have time to make an appointment," she said.

"Maybe you can explain your urgency," Ely said. He touched the odd little cavity in his chin, a self-conscious gesture.

"Can we go in your office?"

He looked at her as if she might be carrying a concealed weapon. Then he nodded, glanced at his watch, and said: "I have five minutes. Only five minutes." An expression passed between Ely and his receptionist: he might have been raising an eyebrow, using some prearranged signal. *You better get ready to call the cops*. Something like that. Dr. Ely motioned for her to step inside; he left the door open.

Eric comes here, she thought. The inner sanctuary. The private temple. He comes here to divulge his secrets and get his maintenance doses of digestible lobotomy.

"You might begin by telling me your name," Ely said and looked at his watch again.

Humoring me, she thought. Plain old-fashioned whitewash job.

"My name is Ellen Campbell," she said. "My husband's name is Eric."

Ely's expression didn't change.

"Eric Campbell," she said again. "He's a patient of yours."

"Is he?"

"You know damn well he is."

"I have a large number of patients," he said.

Applause, applause: so you're successful, big deal. "My husband is a patient of yours. He gets lithium carbonate from you. I've seen the prescriptions."

"What has your husband told you, Mrs. Campbell?"

Ellen stared at the window.

Nothing. How can I bring myself to say that?

"He's mentioned your name," she said.

"If he were a patient of mine, I'd know he's never mentioned me to you because he prefers a course of secrecy for his own reasons, valid or otherwise."

"That's a pretty goddam roundabout way of admitting he's your patient. It's also a pretty tortuous way of saying he wants to keep me in the dark, right?"

Ely nodded.

There was a smirk on his face, a look she loathed.

Ellen could say nothing.

"I can't discuss him with you, Mrs. Campbell," Dr. Ely said.

"I want to know what's *wrong* with him. Is that a crime?"

"I'm sorry. I'm very sorry. I can't tell you anything."

She felt her charade begin to unravel a little, her resolve work itself loose: she'd come in here blindly, she'd charged in here without thinking, half hoping for some kind of help, encouragement, whatever. But she'd learned nothing, nor would she. Ely kept his mind behind a padlock.

"If you weren't so obviously pregnant, Mrs. Campbell, I'd suggest a sedative, a mild sedative like Dalmane, and a good night's sleep. You're obviously distraught. You've got nothing to gain by coming here."

"Can't you tell me, for Christ's sake? Can't you tell me why he needs this medication? Why he has to come here?"

Ely shook his head. His jowls wobbled. He took off his glasses and folded them in the manner of a man about to launch a lecture on something obscure. She turned her face to the side; she felt suddenly humiliated and more than a little angry. Such desperate behavior, coming in here like this, blundering around, learning nothing. Sweet zero.

"You should talk this over with your husband," Ely said. "I can't think of any other course of action for you. You must see that my hands are tied."

She had the unsettling feeling of tears pressing behind her eyes. She fought them back as hard as she could. Your bravado, your bluster—they only carried you so far, kid. So far and no further. And you still have miles to go. She thought of the files again. How could she get her hands on Eric's? It wasn't possible. She could never get around the receptionist. I'm coming apart at the seams, she thought. Just beginning to break up all over again. What the hell happened to that resolve I had?

She heard herself say: *Please. Please tell me. Tell me something.*

The psychiatrist was turning away from her, fussing around his desk, gathering papers together.

"I'm already behind schedule, Mrs. Campbell. I suggest you sit down with your husband and talk to him."

"How can I talk to him when I don't even know him anymore?"

Ely smiled as if in sympathy: he smiled the way all doctors seemed to. The files, she thought again. They were burning away in her mind.

The receptionist had appeared, perhaps summoned telepathically, on the threshold of the office. Think, Ellen. Think your frazzled brains out. Ely was already moving out of the office, striding away with exaggerated steps. A man in a hurry. A man with pressing schedules.

He said something to the receptionist, something like, *Show Mrs. Campbell out, give her one of Al Lewinson's cards, it might come in handy for her*—and then he was sweeping across the waiting room, out the door in a square of sudden sunlight, gone. Ellen smiled at the receptionist.

"I didn't mean to give you any trouble. I'm sorry," she said. "I was worried, that's all. I don't know why I behaved so badly."

Followed by the woman, Ellen stepped into the reception room. The room of files. She paused by a typewriter, glanced up at the thick black folders, noticed they were alphabetically arranged—by letters, not by names. There were several Cs. They each had a number, probably a coded number. Of course: the discretion of a psychiatrist's office would demand that the names of patients not be advertised for all and sundry to see. She felt a sinking sensation, a fall from a great height. C1097. C2234. C8549. On and on, perhaps six or seven with the initial C. Any one of them could be Eric's file. Perhaps there was an elaborate system of coding. Perhaps names that began with the initial C were filed under Z—how could she know?

She pressed her hand to her forehead, faltered, slumped down in the chair by the typewriter. She moaned loudly and heard the woman sigh. *What's wrong? What's the matter? Is it the baby?* Ellen nodded her head back and forth, hands clutched to her belly now. *I don't want to alarm you. . . . I think this might be the moment.* The woman scurried around in a flustered manner. Ellen thought: If you'd been an obstetrician's receptionist you might have known what to do. *Is it the baby? What can I do? Tell me what I can do for you.* Ellen groaned. She hoped she looked suitably strained, tormented. *Water, a glass of water, then call my physician, can you do that . . . ?* The receptionist appeared to behave with the erratic movements of a pinball whanging around a board. She put her hands up to her hair, a gesture of bewilderment, then rushed out of the reception room and pushed open a door across a narrow hallway. The bathroom. *Quickly. Quickly now.* Ellen got up from the chair and tugged frantically at the files, the folders marked with a C.

Fast.

Please don't hurry back from the bathroom. Please don't.

She pulled down the closest one. Inside the stiff front sheet of the folder there was a photograph attached. A woman stared unsmilingly back at her. She put the folder back in place, took down the next one. How could she ever have enough time? She heard the sound of running water from across the hallway. You have to be desperate, kid. You have to be totally desperate.

The sound of the water stopped.

Any moment now—any moment now the woman would come hurrying back. She flipped the folder open. A bald man with a pair of thick glasses. No Eric. She lifted her arm and stuffed the thing back and took down the next one.

It happened horrifyingly. It happened as if she'd hauled out the one card essential to the delicate skeletal structure of a house of cards.

The dark-covered folders rained down on her, scattering all across the floor. Jesus Christ. You couldn't even accomplish this without clumsiness. You couldn't even manage to pilfer a meager file, could you? She heard them thump on the floor—and then she was looking directly into the astonished face of the receptionist who stood frozen in the doorway with a Dixie cup in her hand. Ellen smiled weakly, an apology, bent over, clutched her stomach, groaned, hoped the woman would think she'd lost her balance and just stumbled against the rack and caused an accident, hoped she'd think anything but attempted theft. *My God, what have you done, what HAVE you done?* Ellen shrugged and went down on her knees and scrambled around the fallen folders as if she meant to help put them back on the shelves. The Dixie cup slipped from the woman's hand and threw a shiny puddle across the tiled floor. A comedy of errors. A farce of mishaps. Ellen moaned and muttered something about the baby. The woman stepped over the rivulet of water and reached for the telephone and started to say something about needing a security guard at once, there was a pregnant woman about to give birth, send somebody up immediately, send anybody up. Ellen crawled over the folders, surreptitiously opening them, creating debris and chaos the more she moved. The woman put the telephone down and said, *Please don't touch the folders, you've caused enough trouble, I'll sort them out myself, please sit down and be still.*

Ellen pretended she didn't hear. I'll help, let me help.

Would you please keep your clumsy hands to yourself, you've done enough damage, now go sit down until somebody comes and takes you to a doctor, PLEASE.

Ellen tried to rise, slipped among the folders, kicking several of them open with her foot as she regained her balance: I must look like a pawing animal, she thought, a bear on all fours. She watched the receptionist start to gather folders together, listened to her mutter as she worked, and thought: You don't have much time, Ellen. You better find the folder fast. The woman turned her back, staggering under the weight of a pile of the folders, swaying toward the shelves and still mumbling vague obscenities. Ellen looked around the mess.

She saw it.

She saw Eric's photograph pinned to the outer binding. She put her foot out and kicked the folder and watched it skitter under the typewriter table and then, crawling forward, glancing around to see that the receptionist wasn't looking, she seized the black folder and stuffed it under her smock and then rose, both hands clamped against her belly.

A uniformed man appeared in the waiting room, tapped the glass window, poked his head through: "What was that call about?" he said.

The woman sighed. "This woman is about to give birth. We do not have the facilities here for that. Would you *please* take her out of here and stick her in somebody else's office?"

The guard smiled and raised a hand in Ellen's direction.

"Your water broke?" he asked. He was a small man with a square jaw; he might have failed to make the police department by a matter of inches.

"No, not yet," Ellen said.

"You want me to call a cab? Maybe see one of the docs downstairs or what?"

Ellen shook her head. "I'll be okay. Really. I think I still have time to drive to the hospital. The receptionist got carried away."

"Lady, I'll drive you if you like."

"Really. It won't be necessary."

The man took off his cap. There was a dark ring of sweat inside. "You sure?"

"Sure. Maybe it was a false alarm."

"I hope so. What do you want, boy or girl?"

"Just somebody healthy," Ellen said.

"That's a good attitude," the guard said. "Well, I wish you all the luck, lady."

"Thank you." And she moved away from him, her nerves

singing, she went toward the stairs and began her descent
and hoped the folder wouldn't be missed until she'd had time
to read through it.

She walked across the parking lot to her car, hands still
pressed to her belly. Inside the Opel she thought she was
going to faint. You got away with it, she thought. You blundered
your way into it and out the other side. She reached up
behind her smock and removed the folder and laid it on the
passenger seat.

As she drove she would glance down at the dark binding of
the folder: it burned a smoldering hole in her attention.

She realized she was very dry, needed something ice-cold
to drink, so she parked on a side street and walked into an
ice-cream parlor, a pink place that might have been transported in the 1950s from a Hollywood backlot. She sat up at
the counter, clutching Eric's folder on her knees. No more
leaving things in cars. Not with her history. She ordered an
ice-cream float, a raspberry concoction that foamed, and she
stuck a straw into it. As she put her mouth around the straw,
tasted the sweetness, she glanced to the side, eyes moving in
the direction of the window, the side street—a motion that
was involuntary. Purposeless. A movement that meant nothing.

She realized a moment later that if she hadn't looked she
would never have seen him. She understood that if she hadn't
chosen just that second to glance insignificantly out of an
ice-cream parlor window she'd have missed the sight of him.
She hadn't expected anything, anybody, hadn't anticipated
seeing a familiar face.

But there he was.

There he was crossing the side street.

A woman was walking at his side.

The folder began to slip from her knees. She caught it in
time. The binding swung open and Eric's face glanced up at
her from the photograph.

She felt confused and bewildered. A crack might have
opened in the ground. She might have heard distant thunder
and felt it vibrate through the hot air and somehow enter her
head and ricochet inside like a noise forever trapped in an
echo chamber.

Her hands hung loosely over the folder.

She shut her eyes.

A hallucination. Perhaps a mirage.

Anything but reality. Anything but.

She opened her eyes and pushed the ice-cream float aside.
Then she turned once more to the window and saw that it
was empty now. An empty world.

She dropped some coins on the counter, climbed down
from her stool, groaned as the baby indiscriminately assaulted
her insides, walked slowly to the front door.

You don't have to look.

Always remember—you don't have to look.

That choice is yours.

But then she was outside and the whole day was a sudden
airless vacuum. She couldn't breathe. Her lungs were tight.
She couldn't feel herself walk. Stifled, choked, suspended
somewhere above her own body. And the same distant rattle
of thunder locked in her head.

She didn't feel the sweat that ran from her forehead and
over her eyelids and fogged the lenses of her sunglasses.

She didn't feel a goddam thing.

The side street was filled with parked cars. She looked for
two in particular, didn't find them; it didn't matter anyhow.

Make it unreal. Make it an illusion.

There was a bar on the other side of the street. She moved
toward it. Dreamlike. Trance-walking.

It had swinging doors, appropriate to the wild West conceit
of this dump. She shoved them open slowly. The darkness of
the bar blinded her after the white horror of the sun.

She blinked.

What she saw—

They were sitting together at a shadowy corner table. They
had drinks in front of them. They didn't look up. He was
leaning toward her, his mouth opening and closing, and she
was nodding her head avidly. Her long black hair fell over the
shoulders of her white shirt.

Engrossed. They were wrapped up in each other.

Birds of a feather.

Two birds harping in a gilded cage.

Ellen watched a moment. Why did time suddenly run
berserk, go out of control, why did it stretch as if suddenly all
the clocks in the world were engaged in the impossible task
of marking some chronological babble? Stripped, meaningless: she didn't know how long she watched. They drank their
drinks. They talked. And she heard the echo of an old
comment, the fragment of a dead conversation—*if it works*

*out this time, you'll be the first to know all about it, believe
me. Believe me.*

And then she was out on the street again and walking
without a firm sense of direction, just walking, failing to hear
the sound of her own footsteps. But it was a world of deafness
now, there wasn't sound, everything receded into the kind of
silence you might hear at the heart of a dying flower.

She turned a corner, saw her car, went toward it.

Mindlessly.

Sixteen   *August 15/16*

Ellen sat in the apartment and watched the afternoon darken
to night. She saw the shadows grow longer as the sun
changed angles beyond the balcony door. The room seemed
cold—but it may have been the coldness from within she felt
more. An arctic temperature: it was the infrangible icy surface of betrayal. She sat, she waited, she thought of nothing.
She rocked back and forth sometimes and clutched her belly
as if there were pain inside but it was a pain she was beyond
feeling now.

You see two people cross a side street.

They go inside a bar.

You go after them and you open a door and all of a sudden
you find yourself staring into the kind of room you never
knew existed, never suspected.

The face of your husband.

The face of your friend.

You see two faces together and the sight kills you.

She looked at the black folder she'd gone to so much
trouble to steal. It lay on the kitchen table. She picked it up,
dragged her feet toward the bedroom, sat down on the edge
of the bed and opened the binder.

Flick the pages. Flick the double-spaced, neatly typed
pages of your errant husband's psychic history. She couldn't
read it. Why would she want to read it now, now when it
barely mattered? (The nerves rage. Dead pulses come back
like comatose forces crudely stirred. A winter burns in the

blood.) She turned to the last page, skipping, skipping. There
was a slot inside the back of the folder: a cassette tape. Eric's
voice, she assumed. A recorded session. Secrets for posterity,
revelations doomed to footnotes in some academic treatise,
some unreadable tome.

She shut the folder. She put it in her drawer in the
dressing table among blouses, underwear, socks. You're jumping
to conclusions, she told herself. Be of good cheer. You're
adding up one and one and coming out with the square root
of treachery. Your emotional arithmetic is wrong, wrong.
(Why do you see those two faces together like that? Hanging
on each other's words? Hanging as if words were kisses,
warm embraces? Why do you see his hand flat against her
stomach and sliding down to a place between her legs and
her head thrown back, mouth open, hair swinging, a look
in her eyes of exquisite ecstasy? Why do you see pale flesh in
rooms where curtains are drawn and all the discretions of
infidelity are observed? Why do you see all this run through
your brain like rampant lions? Conclusions.

Eric and Vicky. Oh, didn't it add up, though?

Didn't it add up to something?

You're so goddam sure, Ellen. Why are you so sure?

Vicky and her married men. Eric and the frustration of a
wife whose grace and attractiveness is no more than that of a
dromedary. Why the hell wouldn't they get together? Why
wouldn't Eric seek something on the side for the duration?

But.

But. If it were something else, a deeper thing, a love—
what then?

She rubbed her hands together and walked to the bedroom
window. You thought Anna Rosenberg. You thought the Siren
of the Pool. The Sweetheart of the Tennis Court. Miss
Midnight of the Laundry Room. That's what you thought.
(No wonder Vicky didn't answer her calls, the message. No
wonder. Guilt, shall we say? Guilt of the affair. A world of
married men out there and she has to choose Eric.)

The day was growing darker, the shadows thicker, the
spaces between the fronds of palms more dense. The birds,
sensing dark, were silent in the trees now. She stared from
the window for a long time, thinking all kinds of thoughts she
didn't want to think. Vicky and Eric—you keep seeing them
together, you keep inventing a history of their affair (motels
and hotels and obscure restaurants and the tentative touch of

fingers that leads to the thrust of sex); you keep punishing yourself.

They were having an innocent drink together. Of course.

And more bad thoughts came in with the ferocity of a hailstorm. She could hear them pound, knotted things, things without direction. More and more until the sky of her mind was blackened by them. Stop them, stop the speculations, the wonderings. Stop them now.

They may be in love, she thought.

They may be in love—where does that leave me?

An obstacle, kid. A hurdle in the path of the heart.

It leaves you high and dry and stranded and totally the trespasser upon the stale grave of your own marriage. Lay the lilacs here, lay the carnations there, flowers die as easily as loves. They may love each other with some terrible passion—how could she know?

She walked the room, stalked the dimming light, dreaded the return of Eric. She didn't want to see him, look at him, feel his touch. (An obstacle. The thought was wild. It broke her heart.)

Would he come bounding through the front door shortly, and say, *Guess who I met today? Guess who bought me a drink?* The hell he would. He wouldn't say a word, he'd come in, whistle, put his briefcase down, kiss her: and the touch of his lips would curdle her somewhere inside, make her cringe like an animal fearing the whip of its trainer.

They make a pair, she thought.

They don't need me. I am excess baggage. I am unnecessary luggage. They just don't need me. *Eric, Eric, any time would have been a bad time, but this is the very worst of times.* They don't need me. (People ask for divorces, don't they? They come right out with the question: Will you agree to a divorce? They don't mess around with elaborate plans to drive the third party up the wall, do they? *Where did that thought come from?* The tense strings of your nerves, kid. The taut little cords that carry messages, like Western Union people, from one part of the body to another. The third party. That's what you are, Ellen. *The third party.*)

You could choose to ignore it, couldn't you?

You could turn the switch that puts your memory on to some selective scanning system so that at any time in the future, when you tried to recall these hours, you'd get nothing but a blank. Always a blank, a space, hours lost.

Eric. Eric.

Elaborate plans.

Why did she keep coming back to this notion? This concept of a conspiracy, of something being plotted against her?

She pushed it out of her mind. Everything was suddenly too much, too overwhelming. She wished she had the capacity to go on automatic pilot and dream the rest of her days and perform all functions without ever thinking again. She wished she could pick this moment to faint, to have a breakdown, to let the systems shrivel to tiny disconnected pieces.

A deadly assumption. But deadly assumptions sprang from minds sliced by the razor's edge. *Your husband is insane. Your husband is on a course of potent medication, mental maintenance. He might be capable of almost anything. He might be capable of something deadly.*

She wanted to laugh at herself.

But then she thought—imagine.

Imagine this. Between the two of them, between her husband and her friend, they might resolve to get her out of the way: imagine this—they might hatch some cheapo plot to make her think she was losing her mind. They might steal objects of insignificance. They might play schizo jokes. (Heads together again. Were they dreaming up a new one this afternoon? Were they laughing together and saying *I've got a good one, let's steal her* TV Guide *or send her an anonymous letter?*) They might do things like that—except people didn't, did they? People went to lawyers to see that the due process of the law was observed and a marriage dissolved, because lawyers were the official pallbearers of dead matches.

This builds, kid. This takes you out on uncharted seas, Ellen.

And you can stray on such oceans and drift forever under the killing sun.

All you know, all you *think* you know, is that Eric isn't being on the level with any part of his life. A master of concealment. A twister. Truth isn't truth and lies aren't lies— he makes his own pretzel-shaped reality.

When she stepped out onto the balcony she didn't feel the heat of the day—a strange perception that climate was a state of mind, after all. She looked down into the shadows of the parking lot.

She knew somebody was watching her from the shade down there.

Under a tree, concealed by a shrub, somewhere down there.

She knew it as certainly as she felt her own heartbeat.

She peered through the twilight, leaning against the rail around the balcony. A moment of anger: *Why the hell don't you come out and show yourself? Why do you hide like this, for God's sake? Who are you? Are you Vicky? Are my own mad thoughts taking me in the right direction?*

Whoever you are, in the name of Christ, show yourself.

Show me your face.

The rail pressed against her belly. She saw the blue pool light and the sparkle of water reflected on the palms and the sudden flare of the floodlights going on above the tennis courts. And then she was thinking of a black car, a black car idling in the driveway of her mother's house, she was thinking of the fact that Vicky had a small black car, she was freewheeling among the shorted-out associations of memory. But all the cars in the parking lot were black now in the dead light. They were all colorless, shapeless, still.

She closed her eyes a moment. She thought: All the hurt you feel distills itself in acts of uncontrollable imagination. You see connections where none might exist. You understand that which can't be understood, you fill the empty spaces of your brain with phantoms.

But someone is watching me now.

Someone is watching me from the parking lot.

She stepped back from the edge of the balcony and leaned against the glass door and put her hand flat against her moist forehead. It was a terrible pain, a terrible moment for the baby to kick with such violence. Her eyes watered. When only different pains surround you, which do you choose to assuage first? Which do you pacify?

She wiped sweat from her face with her sleeve and looked back down into the parking lot. The same sensation filled her; the same feeling seemed to extend from her and become enlarged until it had altered the texture of the darkness itself. She thought she saw something move in the palms. Something that flashed white. Something the color of a bedsheet.

But then there was nothing below save for the dark and the noise of swimmers and the distant sound of tennis balls smacking off rackets and a girl squealing someplace. Everything seemed shapeless in some way, without definition: it was as if she were listening to an ill-tuned radio and picking up several channels at one time. The blackness wouldn't yield to her stare, wouldn't give up anything: it was the dark inside a closed box, the impenetrable dark of the sealed coffin. She clenched the handrail and stared at the large palm by the corner of the wire fence and she thought: Anybody could be standing behind it. Anybody could be down there.

But who?

She turned away from the edge of the balcony and went back inside the apartment and, without thinking, without planning anything through, walked along the hallway to the front door, which she opened quietly—as if she were afraid of somebody eavesdropping on the squeal of hinges—and stepped from there to the stairs. Slowly, slowly, she descended. Now the heat seemed to be growing all around her. Why are you doing this? Why are you going out there? You pursue more phantoms. Nobody is watching you and McDonald has got it all wrong. There are no plots, no practical jokes, no thefts, your husband isn't having an affair with your friend—the world is in the proper order.

She stood in the unlit parking lot.

She looked beyond the cars to the fence, the stunted palm, the still shadows under the fronds.

And then she moved toward it.

She moved cautiously. She thought: I am going out of my mind. This is what a breakdown feels like, a vacancy of the heart, an airlessness within the brain, a sense that nothing matters because nothing exists.

There was a movement under the leaves. A dart of white, visible as the motion of a tiny cockatoo might be—a flash, a flurry of white. (Somebody in white—she'd seen somebody weeks and weeks ago standing in this very place in the dead of a sticky night.) She approached the palm which, bending as if it were dying from heat exhaustion, threw a spread of thick shadows across the ground.

Then she stopped.

She saw it vaguely through the darkness, through some half-lit passage in the clenched shadows, half hidden by broad fronds and thick branches; she saw it shimmer a moment as if it were ethereal, composed of nothing but pure white light. She saw the face and the black rings beneath the eyes and the black gash that was the mouth. She stood perfectly still in the manner of a man stalking a bird or a butterfly, that frozen moment when the binoculars are poised or the net is stiff and motionless in midair: she stood perfectly still and she watched.

The lips moved. The black lips moved.

The mouth became a circle, a vacant hollow.

The dark of the eyes suggested a bottomless place, a sea with more fathoms than anybody could measure. And then she became aware of something else—more than the single bell-like note of familiarity she experienced—she became aware of the whiteness of clothing, a full-length milky paleness that reminded her of a bridal gown, a robe of some kind, a garment of betrothal. She wasn't sure what. And something else, a dark object held in midair by pale hands, an object that looked for all the world like a spray of small pathetic flowers, a bridal spray, the flowers a bride might clutch, as if out of hope, at the foot of the aisle.

She swayed slightly, closed her eyes, felt something grip her gently by the arm.

She turned her face and saw Eric standing beside her.

She said nothing, she raised her arm, pointed to the shadows under the palm.

"What?" Eric asked. "What is it?"

She said, "Look, look over there—?"

But there was nobody, nothing, a space where somebody had been, a flat expanse of dark, evacuated of its stunning whiteness, an emptiness such as the kind you might see through a telescope on a cloudy night.

Eric turned his head round. "What is it? I don't see a damn thing."

"Somebody was standing there—"

"Ellen," and the tone was filled with warning, with impatience.

"Somebody was—" *Eric. She remembered Eric.* She dragged her arm from his grip and moved away from him and said, "Don't touch me." And she was conscious of a scene coming, a slice of hysteria cut from her behavior, an act to be played out here in this black parking lot.

"Ellen, what's wrong with you?"

She said nothing, she tried to swing away from him, but he caught her hard and forced her close to him. "Jesus Christ, Ellen, what is wrong with you? What's gotten into you these last few days?"

"Don't you know? Do I have to answer that question?"

There was a look of pain on his face, his features lit by the faint glimmering light from the pool. She couldn't stand to look at him; she turned her eyes toward the palm tree. What had she seen? What kind of hallucination had that been? No, Christ, no; it had been real.

A woman had been standing there as if dressed for a wedding and on her face was the most sorrowful look Ellen could ever remember seeing. Sorrowful—but that wasn't the word, that wasn't exactly it: if there *had* been sorrow, it was a look touched by madness as well, a madness in the blackness of the eyes, the dark mouth, the drooping flowers.

"Ellen, please," he was saying.

She didn't turn to him. She didn't want him to touch her. The baby moved suddenly, almost as if it were plunging downward between her legs. Dropping, taking position. Eric reached out for her again but she stepped back. How could he have missed the woman under the tree? Unless it was part of his plan—but he had no plan, there was no conspiracy, nobody was acting and plotting against her. Remember, Ellen, remember you're dealing with a man who might be quite out of his mind.

Jesus, which one of us is mad? Are we both?

She moved toward the tree, brushed fronds aside, saw nothing: Eric was behind her, trying to grab her by the shoulders.

"Ellen, please, please, let's go upstairs, you're not well—"

"Yeah, I'm sick, I'm sicker than hell. God knows, maybe I'm even as sick as you, Eric."

"What is that supposed to mean?"

She didn't answer him. She circled the palm tree—only vaguely conscious of how absurd she might look to anyone passing. She could hear Eric coming up behind her. She swung around, one hand raised to grip the wire fence as if for support, and she said, "I suppose that was Vicky under the tree, huh? I suppose that was her in fancy dress?"

"Vicky?" He paused. He pushed a broad frond away with the flat of his hand. "What are you talking about, Ellen?"

Nobody. She didn't see anyone. She might have dreamed the presence; she might have encountered an apparition. And even the sound of her own voice now, the words she was saying, didn't seem altogether real or sensible to her. *You and Vicky, your little game, don't you think I know?*—and she stopped, she had to silence the shrillness in her voice and stem the flow of her thoughts, thoughts that were leading her ever further away from certainty, from the things she knew and felt safe with. Eric had his arm around her shoulder and was saying things in a soothing voice the way a nanny might talk to an agitated kid.

My world is falling to pieces.

My whole world is just crumbling and my nostrils are filled with the smell of wreck and decay.

Eric is touching me.

He's *touching* me.

She shrugged his hand away from her shoulder, walked a few steps in front of him. The pain was burning between her legs.

Eric came up from behind. "Ellen, I don't understand you. I don't know what you're talking about."

She couldn't speak to him, wouldn't speak. Why waste her words? Why try to communicate with a man whose whole world was shot through with lies, deceits? A complete waste of breath. She entered the building just ahead of him. This falling sensation. She held her stomach tightly and felt calm all at once, a moment of madness past, a dangerous moment behind her. You only need to think of baby now, just think of baby, nothing else matters in this whole twisted world but the safety of the baby.

It's your only responsibility.

Nothing else is of any importance—neither lies nor infidelities, neither illusions nor hoaxes.

Only baby matters.

Keep that thought uppermost in your mind.

Never lose sight of it. Don't let it slip. Your anchor. It holds you to a practical world of black and white and common sense.

Baby. Let the baby preserve your sanity.

Baby.

Hold it. Just hold it and love it. Suffer pain on its behalf. Nothing else means a damn.

Baby is life. Life itself. The only positive force.

Beauty and life.

"I don't understand anything you've been saying," Eric said.

You don't matter.

I should have seen through you before now.

"I just don't know what's come over you," he said.

She began to climb the stairs. She wondered if, in her absence, something else might have been stolen from the apartment. She thought: Maybe they've taken the bulb from the bedside lamp. Good luck to them. Good luck to them, whoever they might be. A light bulb—they might as well. It didn't matter to her now.

Concentrate on nothing but this life inside you.

Nothing else.

She heard the sound of Eric's voice, whining, wheedling, pleading. The words didn't reach her brain. She thought: A light bulb to illuminate all the other stolen junk. A blue shirt and an old doll's face and a couple of library books I borrowed and never returned.

They might need a light to sift through that collection.

Whoever they are. It doesn't matter now.

She stopped, breathless, outside the door of the apartment, which she'd left open. She could still hear Eric coming up the steps at her back, his voice going on and on; she derived some kind of satisfied amusement out of the fact she wasn't really listening. For the first time in their marriage, his words meant absolutely nothing.

She walked inside the bedroom and slammed the door behind her. She heard Eric open it: a lock, I wish to God there was a lock on the bedroom door. She sat on the bed and stared down at the rug. He was going on and on. She heard Vicky's name recur in his one-sided conversation, but she wasn't really listening. She wanted to look at him with all the coldness she felt and say: *I don't know you. I don't even care*.

She glanced at his face and looked away. The baby moved once more. My love, she thought. And the thought ran through her veins. My sweet baby.

Why did Eric keep talking like this? Didn't he understand he wasn't getting through? What difference did his words make? She covered her ears with her hands. Make him stop, somebody make him stop.

Aren't you interested to know I had a drink with Vicky only because I've been concerned about you recently only because I wanted to ask her advice about you and your behavior and there isn't anything going on I just wanted to talk to her about the weird way you've been acting the strange things you've been doing the way you've been watching me never taking your eyes off me maybe because you're under some

*strain I can understand that but it's hard for me it's hard on
me why the hell do you make it so hard for me how could you
imagine anything was going on with me and your best friend
I love you love love you*

In and out, fading and breaking, his voice went on and on.

She distanced herself. She made herself absent. She imagined the white beautiful face of a baby lying in a crib, saw its
small lovely mouth at her breasts, felt its warm hand lying in
her fingers. Then she was conscious of Eric falling silent. She
took her hands from her ears. She watched him shake his
head and turn and go out of the room. He closed the door
behind him.

She lay back across the bed for a while and gently rubbed
her stomach. The baby will save your life, she thought. The
sordid affairs of the world can go on and on—the purity, the
newness of this baby is the only thing that matters.

The purity. The newness.

A new life.

Everything else is a strain.

She closed her eyes and thought about the woman she'd
seen under the tree. She thought about the face. The eyes.

Those eyes.

It hardly seemed to matter to her now that the face was
familiar. Familiar—in some way, yes.

She listened, hearing Eric clatter around angrily in the
kitchen. She thought: Maybe he's mislaid his precious pills.
Maybe he has an attack coming on.

She went to the closet and opened it.

She stared at her clothes, thinking: How can I stay here
now? How can I go on living here with a man I don't know?
She hesitated only a moment before she hauled out a couple
of garments and stuffed them inside an overnight bag, then
she went to her drawer in the dressing table and removed
some underwear, stashing them on top of her clothes. She
hesitated a moment over the folder—did she need it now?
Did it really matter?

She paused: Where are you going anyhow? Where can you
run to?

She shrugged and dropped the folder on top of the rest of
the stuff in the bag, then she moved toward the bedroom
door. The TV was playing loudly now—as if it were a manifes-
tation of Eric's anger. Or his madness. She went quietly along
the hallway and just as quietly unlocked the front door.

A moment suddenly—of sadness? sorrow? You don't just walk out on the spur of the moment without feeling something, but whatever it was she experienced it passed in a flash and when she closed the door behind her she felt numb, nothing else.

She had everything she needed. She might be walking out on a life, but she had everything she needed.

Cross the dark parking lot, open the door of the Opel, start the engine, slip the car into reverse. These wheels will take you to a safer place—perhaps not sanctuary, but a safer place. So she drove to the edge of the parking lot with her headlights piercing the dark.

It was then she almost lost control.

The wheel spun from her hands as the lights pinned the shape of a woman in a long white dress, face covered with white makeup, eyes and mouth as black as the desert night. Ellen twisted the wheel, braked, felt the Opel go into a slight skid, but by then the figure had moved away and was lost in the deeper shadows of the parking lot. Something flew in front of Ellen's face, something moist and perfumed that landed on top of the overnight bag on the passenger seat. Moist and perfumed. For a long time she didn't move, she simply sat behind the wheel with her head inclined forward, breathing badly, unsteadily, her pulses going crazy.

Madness—you're circled by insanity. You might have made a ring of the covered wagons of lunacy around you, only to discover there was no protection to be had. Madness. She shut her eyes and sniffed the scented air, then reached for the overhead light and switched it on.

It was a bouquet of flowers that had been thrown through the window. A damp bouquet of various flowers.

She turned off the light and drove forward, thinking: A mad woman is out there haunting me. Somebody crazy who knows where I live and who knows where I'm going, who knows my erratic schedule as well as myself.

You have to go there.

You don't have anyplace else to go.

You can't return to Eric and that tense apartment, the straitjackets of those rooms.

So she drove circuitous routes and narrow side streets; she drove with a paranoid's sense of direction, as if even now she thought she was being followed. When she reached the home of her mother in Paradise Valley it was after midnight. She parked the car in the driveway but didn't get out at once.

There was no pride in any of this.

There was no dignity to salvage.

An emptiness. Only that. You run home to mother because in your time of fear you have nowhere else to go. The circular life—you leave home, you return.

She opened the door and reached for her bag and the overhead light snapped on. For a terrible moment she was possessed by the notion that somebody was crouching in back, huddled on the floor. Nobody. She even looked to be sure. Then she stared at the flowers. A wreath. A bouquet.

Violets. Carnations. Roses.

She picked them up, then let them fall from her hand.

She got out of the car and stood in the darkened driveway with the bag at her side and she thought: How long has this person been following me?

And then she turned, startled by the sound of a movement behind her. She peered through the darkness, trembling, every nerve in her body activated. Somebody moving through the night, somebody behind her.

She opened her mouth to say something. She heard her own unintelligible whisper.

"Ellen? Is that you?"

Hattie. Hattie Dalrymple. It was only Hattie. In her hand she held something that shone dully in the feeble light from the house.

Shears. Garden shears.

"Ellen, whatever are you doing here?"

"Hattie," and her voice was thin, reedy. The shears. Why did Hattie have those sharp things in her hand? She felt dizzy, knees weak, the bag in her hand unbearably heavy. She couldn't take her eyes away from the garden implement. She watched Hattie approach then felt the woman's hand on her shoulder.

"Ellen, what's wrong with you? You look terrible. You better come inside, lie down. Here, let me take that bag."

Thank you, Hattie. Thank you. But why are you holding those shears?

Hattie swung the bag in one hand, lowered the shears in the other. "If I didn't know better, Ellen, I'd say you've run away from home."

Dizzy again. Scared. She let Hattie lead her toward the house, open the door. A flood of electricity blinded her. She pointed to the shears and Hattie smiled.

"Your mother has some odd superstition that it's better for roses to be trimmed during the dark. Don't ask me why."

Ellen nodded feebly. From somewhere within the house she could hear her mother's voice and the tap-tap-tap of the walker touching ceramic tiles. She was weak now; her limbs might have turned to a viscous liquid. The baby pushed, shoved, stretched as if bored by its confinement.

"Hattie?" Her mother's voice. "What the devil's going on out there?"

"It's Ellen," Hattie called out.

It's only Ellen, it's only me.

It's only your daughter come back to the fold.

See how she runs. See how she runs away. She doesn't know she can't run. She has nowhere to go. Nowhere in all the world.

You watch her stand in the night, shaking to death. You can smell the fear upon her. You see how her fat belly trembles. You think: One more thing.

Her scared face gives you pleasure. The terror in her eyes delights you. You feel a power rising inside you, a sweet sense of control.

Just one more thing.

Then everything is complete.

Soon.

Seventeen   *August 19*

≈≈≈≈≈≈≈≈≈≈≈≈≈≈≈≈≈≈≈≈≈≈≈≈≈≈≈≈≈≈≈

Her mother had Hattie make up the spare bedroom for Ellen. No questions were asked, and Ellen—thankful for such a small mercy—gave no explanations in any case. She hung her clothes in an empty closet, a few pathetic garments, a couple of blouses. She stuffed her underwear in a drawer Hattie had lined with old Christmas wrapping paper. She put Eric's folder under the bed, and although she tried several times to open it and read the typed pages, she didn't have the heart. And all the time the baby kept dropping, as if pressing now to be born, to be released from the captivity of the womb.

Eric telephoned a couple of times a day and each time she refused to speak with him; there was one part of her that wanted to talk with him badly, but she realized she didn't have anything to say. During those solitary moments when she lay in the spare room and flicked through magazines, she wondered if perhaps she was being too hard on him. But the lies, the suspicions, the recollections of Eric and Vicky made her think she was doing the right thing. The right thing—how could you ever be sure of that? She lay on the bed and listened to her mother play ragtime tunes on her tinny piano and she thought about her marriage, she thought about its deterioration, she pondered her future. You could go back to Eric, she might say to herself. Go back and tell him you know about Ely and forgive him about Vicky (even if he disclaimed that affair, thought it preposterous) and put your marriage back on something resembling the right tracks. How the hell can I go back? How could I ever be sure he was being truthful? How could I sit in that apartment on a night when he said he might be working late and not construct alternative scenarios for his lateness.

So she refused to take calls from him until she felt she'd reached a decision of some kind—although the prospect of a decision seemed to have all the shimmering distance of a mirage under a hot sun. She was tired most of the time, feeling the baby turning inside her, twisting and dropping as if in some state of hyperactivity before birth. She was tired and afraid of the pain. She couldn't imagine something as large as a newborn child passing through the narrow opening at the top of her legs without hearing the sound of her own flesh tear. You can't go into the last hurdle feeling this sense of fear, she thought. With Eric the fear might have been tolerable: alone like this, it was terrible.

On her third day at her mother's house, she telephoned Patrick McDonald. She had been putting him at the back of her mind, trying to forget the events he invariably reminded her of—but when she thought of the woman under the tree and the flowers inevitably rotting on the seat of her car she felt another kind of fear, a different fear. When he answered the call he didn't sound surprised to hear her voice.

He said, "How's the baby?"

"Pressing," she answered.

"I suppose you can expect it any day now."

"It isn't really due until next month—"

"Ah, they're such contrary little buggers. They have this bad habit of choosing their own time."

A silence. She could hear him strike a match. There was the sound of smoke being exhaled. Then he said, "So what's new, Mrs. Campbell? Anything happening in the monkey-puzzle tree of your life?"

Monkey-puzzle tree: those tortuous branches. She hesitated a moment and then she heard herself telling him about the woman in the bridal outfit, she heard herself speak about the bouquet thrown into her car—the voice didn't sound like her own somehow, nor did the events she related seem in any way connected with her life. He was silent again as if absorbing this new information.

"Alice in bloody Wonderland," he said. "I sometimes wonder what you'll surprise me with next, you know that? Now you've hit me with a woman dressed as a bride who seems to want to give flowers away. This person's been on your heels for a long time," he said. "Don't you have any idea who it might be? Don't you have any idea at all? Think hard."

"I've thought about it, believe me. I can't figure it out."

"You're missing something, Mrs. Campbell. You're leaving something out. God knows what, but I'm sure it's staring us right in the face."

Staring me in the face: sure—but what the hell was it? What had she overlooked? Eric, she thought—why didn't she just go the whole way and tell McDonald about Eric, about his shrink, about Eric together with Vicky? But when she considered this prospect she saw some dreary soap unfolding in front of her eyes and she didn't want to unload it on the cop.

"I don't know what to say, Mrs. Campbell. It's got me beat, I admit. Somebody's playing a silly game—I just wish I saw some pattern in it. Why the hell would a woman go around dressed up as a bride, for heaven's sake?"

"I wish I knew. Maybe she lost her way when she was going to church—"

"She must *really* have strayed," he said.

"I guess." She realized she'd been secretly hoping he'd come up with answers, but he didn't have any. She felt alone again, disappointed, let down in some mild way.

He said, "Listen. Do something for me. Think hard about everything that's happened. Try to remember if there's anybody who might want to harm you. Go over the pattern of events and see if you can find something that stands out. I'll do the same. And if anything occurs to you, you've got my number. Okay?"

"Thanks," she said. Her voice was flat and dry. *The pattern of events*. What pattern? Maybe cops were trained to see designs in things, maybe they were taught to look for logical wholes. A pattern—there wasn't one. And who would want to harm her except for—

She stopped dead in her thoughts. Open your hand, let that particular bird fly free. When you come back to Eric you come back to despair and you don't need to feel like that. You need to be strong for the baby. So why did she keep returning to the notion of Eric and Vicky involved in some deadly charade? Why did she imagine Vicky standing under that palm? Throwing flowers into the car? It was a fearful stretch of the imagination. It came out of hurt and betrayal, out of fresh wounds and new scars.

In the living room her mother was sitting at her piano. A cheroot hung from her lips and her head was tilted back, eyes screwed up against the rising column of smoke. She was tinkering at the keys, hitting bum notes as frequently as the right ones. The room was cool and the awnings beyond the windows created shade. From the kitchen there was the sound of Hattie Dalrymple chopping something with a knife—celery, carrots, something crunchy. Her mother swung around on the piano stool. For a moment she surveyed her daughter. Then she took the cheroot from her mouth and stubbed it in an ashtray on top of the piano.

"How are we today?" she asked.

Ellen said, "Fine, just fine," but she knew her voice was glum. She flopped into an armchair and spread her legs apart, noticing how thick the ankles were, how flabby the calves seemed.

"Your husband called twice this morning," her mother said. Frail smoke was breaking around her face. "I told him you didn't want to speak to him. I assume you approve?"

Ellen nodded.

"This falling out..." Her mother paused, then laid her elbows on the keys. There was a harsh chord. "It's none of my business, dear, but if you want to tell me, I'm here."

Ellen looked at the older woman. It was impossible to confide in her, hard to speak the truth: it was a depressing recognition—*I can't be open with my own mother.* She rose from her chair and walked restlessly to the window, stared out at the back yard, the land turning to an expanse of desert under the cloudless sky. *Anybody who might want to harm you . . .*

Anybody.

Think hard, Mrs. Campbell.

Think hard.

She could think until her mind was bruised and raw, until she'd run all her thoughts dry as desert streams.

She could think until the clap of doomsday and never come up with the name of somebody who might wish her harm. (Eric, Eric—the wheel keeps turning that way, it keeps revolving toward him. Even Eric—she couldn't imagine even Eric wanting to harm her. Could she?)

I could have given him a chance, she thought. I could have heard his case out and then delivered a judgment. I rushed into this flight back to the nest. I could have tried to understand his psychiatric problems, whatever they might be. His pain, his burden, whatever. I didn't. I didn't give him a real opportunity, did I?

Think hard.

I'm thinking, goddammit. Can't you see I'm thinking?

She had to lie down.

She lay on her side, her head hanging over the edge of the mattress. Her fingertips dangled on the uncarpeted floor. The folder was inches away, she knew that. She also knew she wanted to turn those typed pages and read about her husband, read about his condition, his life, his anxieties—read about the inner man. You only have to open the folder. You only have to scan the pages. If you dare.

She stuck her hand underneath the bed and her fingers encountered the stiff binding. As she attempted to raise the folder, drag it into daylight, there was a searing, burning sensation in her womb. She clamped a hand over her mouth to hold back the scream she knew was rising inside her.

It passes, Ellen. Even this pain passes. She wished there were something she could take, but then Phelps's voice came back with all the chilly echo of authority: *No needless chemicals, Ellen. No needless chemicals.*

It passes, remember that, all pain passes.

She tried deep breathing now, relaxing her muscles, waiting for the pain to go away.

The folder was open. Eric's photograph. She stared at his face and wondered why it looked so unfamiliar. *Who are you? Whom did I marry?*

Eric. Oh, Eric. Why does it come down to this—discovering the truth about you in some sterile binder? Why couldn't you have told me yourself?

At first she thought it might have been written in Arabic script, a foreign language calculated to protect privacy. But as she looked she realized the entire psychiatric history of her husband had been written down with a shorthand machine, a typewriter like the ones court stenographers use. Everything was inscribed in shorthand. A security measure. Confidentiality. And for her purposes utterly useless. It might just as easily have been braille. She turned the pages hastily now, bending them as she flicked.

I went to all this trouble to steal something I can't even read.

When she threw it aside she heard something skidding across the tiles. The cassette tape had fallen free and was lying some distance from the binder.

The tape. She'd forgotten the tape.

She rose from the bed and bent to pick it up.

The pain, God, the pain.

She straightened up. How much lower could the baby drop? Please, not now. Not now. She clutched the cassette in one hand and went out of the bedroom. She moved along the hallway: her mother was at the piano again. *Clunk clunk clunk.* All the meters of the ragtime age were dying under her thick fingers. She looked inside her mother's bedroom. Somewhere, she had a portable radio with a cassette player. But where? There were plants and books all around the large brass bed—but no sign of the player. She looked around quickly, then entered the adjoining bedroom, Hattie's. A bed, an old trunk with initials carved on the side, newspapers stacked on the floor. No cassette player. She stepped into the kitchen: Hattie was carving the wings from a chicken, singing to herself as she cut. The radio sat on the kitchen table, a man's voice in the middle of a narrative.

"Hattie, can I borrow the radio?"

"I'm listening to something—"

"Please, Hattie. I want to *borrow* it."

Hattie wiped her hands on her apron and looked at Ellen and said, "Sometimes you're really your mother's daughter, aren't you?"

Ellen picked up the radio and carried it back into her bedroom. She inserted the cassette, turned the switch to TAPE, then sat on the edge of the bed to listen. At first there was nothing but a scratchy hissing sound and she began to wonder why a blank tape would have been included in Eric's folder, but then she heard a voice she recognized as that of Ely. A flat monotonous voice clearly reading from prepared notes. (Maybe he'll start to *talk* in shorthand in a moment, she thought. Then what?)

Subject, Eric Campbell, Caucasian male, age thirty . . .

Subject. How cold. How objective. Caucasian male. She reached out and turned the tape off. She was scared; suddenly she was scared—she didn't want to know anything else, didn't want to listen to what was on the tape. First you spy on your husband, then you eavesdrop on his secrets. What kind of person are you, Ellen?

A frightened one. That's what you are. *Dead scared.*

She reached out, her hand shaking, and she pressed the TAPE button again. The quality of the recording was poor, very poor, a well-paid shrink should have been able to afford something better.

. . . a brief résumé of this subject's history would involve the recurring self-accusation that he should have been married to someone else . . .

She switched the tape off. She was sinking, falling into a black place. She didn't need to hear this. Didn't want to hear it. Why should she go on punishing herself?

Someone else.

Someone else. A woman in a white gown. A bouquet. She walked up and down the room. Connections. Like what? They shimmer. They blink in and out like the orchestrations of neon lights.

She stopped beside the cassette player and stared at it, her fingers hovering over the TAPE button. Press it. Go on. You've come this far. You can't hide from it any longer.

. . . the history of this subject's relationship with his present wife is suffused by a deeply rooted sense of guilt concerning X, a woman he knew prior to his marriage . . .

X. No names. Just a dehydrated symbol. Just the clinical ascription of a letter, as if a human being might be reduced to a random fragment of the alphabet. Jesus. What gives people like Ely the right to distill a person like this?

. . . the symptoms of his condition manifest themselves in classical ways, in extremes of mood . . .

Ely cleared his throat here. She could see him raise a hand to his mouth and politely cough.

. . . extremes of mood which he is frequently unable to deal with or to keep under control. He goes from elation to depression without intervening stages. Classical too are his recurring nightmares concerning X and the violence involved in that relationship . . .

Nightmares. He doesn't remember his nightmares. *The baby should live.* His nightmares concern the baby, paternal anxieties, fear—that's what his nightmares are all about. What the hell do *you* know, Ely? And violence, what violence? She stared at the tape, suddenly wanting to rip it from the cassette player and smash it, twist it and twist it until it was beyond salvage.

I don't need to hear all this.

She listened to the sound of her mother on the piano. *Chink chink chink*, a ragtime melody.

The baby dropped. It lurched, falling, inside her. She held her stomach tightly. Sweet child, dear child, be still. Sleep softly now. It fell again, this time as if from some great height. It jarred against her pubic bone, shaking her badly. Sleep, my love. Sleep, be still.

Her mother's piano playing became louder, more erratic, a berserk accompaniment to the tape. But now the tape was silent, there was only a hissing sound, and she imagined it had come to an abrupt end. Was that all? Wasn't there anything more? Was she to be left with more puzzles? And then the hissing sound changed and she heard Ely say, *Sixteenth of July, 1981. Subject Eric Campbell.* A click, as if the tape had been momentarily stopped. Then Ely cleared his throat and said: *Did you take the medication I prescribed?*

Ellen didn't move.

The next voice you hear. The next voice.

No. I don't like taking chemicals.

His voice. *His* voice.

Eric. Eric answering Ely's question.

It was spooky, frightening, it was like listening to voices transmitted through ether, through the machinations of a spiritualist in a darkened room. She felt scared, she felt utterly alone. And the piano was rising in an insane crescendo, hammering at her eardrums.

Why didn't you fill the prescription? I only prescribed them for your help. Don't you trust me, Eric?

I trust you. I don't want to take those pills, that's all. I'm not sure what they're supposed to do.

They would help you control your moods of depression. They might even help with the nightmares. I think you're being a little hostile, Eric.

Silence.

She put her hands to her ears and longed for a whole world of total quiet, an absence of everything that shook or rattled or vibrated through spaces. Stillness—Jesus, how she longed for stillness.

I'm not being hostile. I don't like chemicals. That's all.

Tell me about the nightmares. Have you had one recently?

A week or so ago.

And what do you remember of it?

Pause. Papers being ruffled. Something banging on the surface of a desk, a chair creaking.

I don't remember much. I remember a church. A kind of a church. Everything's different in dreams. She's standing there in her bridal gown and she has flowers and an organ is playing and I'm watching from a balcony. Someplace above, I don't know where. And suddenly it's a different place. It's like months have passed. Maybe years.

Ellen pressed her face against the warm window. The pain in her stomach was intense now, a wild rage, something she had no control over, a fire licking and burning. The bridal gown. The flowers. What are you talking about, Eric? Who is this X you're talking about? This woman in a church.

Years, Eric said. *Then I look into her face and I see cobwebs in eye sockets. I see the skin rotting from bone. There are things crawling just under the surface of the skin. Then I think . . .*

Pause. A telephone rang a couple of times. Another pause. The tape clicked.

Ely's cold voice: *You keep blaming yourself, Eric. And blame involves energy of some emotional kind—where does all this energy go, Eric? You throw it into your work. You shove it into your nightmares. You don't let it out, do you?*

It was my fault—

How can it be your fault if you fell in love with another

*woman? You can blame yourself because you didn't have the
courage to say you weren't going through with the wedding.
But it's in the past. This is another life you're leading, Eric.
You can't haul yesterday's luggage around with you forever.*

A wedding, Ellen thought.

A wedding, Eric's wedding, except he didn't attend.

He didn't turn up because he'd fallen in love with me.

And a woman waited in a silent empty church. Surrounded
by flowers. By organ music, endlessly repeating the same
tune. And the groom doesn't show.

A wedding.

Eric said: *If I can't blame myself for jilting the woman, if I
can't do that . . .*

Silence. A buzzing sound like that of a fly winging too close
to the microphone. More silence. She could imagine Ely
staring at Eric, hands clasped, eyes cold. Ely waiting.

I blame myself for her accident.

*Accident? It might be a step in the right direction if you
stopped calling the incident an accident, Eric. It wasn't an
accident and you know it.*

Accident? Ellen suddenly moaned: the turmoil in her
womb was unbearable now. She felt her legs give way; she
slipped to her knees on the floor, moaning, her eyes water-
ing. Accident? What the hell were they talking about? Eric
had fallen in love with her and because of that love he'd
canceled wedding plans and he hadn't told her, he hadn't ever
mentioned anything about another woman, about any accident.

Eric's voice: *Okay, it wasn't an accident—*

*It's better to face it, Eric. If you don't face it now, you'll
have to come to terms with it later. When we bury things
away, you know what happens to them? They're like simple
wounds you fail to dress, so they fester, and if you don't catch
them in time—suddenly you're looking at gangrene, you're
looking at amputation, Eric. If it wasn't an accident, what
was it?*

It was an attempt at suicide.

Suicide.

Ellen made a fist of her hand and put it to her mouth and
bit on the knuckles to ease the pain that was driving through
her. The eruptions from inside, the pushing and stretching
and pulling. I'm coming apart, coming apart from inside.

*A certain grotesque attempt, you must admit—if suicide
was what she was attempting.*

Suicide. Waiting broken-hearted in a church, flowers wilting, wanting to crawl into a hole, weep your humiliation and your pain away. She moaned again and crawled toward the bed and each movement she made seemed to burn through her body.

Eric. This woman filled a bathtub with water. She was three months' pregnant. She had a fetus in her body.

I didn't know that at the time . . .

It doesn't matter what you knew or what you didn't know. She filled a bathtub with water, Eric. She came home straight from the church. She didn't take off her bridal gown, Eric. I want you to look at this picture, I want you to imagine it, Eric, you need to face it, you don't have to keep burying it away. She gets inside the tub and she takes a knife. She takes the knife and she makes an incision. She cuts from a point below the navel to a point above the pubic bone, Eric. Try and picture it. Try it. She takes a knife and she performs a crude and impossibly dangerous caesarian section on herself. Can you see the blood? Can you see the fetus come out of all this blood and die in the water?

Don't—

Don't what, Eric? Don't narrate all the graphic detail that's already buried away inside your brain? I'm only getting you to force it out, that's all. I'm only getting you to look at it. Face it. Shove your face right in it, Eric. If you don't, you'll never overcome the guilt that's destroying the fabric of your personality. Never. Just face the fact that she almost died. Face the fact that your child was aborted. Face the fact that she was saved and rushed to the hospital. Face those things.

Ellen stretched her arm out and killed the tape.

A knife in water, a knife slashing the layers of skin, laying bare the womb, bruised bloody skin flapping, blood-red misshapen fetus floating upward in blood-red water.

Oh, Jesus, Jesus, I can't hear anymore.

Can't listen.

A knife burning through flesh. A dying bride.

The pain swooped in on her again. It might have been a huge enraged bird panicked and trapped in her womb. Nothing ever felt this bad, nothing ever.

A knife in skin.

Deep. Deep.

A heart broken.

The pain intensified, grew loud in her ears, sang a frantic

melody in her head. Things gave, splintered, the sky blackened, the bright sun turned green. Her eyes streamed water, eyesight blinded. Eric, you could have told me, you could have let me know, I could have withstood it, taken it.

The woman, the poor woman, you might have told me about her, you might have told me who she was.

Who? Who was X?

She got to her feet. Suddenly the piano playing stopped. Suddenly everything was deathly quiet.

Then her water broke.

Part Three

The Delivery

❋❋❋❋❋❋❋❋❋❋❋❋❋❋❋❋❋❋❋❋❋❋❋❋❋❋❋❋❋❋❋❋❋

Premature, premature by two weeks, ten days or whatever the time period might be: but she remembered Phelps saying to her once—*You can never know these things for certain, you can always be off by a number of days either way.* She could feel faint contractions as if they were the pulsations of a large jellyfish in the dead center of her body. They were coming regularly and with each contraction there seemed to be more pressure exerted against her stomach, more pressure forced against the pubic bone and the base of the spine. Baby baby baby, she kept thinking. It was all she wanted to think about now, the only responsibility she needed to have—why would she need some poor deranged woman, some ghastly self-laceration, an empty church, the memory of a psychiatrist's voice on a tape: you only need to think about getting through this birth, producing something beautiful and healthy, a well-made child. And she realized she wanted Eric to be with her, despite it all she wanted him to be there, holding her hand in the back of this antique vehicle—why would she need the fussing of Hattie Dalrymple and her mother, kind though they were trying to be? You don't need a damn thing except to get to the hospital, where you'll be safe, the baby will be safe; they'll put you in a delivery room and take care of you through all your pain and deep breathing and pushing and grunting. She leaned forward to Hattie and asked, "Did you call Phelps?"

Hattie said, "Of course I did. He wasn't there."

"Wasn't what?" Panic in the voice.

"He was out of his office. I talked with his nurse. She was very pleasant indeed. She said Phelps would meet you at the hospital."

Then her mother was cutting in, saying: "I don't know how many hours I spent after your water broke, dear. It must have been almost a whole day. Of course, they told me afterward they didn't think it was safe for me to have another baby, my

187

frame wasn't sturdy enough. I can't really remember it clearly now."

"Mother, please. If you want to talk to me about childbirth, think of something happy. Can't you do that?"

Ellen's mother turned around in the passenger seat and smiled at her daughter: "It was quite a pleasure to see you for the first time. I recall that as being a pleasant moment."

Ellen sat back with her eyes shut. *A knife carved through a woman's stomach. A fetus floating in dark red water.* Eric, Eric, why couldn't you have told me? Why? Were you ashamed, did you think I'd feel any less for you if you'd told me the truth? *The baby shouldn't die.* Only he'd been thinking about a different baby—not *their* baby, not the one she was on her way to deliver.

When another contraction went through her she doubled over and held her stomach and tried to remember: You're having a baby, it has to be the most magnificent moment, a moment you'll remember the rest of your life—you don't need the revelations of a shrink, the secret details of your husband's past—you can relegate these things, put them away for later scrutiny, you can hide from the sharp edge of reality, the baby is your only reality for now.

Hattie said, "You did say it was Scottsdale Memorial, didn't you?"

"Yes," and Ellen couldn't keep a faint note of impatience from her voice. That same pressing pain, that same rippling and tightening of the stomach muscles—but now the tightening seemed to involve the legs and the upper part of the body, as if the contractions were coming from every conceivable angle. She twisted her head as Hattie turned the Bentley on to the Scottsdale Road; they were hitting the midafternoon traffic now, the curse of the commuters who clocked out early, the housewives doing some late shopping.

She pressed her hands flat against her stomach and she felt something moist between her legs, a discharge of some sticky kind. The ignominy of childbirth, the breakdown of systems, the general change in the body's behavior—she realized she was on an unpredictable course now, she'd reached a point that was beyond her experience. And it was a place filled with fear. Don't be, don't be afraid, kid, you'll come through all this without trouble, you'll make your way out the other end. Other women do.

Other women. *A woman waits in a church. A bridal bouquet falls to the floor. A foot carelessly tramples it.* And your love doesn't turn up. Your love doesn't show. A whole spidery affair collapses with the sound of unbearable silence.

And then she was suddenly thinking of Vicky.

Why now?

Vicky, maybe Vicky had been the one, maybe it was Vicky he'd left waiting in that church—but how? how could that be? *Vicky was her friend.*

A terrible scar on the stomach. A scar. The scar left by a knife.

What was it about a scar that seemed to make an alarm ring inside her head?

A blonde girl standing by the wire fence around a swimming pool, a blonde girl who didn't wear a bikini even when all her friends were doing so, a blonde girl with a dazzling smile and a one-piece bathing suit. Hiding what? You see Eric inclining his head toward the girl, you see sunlight creating a nimbus around both of them, you see a certain intimacy in the way they stand together, you see too many things, too much . . .

Dream, float into the dream of pain, let yourself drift into unconsciousness.

Vicky's married men.

Vicky and Eric together.

Vicky being mysterious about her most recent love. The phone calls that went unanswered. Why hadn't she returned those calls? Why hadn't she?

Vicky—

You don't need these thoughts now.

Then you see a mattress slashed and a beheaded doll laid in the slit, as if that gash were the opening through which a baby might emerge, some travesty of her own body.

The bridal gown.

A baby.

The woman left forsaken in a church.

It adds, in a wild way it adds, in the berserk arithmetic of insanity it adds up to something.

But what? Exactly what?

Too tired, too sore, to think. Drift, Ellen. Make believe there's no pain, nothing hurting you. Drift away from it all.

The motion of the car vibrated through her.

* * *

Soon.

It has to be soon.

Didn't he promise you so many things and how he'd love you forever and hold you in his arms and care for you and nourish you and didn't he tell you nothing could interfere with your love, your loving?

He knew you'd always come back.

You knew you'd be together.

Soon now.

You'd forgive him, if there was anything to forgive.

Why don't I get Hattie to stop the car so I can call Eric and have him meet me at the hospital?

Why don't I do that?

The answer is obvious, Ellen.

Obvious, even if you don't like it.

You still can't trust him. Even now, even as the contractions of his child stun your nerve endings, even now you still don't really trust him.

The hospital isn't far, she thought. They'll know what to do about my pain then. They have all kinds of aids and devices in hospitals, don't they?

She vaguely listened to the conversation between Hattie and her mother: it wasn't exactly tactful.

I remember my cousin Daphne had a baby with a clubfoot.

And then Hattie: *My niece's first died after three weeks. Spina bifida, I think they said.*

Then, as if they remembered who was seated in back, they talked about the weather in an idle way.

I don't need to hear bad things, she thought. And then: Oh Eric, I need you. I need you and I don't need you and I feel so alone.

Something is wrong, she thought, the baby is coming out buttocks first, something is either wrong or going to go wrong, I just know it, I just know I'm not equipped to do this thing properly, they'll have to do a C-section and lift it out of its bed of mucus and blood. No, Ellen. You have to breathe deeply and relax. Good old Phelps. You knew a thing or two apart from the benefits of chamomile tea, didn't you?

Chamomile tea. McDonald.

She didn't have time to think about McDonald now. So

why did his voice come back into her head, his exhortation to Think Hard, Think Hard. *My head will break open as surely as my body is about to.*

Think hard.

The only thought was fear. A blank shapeless thought, a feeling. *You're afraid, Ellen, but every expectant mother feels that way. You show me a pregnant woman who isn't afraid and I'll show you somebody who doesn't give a damn about her baby.* She leaned back and tried to draw some comfort from the seat of the car, tried to sink deeply into it, but then everything seemed very confused in her mind suddenly—all the pain, the surprises, the fear, Eric's life and his history, the woman in the white gown. The psychiatrist's tape. The voice of McDonald. Everything became confused and garbled.

Think babies. Think of the joys of breast feeding. *Think hard.* Leave me alone, McDonald. Leave me in peace at a time like this. Don't talk to me of patterns, shapes, wholes—I have this baby to deliver.

By tonight, by tomorrow morning, she would be a parent. Eric would be a father. It could have been a happier state of affairs. (Call him. Get Hattie to call him. Tell him what's happening. I love you, Eric. I didn't stop loving you. It might have seemed like that, but I didn't stop. Why am I thinking of some unknown girl slashing her body? I don't want that picture at this time. I don't have to entertain it. My mind is my own. Keep off the grass. Trespassers will be prosecuted. This land is posted. Stay away. A warning to all intruders. Think hard. Damn you, McDonald. Damn you for interrupting me when I'm trying to keep body and soul together.)

Everything was receding now, everything racing away from her. She ceased to have any existence save for the regularity of the spasms in her stomach. Soon, soon you'll be a mother.

Hattie was drawing up in front of the hospital. It looked larger than it had before to Ellen—a huge temple, so many windows, so many people flitting in and out.

Hattie helped her out of the car. She could hear her mother tap-tap behind slowly. "Don't wait for me," her mother was saying, "I'll catch up with you, don't wait for me." Ellen leaned against Hattie as they went together through the door.

"Hattie, I think it's wrong, it feels wrong," she heard herself say.

"Nonsense, Ellen. It's going to come off like a charm."

"Will you do something for me? Will you call Eric and tell him?"

"Gladly. It's right to call him now. I'll be delighted to call him, Ellen. Delighted."

"If he isn't at home, call him at the office. It's in the book. Will you do that for me?"

"Promise," Hattie said.

"Will you do it now?"

"It's as good as done."

Then she was standing in front of a desk and giving her name and the particulars of her life to a receptionist who'd seen too many pregnancies. After, she was taken into the labor room, a place with an upraised bench, she was told to sit, and somewhere in here Hattie disappeared. Calling Eric, of course. Didn't I just ask her to do that?

A nurse came in, checked her pulse, timed the contractions, told her to relax. Relax, she thought. Everybody tells me to relax, unwind. Take things easy, sure.

A familiar face, she needed to see a familiar face about now. She lay back on the labor bench after the nurse had left and wondered if she could get lost in the crazy shuffle of a hospital and be destined to give birth on her own and, like a dog with pups, lick her baby clean.

She heard the sound of her mother's walker; then her mother was standing over her and muttering words of comfort. The overhead lights made her blink—why did they have to be so strong?

"It's going to be okay, Ellen. Take my word for it. You're going to be fine."

Then her mother too was gone.

Time passed. She wasn't sure how long. The ache of the spasms flooded her. She lay with her arms at her sides, afraid, afraid of the notion nobody would come to help her, scared by the idea that she'd been forgotten. One pregnant woman in a vast hospital—what difference did it make?

You could get overlooked. It wouldn't be the first time.

When the door opened next she heard a familiar voice and she looked up to see Nurse Grabowski come into the room. The smile—she'd never seen such a warm smile before now.

"My, Ellen—you've given us all a scare. Naughty of you. You weren't meant to produce until next month. My, my. The doctor is on his way."

Grabowski was taking her pulse, timing the contractions, nodding her head. "You've still got some hours in front of you, Ellen. I think you might have been a little more considerate, don't you? Couldn't you have held back until the due date?"

"Do you think it's going to be okay?"

Grabowski laughed and said, "It's going to be fine. We're old hands at premature deliveries, honey."

An echo. The echo of a nightmare.

Hadn't she said just those words in a dream? Word for word?

"You're in terrific hands, Ellen. The very best," Grabowski said. "You don't have a thing to worry about."

Ellen felt herself drift again until the next contraction and then she started: the dream—she couldn't remember the dream in any detail now. Coincidence, nothing else. She looked across the room and saw the nurse washing her hands in a basin.

"It's painful," Ellen said.

"Oh, who's the *baby*, Ellen? You or the little person in there?" Grabowski came to the table and looked down at her. "I told you before, you're in the best of hands. Now take your air in real slow, then let it go even slower. You'll be okay." And the nurse's hand patted Ellen on the shoulder. When is Phelps coming? she wondered. When is Phelps going to get here?

Ellen tried to relax. She tried to imagine she was someone else. But the air seemed unbreathable to her, sterile, the kind of air you might imagine trapped in the cotton head of a Q-Tip. She closed her eyes and listened to Grabowski move around, wondered what the nurse was doing. There was the sound of a woman sobbing somewhere nearby. The labor room, Ellen thought: the room of pains. A torture chamber. Weren't they going to move her to the delivery room at some point?

She heard her mother come inside, the metallic sound of her walker hitting the floor. As she raised her head and looked at the older woman, another contraction hit her as if her flesh were soft dough and the muscle a large hand kneading it viciously. Through the open door there were people walking back and forth along a corridor, nurses with charts, bedpans, orderlies pushing somebody on a stretcher, a doctor rushing in a flapping white coat—there were voices booming out of loudspeakers, *Dr. Candless to surgery, Dr. Nair to room 337.*

"How are you, Ellen?" Her mother was standing over her and tapping her lightly on the hand.

"I've been better." Ellen groaned again.

"It won't be long now."

As if I were waiting for a bus. She makes it sound like that.

"I'll be in the waiting room," her mother said. "If you need me, shout."

Then she heard her mother go out again and Grabowski was back fussing around her, checking the pulse another time, timing the contractions. How long does it all last? Ellen wondered. How many hours do I have to go?—then she remembered horror stories about women being in labor for thirty-six hours. Imagine thirty-six hours of this: imagine going crazy with the pain and the boredom and the impatience. She was glad Grabowski was here—at least now she knew she wasn't going to get overlooked, the system wasn't going to let her slip between the cracks.

There was a long sleepy period without contractions next—they simply ceased coming with anything like their recent regularity.

Ellen yawned: "God, I feel so tired."

"Maybe you can try to sleep. I doubt it, though," and Grabowski smiled.

Ellen shut her eyes and tried to imagine she wasn't in a hospital, tried to think ahead to a point when the child was born and washed, dressed and named, a point when she was carrying the baby out of this place. It was something to look forward to. She yawned a second time, wished she felt more alert, tried to turn on her side—but it seemed to her that her body was too heavy and sluggish for the effort.

Yawning, yawning: Christ, how she wished she were through with all this. A contraction again—this one seemed very low in her body.

She moaned, and Grabowski moved to her side.

"You okay?"

"I think so," Ellen said.

"The baby's depending on you, Ellen. Keep up your strength."

I'll try, Ellen thought. God, I'll try.

*   *   *

*You remember how you lay together in the warm grass above
a lake and there were trees just filling the sky as if they were
shouting about your love to the heavens oh you remember so
many things.*

And he knew you'd always come back.

He knew it.

You don't want to let dark clouds cross your memory now.

*You don't want to remember the knife in your flesh, the
blood in the bathtub.*

You were very sick then.

You're better now.

Alone with her pain, she wondered if Hattie had reached
Eric and how soon he'd get here. Please make it before I go
into delivery, she thought. Please make it soon.

She wanted to get up and walk around the room but she
didn't have the energy for it. When the door opened she saw
Grabowski come inside: she was carrying a hospital gown
across one arm.

"I want you to put this on, Ellen."

"Only if you close the door," Ellen said.

Grabowski smiled and knocked the door shut with her foot.
Ellen saw something sharp in the nurse's hand.

"What's the razor for?"

"You've heard of preparations, I guess."

Ellen nodded.

"Well, I'm going to prep you. Don't look so alarmed. I've
done this a few times before as well and I'd say my hand
slips—oh, maybe once every twenty times."

Ellen struggled to get her smock off, threw it to the floor
and put on the clinical gown Grabowski gave her.

"You could help me by opening your legs a little wider,
Ellen," the nurse said.

"Is this really necessary?"

The nurse began to work with the razor between Ellen's
spread legs. "It cuts down on the possibility of bacteria.
Those little menaces like living in pubic hair. We wouldn't
want baby to catch anything nasty at once, would we? It
wouldn't be the best possible welcome to the world."

"I guess," Ellen said unhappily. It was an odd sensation
having a woman shave your pubic hair. When Grabowski was

finished she stood with her hands on her hips and looked at Ellen.

"Now we have to hook you up, Ellen."

"Hook me up?"

"The old IV connection."

"Do you have to?"

Grabowski nodded and began to haul out of the corner a wheeled contraption from which there hung an inverted bottle and a long tube. "Think of this as your friend, Ellen. It's only glucose and water, but it could turn out to be very useful."

It was attached to Ellen's arm with a piece of tape: she watched the tube run from her flesh to the bottle. A bubble appeared in the liquid, rose upwards, popped.

"Now you're ready," Grabowski said.

Another contraction. How many more? Ellen wished she didn't feel so sleepy. And Grabowski hadn't been too gentle between her legs because now she felt sore and exposed down there. She closed her eyes.

"When the time comes, we'll have you wheeled to the delivery room," the nurse said.

"I hope it's soon."

Grabowski smiled: "I hope so too."

Time passed slowly. The contractions came and went. Sleep seemed as pressing as the need to give birth somehow; she just wished she had a couple of minutes now without any pain so that she could close her eyes and drift away, but each time she tried the pain woke her. She realized she'd never felt quite so alone before. Where is Eric? Is he on his way and stuck in the insanity of traffic? When she was lying down again she asked, "Has my husband arrived?"

Grabowski shook her head: "When he does, I'll drag him in here immediately. Just try to relax, Ellen."

Imagine he doesn't come, she thought: imagine he's decided that the marriage is over. She thrust the thought aside— who needs more insecurity now? Then she wondered again if Hattie had managed to get in touch with him. Maybe not. Maybe Hattie hadn't even tried. But why wouldn't she? My mother, Ellen thought, perhaps my mother somehow prevented Hattie from calling Eric. I don't need that thought either.

Grabowski was standing over her and looking down. This is

just like my nightmare, Ellen thought. Exactly like my nightmare.

"I want you to try pushing a little, Ellen."

Pushing?

"Gently. Help the baby. Let me see you do that."

Push. Almost exactly like the bad dream.

She drifted in and out of consciousness. She thought of the instruments in nurse Grabowski's hand, the garden shears in Hattie's. Sharp instruments, somebody slicing their own belly, the thought of the black car, the white face under the palm. Dressed for a wedding. A wedding without a groom. Random thoughts, things on a zigzagging tide.

She opened her eyes and saw Phelps come into the room. He approached her, smiled, touched the back of her hand. She tried to smile back but she knew her look was glazed from the repeated pain.

"How are we, Ellen? Eh? Coming down to the old finish line, right?"

Ellen opened her mouth but her lips felt too dry for speech. She watched Phelps go and whisper with Grabowski in the corner of the room and she wondered what they were saying—had his trained eye spotted something wrong? It had to be that. Something going wrong. But when Phelps turned his face to look at her he was still smiling.

Like the dream again.

There was a sudden savage downthrust of pain just then and she rolled her face to the side: how long have I been lying in this labor room? An hour?

Two?

She wasn't sure. She felt confused again. She opened her mouth to ask if Eric had arrived but cotton might have been sticking to her palate. As if by some instinct Grabowski came to the bench and allowed her to sip a little water from a plastic cup. It was lukewarm, it didn't matter. Hoarsely, she asked about Eric, but Grabowski was already taking the cup to the sink and didn't answer her question. *Is something wrong? Can there be something wrong?*

No, Ellen. Just push gently like you've been told. Don't let your mind play more games, you don't have the mental energy for games now. She arched her hips and pushed and Grabowski, watching her, smiled and said, *Good girl, Ellen, good girl.*

How much time had slipped away in this sweaty room?

"You're doing just great, Ellen, wonderful," Phelps said as he left the room—and she wondered why he was going out again so soon; for a moment she felt abandoned, almost as if Phelps had remembered another appointment suddenly and was rushing off to keep it.

"He'll be back when you're ready," Grabowski said. "Don't look so *down*, Ellen. Everything's going great."

"You're being very patient, Ellen. Just keep pushing."

She raised a hand and wiped sweat away, then she felt something trickle between her legs.

"What is that? Is it blood?" she asked.

"It's called a pink show. It's normal."

Ellen strained to look down. She saw a small smear of pink against her skin. It looked like watery blood.

Eric, what is keeping him? Maybe he decided not to come, maybe he had reasons of his own, couldn't make it, something along those lines—or perhaps he wasn't in his office nor at the apartment and Hattie couldn't get through to him.

She was very scared.

She wondered if they left things to the last moment before they carted her off to the delivery room. She wondered if they enjoyed the suspense of that. Where the hell is Phelps anyhow?

Drift. The ebb and rise of slats of wood on a sea. The motion of weed upon a tide.

The blue shirt floating in the pool.

X. X got inside the apartment a couple of times. Eric's history. If it was X, if if if—if it was the same poor woman, deranged from looking too long upon the corpse of love. Why did she steal the things she stole? Why those things?

The clean apartment.

You might understand that in a twisted way. *She thinks she's his rightful bride. It would be part of her marital duty to clean his home. Her function as Eric's wife.*

But those things she took.

Those odd things.

A blue shirt. (A fit—maybe she destroyed it in a fit of jealousy. But why *that* shirt? And why cut off all the buttons?) Was it all random, all done on the spur of a mad moment?

A shirt.

The face of an antique doll.

Library books.

Patterns, Christ. McDonald was out of his tree. What patterns? She couldn't think of any: she couldn't think of a single meaningful mosaic. Over to you, McDonald. Over and out. You can have it all.

His rightful bride.

Then what is my place in all this insanity?

She heard Phelps's voice in the room. He was wearing his white coat now, his stethoscope dangling from his neck.

He asked her to part her legs a little. She did so, then felt his fingers enter her—she grimaced and moaned. "Sorry if that was a bit rough," he said. "But I think we're about ready."

Ready? At long last?

"Fine," Grabowski said.

Now there was somebody else in the room, an orderly in his hospital greens. Then she was being wheeled along a pale white corridor, passing under a sign that read DELIVERY ROOM, going through gray double doors and into the room where she would give birth to this child.

Soon, Phelps was saying. *Very soon*.

And Grabowski was muttering *Push, push*.

This isn't a dream, Ellen, this is for real.

You have your pubic hair clipped and someone sticks his fingers inside you and pale blood runs down your thighs and you cry with the pain of it all and you undergo the creepy looks of strangers and you open your thighs wide to give birth in a room filled with people you barely know, Grabowski and Phelps, an orderly in a green jacket, people who were wearing masks. Masks now, half their faces eclipsed in a sinister way. Spooky. Humiliating and spooky. Why did you ever dream of something warm and pleasant? And soon there will be blood and mucus and a child, then the placenta coming after like a second kind of birth—the body seemed nothing more than a system of discharges, a producer of effluence. How could a beautiful child come out of all this horror?

Phelps and Grabowski, masked now, stared down at her.

Then Ellen felt her legs being raised and placed inside stirrups that hung from a point overhead. The final disgrace—to be so exposed, bald and exposed, in this sterile room.

Phelps was feeling her between the legs again. Two fingers opened her up.

She might have been a wishbone about to crack.

She opened her eyes. At the foot of the table there was a large mirror: I can look, she thought. I can watch this child emerge from my body. I can see it all.

Somewhere along the way the attendant seemed to have disappeared and now she was alone with Phelps and his nurse.

She overheard words like *dilated* and *position* and *oxygen*.

Then Phelps was looming above her with something in his hand.

It was the dream all over again.

"I'm going to have you breathe some oxygen for a few seconds, Ellen. Don't panic when I hold this against your face, okay? Everything is going just great. No problems. Take a few deep drags on this."

It was clamped upon her face. She breathed and she felt she was floating high above the room now, looking down on this shabby little world of masked people.

It wasn't like the dream at all, she thought. In the dream there had been a third person, an invisible stranger who held her hand. Wasn't that the way it had been? Here there were only two people in the room beside herself. Phelps and Grabowski. Good old safe familiar Phelps and his sidekick.

I'm in good hands.

The best.

Everything is going to be just terrific.

The oxygen was applied again and now the seizures of pain were no longer a part of her, they were remote from her, manufactured out of the ether, materializations that didn't touch her.

Think hard, Mrs. Campbell.

Why did she feel it was too late to call Patrick McDonald? She concentrated on floating away.

She thought: A blue shirt and an old doll and a couple of used books from a library. The conglomeration of things made her feel even more silly than before. Oxygen—it was a decent high, it was pretty good.

A blue shirt.

An old doll.

Borrowed books.

What pattern?

Wrong.

She wasn't floating any longer. She was tumbling fast from

her perch in the ceiling. She saw her legs sway in the stirrups.

Wrong.

Something is wrong.

She stared between her upraised legs at the mirror and thought she saw a movement down there, a shadowy movement. Baby baby.

Why is something wrong.

Something blue.

Something old.

You see patterns, you have to look for them and sift them out of the whole crazy mosaic of events, but sometimes when you look you see them real close and they frighten you.

A woman in a bridal gown.

Brides. Weddings. Traditions.

Something old. Something blue.

Wrong, you have to be wrong.

Something old. Something blue.

Borrowed.

Old and blue and borrowed and something else lingering just behind it all—something else taking shape out of the doped mists in her brain. *I am coming down and I am terrified*, she thought.

Your perfect pattern, McDonald.

Old and blue and borrowed and

And what?

She looked between her legs and she grunted and pushed and forced herself hard, straining until her spine seemed to slip out of joint. She saw a head emerge in the mirror, a bloodied head.

Baby, baby.

A new life.

Something new.

Keep it coming, Ellen. Keep pushing. I can see a perfect head. Beautiful, beautiful. It isn't like the dream, Ellen thought. It's different from the dream now. The baby is beautiful.

Something new.

The woman had taken the other things and now she was going to take something new.

Fragmented images in the mirror, an arm curled and pink.

A slight down of hair on a fragile skull.

Ellen tilted her face back for a final push, a last thrust. And wondered through all this pain whether the process could be reversed, whether she could somehow draw the baby back inside her, where it would be secure and safe from the harm of madness.

Come back inside me. Come back.

The mirror darkened. Phelps's head moved in front of the light and the image vanished a moment and she panicked because she couldn't see the baby.

A cry—did she imagine the cry?

And now you are going to deal with the last part.

You are going to deal now with the last thing of all.

Ellen opened her mouth. She stared at Phelps and Grabowski. They were busy between her legs.

She wanted to tell them, she couldn't find the strength, there were no words on her lips.

New.

The new life.

The pattern.

"It's a boy, Ellen. It's a healthy good-looking boy."

Phelps, she wanted to say. Don't let the baby go. Then she saw the infant—a crying naked baby. And Grabowski was smiling, a smile of pride, a beaming smile, almost as if she herself had just given birth. The baby moved in Phelps's arms. Ellen stared at it. Bells, there were bells ringing, clanging, inside her head. They might have been lights, red lights, lights of danger. She began to shake, wild adrenalin racing through her with the speed of an unfettered wind. She'd never heard her blood roar so loudly.

Phelps is holding the baby, Grabowski is smiling. There isn't any danger here, not in this safe room, none at all.

Then why—

Why do I smell it and sense it and know beyond all doubt that the child is in peril, why do I know that, where does that instinct come from, where?

She moved her eyes from Phelps, from the baby, from Grabowski, to the closed door of the delivery room. Was that a shadow she saw against opaque glass, somebody standing just outside the door?

Give me my baby, Phelps. Give my baby to me.

Phelps, still beaming, did not move. The nurse, smiling, smiling, stood very still. Didn't they see? Did neither of them

see the motionless shadow pressed against the outside of the
door? Were they blind? So goddam blind?

Scream let me scream let me scream.

The cry of a baby.
   The soft pink flesh of a baby.
   He will be happy to see you with the baby.
   Happy to see you again, to love you again.
   So happy.
   *And then the parting will never have mattered. You will
forget. The absences. The sickness. The time he visited you
when they said you were sick. They said, they, they, they.*
   They never knew.
   And you will not go back to him empty-handed.
   You will take pages of books.
   The buttons of a shirt.
   Broken pieces of old china.
   And finally this baby, beautiful in death, in destruction.
   This baby. Your last gift to him.
   And everything will be happy again.
   And you will be his true bride.

Her eyes watered, her mouth hung open, her throat was dry
as a bleached bone. She raised one hand in the air and she
pointed toward the door, toward the shadow, but neither
Phelps nor Grabowski was looking at anything but the baby.

Grabowski was saying, "Oh, he's perfect. He's just perfect.
Just what we wanted."

Please, Ellen whispered.

Oh please. The door is opening, opening only a fraction,
the shadow moves to the edge of the opaque glass.

Please look.

But they weren't turning round, they were smiling at the
baby.

My baby.

You fumble for the knife.
   Knife. Sharp. Concealed under your clothing.
   *It pricks your finger and draws blood and the pain brings
old savage memories back to you.*
   *You get the knife, clasp it, pull it out from under your
clothing.*
   Now now now, the time is now.

For you, darling Eric, a dead baby.
For us, a new beginning. A new wedding.

The door opened wider: the shadow, lit from behind by the
cold fluorescence of clinical light, fell into the room. Ellen
tried to sit up. For a moment she caught Grabowski's eyes—
the expression there was beatific, proud, the eyes glowing.
*Grabowski, please, turn and look, somebody is coming into
the room.* Somebody who wants my baby. Please look.

The knife. Cold steel in white air. Cold killing steel.

Phelps leaned forward and gently laid the baby in Ellen's
arms. This soft wonderful love, I carried it for nine months,
nobody is going to harm it. Phelps said something like, *fine
fine well done*.

These were the last words of his life.

Through the air there was a flash of brittle steel. Ellen
heard it whisper, saw the blade reflect the sizzling overhead
lights, watched the metal make a faint rainbow as it arched. It
arched, became liquid as a thundering waterfall, arched and
twisted and found its own cruel, inevitable trajectory. Blinding steel. Blinding as metal freshly forged, glowing still from
the heart of a terrible furnace. Searing. Searing. And the
blood made a sudden fountain, a grotesque column of red—
the knife, the scalpel, whatever, slid through his neck and he
made a quiet moaning sound as he slipped—slipped first
against the delivery table, a look of shocked recognition in his
eyes, then to the floor, where he rolled over and tried to
clutch the wide slit in his neck. She could hear him: she
realized she'd never heard anything more final in all her life.
The moan, the dying strain—it might have come directly
from his heart, as if the heart had a voice of its own.

She stared, eyes frazzled by overhead lights, burned by
movements of white, so much whiteness, so many pools of
red. You're dreaming this, she thought. *This is where you've
been before, this is just another extension of the nightmare.*
The baby, maybe the baby isn't real either—but it was crying
against her breasts, small curled hands fumbling awkwardly.
You couldn't dream that cry, couldn't dream the feel of this
infinitely vulnerable person, this *new* person, huddled against
you.

Grabowski took off her mask.

Familiar. Maybe that was still another echo of a dream.

The door of the room was wide open, she noticed from the corner of her eye, a fragmented perception, because she was looking now into the light of Grabowski's eyes, seeing there some bottomless, nameless thing. Grabowski, she thought.

Maybe Ellen screamed the name. Maybe she imagined screaming. She was immersed in a world without senses, a silent place, a sightless place. Then everything was slow.

You want the baby. You want to take the baby to him.

The last of the wedding souvenirs.

The last tradition.

You need the baby.

You had to wait.

Now the waiting is over and you have love to look forward to.

She wrapped her arms around the baby, swung her body to shield it, listened to its cries pierce her ears. And suddenly she realized something more important than anything else in the whole goddam world. *I'd die for this baby. I'd gladly give my life for him.* She looked into Grabowski's eyes: they were empty, they were vacant, and yet there was determination on the face, an expression of some anguished madness.

You! Ellen thought.

You! You slashed your stomach. You waited in a church. You. Dear God, you.

This precious new life: you can't have it.

Never. You can never have it.

She couldn't take her eyes away from the woman.

A moment—everything might have stopped suddenly, run down, clouds stilled in the sky and the sun frozen in flight and the tides chained and captured. Those eyes, those lost dark eyes, she realized she was looking into the outer edges of love, seeing that place where the heart lost all reason, where love was insanity's companion, where reality was something you touched only if you wanted to alter its course, if you wanted to change and corrupt it.

Not this baby, she thought.

No matter what you do, you will not harm this child.

She saw steel glitter again in the light and the woman's arm began to rise. Move, Ellen, move—turn away from the hypnotic glitter of this falling thing. This killing blade.

And she rolled on her side, surprised by her sudden feeling of hollowness, emptiness, lightness, she rolled and arched her body to cover the child who lay beneath her now. A beautiful baby. More beautiful than she might ever have dreamed. More wonderful than anything her imagination had constructed. Love filled her. It was a love you'd die for without question.

She could sense the knife falling. But it would slice into her, it wouldn't touch the child, at least it wouldn't pierce the soft flesh of this child.

It would kill only her and that didn't matter.

She could save her baby.

Even if it was the last thing she did.

She made a tent of her body over the infant. A fragile tent, a frail shield, too frail to do more than delay the inevitable. She tensed—terrified—waited, waited. Waited and waited with her eyes shut for the instrument to fall against her exposed spine.

Somewhere she heard a door creak open. The shadow beyond the glass—who had been waiting there? That didn't matter now. That just didn't matter a damn. *I am going to die.*

Waiting, waiting to die.

Listening to the baby cry beneath her.

Waiting, listening.

And nothing.

Nothing happened save for the sound of something metallic striking the tiled floor.

Why?

Eric was in the room, somehow Eric had come inside the room and was speaking softly to the woman, stroking the side of her face with his fingertips. (Eric, Eric, the shadow beyond the door.) Stroking, it might have been a gesture of intimate love, a private act of sharing. Ellen held the baby in her arms and looked across the room. Eric was rubbing the woman's arms. Then he leaned forward and kissed her lightly on the forehead and Ellen shut her eyes and held the baby harder against her body. It didn't happen—withdraw from it, I dreamed all this up, I created it out of the delirium of my condition, my fevered state. It didn't happen and Phelps will come through the door at any moment. And Grabowski—Grabowski didn't do anything, she isn't the woman of Eric's guilt, I made it all up, hacked out my own tormented fiction.

When she opened her eyes she could see Phelps on the floor, eyes open, mouth slack, one hand twisted under his body.

Don't look. *If you didn't dream it up, you don't have to look.*

But it's real. It's real. You lived through this pain.

You are holding your baby.

And X is Grabowski, Grabowski who steered you through this pregnancy, who gave you advice, who was kind to you.

And out of it all, this new life, this boy.

She felt tears come into her eyes.

"Dear Irene," Eric was saying.

The nurse didn't speak. What kind of history had they shared? What kind of love had delivered this poor woman into such murderous madness?

Now he was touching her, consoling her, talking her out of her fantasy. He was being slow and patient and kind, he was being considerate; she was reminded of someone trying to defuse an unexploded bomb.

But this one has already exploded.

She stared at the open doorway: there were several orderlies and nurses standing in the corridor. Warily, they began to edge their way into the room. A young man in a white coat picked up the knife from the floor. Somebody else laid a sheet over poor Phelps.

Poor Phelps.

Then, from out of nowhere, there were two cops.

Eric said, "Irene, I want you to go with these people. They'll look after you."

"When will I see you?" she asked.

"Soon. In a little while."

"Promise?"

"I promise," Eric said.

They kissed.

Their lips touched.

The woman turned her face and looked at Ellen.

What was in that look? Ellen wondered.

What did she see there?

It wasn't emptiness, hollowness, it wasn't the strange dis-

tant light of madness. It was the sharp look of triumph, the
look that cuts, the look that says: *He's mine, he'll always be
mine, he'll never be yours completely.*

Flanked by the cops, the woman left the room without
looking back.

I imagined that expression, Ellen thought.

I only imagined it.

And she held the baby tighter against herself, glancing
over his fragile skull at the face of her husband.

He looked weary, pale, like someone who has traveled a
long and arduous journey.

This is your son, Ellen thought.

I am holding your son in my arms.

They put her in a private room. At various intervals they
brought the baby in, then they would take it out again. They
had to weigh the infant, check it, test it, they had to make
certain it was healthy. She understood all this: what she didn't
understand was the sense of emptiness she felt each time
they took the baby away. It was new sensation, something
she'd have to get used to—a new protective sensibility that
had stirred inside her, a new sense of loss and anticipation.

Eric came with flowers. He put them on the bedside table.
He kissed her on the side of the mouth. She looked at the
flowers—long, fragile lupines. When he saw the baby for the
first time, when he was allowed to hold it, he did so with a
gentle clumsiness, as if the boy were made of fragile glass. It
was the look on his face that enchanted her—she couldn't
remember ever having seen him appear so tender, so totally
involved, so proud.

Proud, she thought. It made her feel good. When a nurse
came in and carried the baby out, Eric sat for a long time in
silence, his hands dangling between his legs. Ellen watched
him: it surprised her all at once to realize she wanted him,
she wanted him with a terrible urgency, wanted his love. But
there was a waiting period, a time of enforced celibacy—she
recalled Phelps telling her that once.

Phelps. Poor Phelps.

Eric said, "It never occurred to me. It never crossed my
mind to connect Irene with what was happening to us. How
could it? I didn't know she'd been released. I never imagined
her coming back into my life..." He stared silently at the
floor, rubbing his fingers together nervously. She realized, as

she saw him take a handkerchief from his pocket, that he was crying. What kind of tears? she wondered. Fear? Relief? Simple pride about the baby? She reached out and held his hand; his fingers were soft and warm. When he spoke again his voice was broken. "I know I should have told you a long time ago. I should have told you everything. But sometimes... I don't know exactly how to say this. Sometimes it seemed to me that none of it had ever happened, it was like a dream. And sometimes I was just so damned scared I'd lose your love if I told you about Irene."

"You could never lose my love," she said. She rubbed his knuckles. I want you, she thought. *I want you so badly.*

"It doesn't matter now," she said. "I found out the truth the hard way, didn't I?"

"The hardest way," he said.

She stared past him at the slices of dark through the slatted blind at the window. She closed her eyes—she didn't see the knife go in Phelps's neck, what she saw instead now was an image of a heart-broken woman slicing into her stomach with a sharp instrument, a fetus dying. *Old and blue and borrowed and new.* Somewhere in that woman's deranged version of reality there was a dream wedding, she and Eric reunited in vows of blood. Blood: why couldn't she get that picture of Phelps out of her mind now? It lay inside her mind like a stain.

She looked once more at Eric and wondered what he'd suffered, she considered the strata of guilt, the quarry of self-recrimination being dug deeper and deeper still. She tried to imagine keeping such pain a secret, locking it away inside some closed door of the brain. It breaks loose, it always has to break free, you can never contain that kind of pain.

"What do you feel for her now?" Ellen asked.

"I think I feel a kind of love. A kind of pity. It's so hard to say. I know this much—I'll always feel responsible for her somehow. Some part of me will always feel like that."

Some part of you, she thought.

Some part of your history I can't change, I can't go back and erase, something in the past I have to live with.

"I went to see her once after she'd tried to mutilate herself," he said. "Just before you and I were married. I don't know why I went. Just that same old sense of guilt, I guess. She was locked inside a room and they had her on some

strong medication. She looked at me for a long time—then
suddenly it seemed she recognized me. I always remember
what she said." He paused, there was an appearance of
absence on his face, almost as if he was remembering a
dream. '*I'll always love you*,' she said. '*I'll love you until the
world ends*.' That's what she said."

Until the world ends, Ellen thought.

*You left her waiting in the church. You left her because of
me. And I never knew, never knew.*

"What will they do with her now?"

"They'll send her back to Maine, I guess. Back to the
mental institution."

Strong doors. Heavy keys. Stout locks.

Why do I feel so sorry for her, even now? Ellen wondered.

Eric said, "I'll never be able to tell you how bad I feel
about this."

"I'd like to try and forget it all," Ellen answered. Forget it
all—was that possible? Was that ever going to be possible?
She had to make it so, she had to work hard at it.

The door of the room opened and a nurse came in carrying
the child. She laid the boy in Ellen's arms. For a while there
was silence in the room. Then Eric, looking over the baby's
blanket, said: "He's beautiful. He's so beautiful."

"He's even got ten fingers and ten toes," Ellen said. "I
counted them."

Eric smiled. "He's got your looks, love."

"I thought he had *yours*."

Eric lightly laid the tip of his index finger on the baby's
cheek, the soft new flesh.

"Have we thought about a name?" he asked.

"I'm considering."

They were silent for a while. The baby yawned, moved its
tiny fingers. The door of the room opened again and Ellen
looked up to see McDonald standing in the doorway, a small
bunch of flowers held awkwardly in his hand. He approached
the bed slowly, looking a little more crumpled than usual, his
off-white suit creased and stained here and there with smears
of cigarette ash. He laid the flowers on the bedside table. He
didn't sit; instead he stood by the side of the bed with the
nervous look of a chain smoker trapped in an elevator,
surrounded by signs of tobacco prohibition.

"Lovely baby," he said in a quiet voice. "Congratulations.
Both of you."

Ellen smiled at the cop. He was shaking his head from side to side. A momentary expression of exasperation crossed his face.

"Call me dense," he said.

"Dense?"

"All my life I've been trained to look for patterns." He spread his hands, looked at them. "Then when one stares you in the face, you overlook it. I should have seen it. I should have seen right through it."

The cop leaned closer to the baby now. His shadow fell across the child's face. He said, "I love them when they're just born. I don't know what it is. Maybe it's because they're so soft and vulnerable." He seemed a trifle embarrassed at his own words. His shyness touched Ellen: she realized suddenly how much McDonald's support and concern had meant to her—what did it matter if he hadn't solved the puzzle in time? What did that matter? There was an ending. The baby was alive, healthy.

"Have you thought what you're going to call him?" the cop asked.

Ellen leaned back against the pillows with her eyes shut for a while. She played with the name in her mind: she could hear it and it sounded just fine.

She opened her eyes and glanced for a second at Eric.

"We just decided," she said. "Just before you stepped through the door."

She hesitated, enjoying the faint look of bewilderment on Eric's face.

She said, "We've decided to call him Patrick. Patrick Campbell."

McDonald rubbed his jaw with the palm of his hand. He smiled and turned toward the door, where he paused. "I like the first name," he said. "I like the first name a whole lot. I'm not so sure about the last one, though."

"Ancient history," Ellen said.

McDonald nodded, as if uncertain about her remark. "I'll be back in my official capacity later. Right now, though, you've got a roomful of visitors. Personally, I think you'd be better off resting." He was quiet as he opened the door. Then he said to himself, "Patrick Campbell," and smiled as he went out.

Ellen gazed at the open doorway. In the corridor beyond she could see her mother sitting on a bench with Hattie standing alongside her; she stared at them and smiled. And then she noticed Vicky holding a large bunch of flowers against her body. Eric got up and shut the door very quietly.

"Later," he said. "Right now I want to have you to myself."

She watched him cross the floor. He sat on the edge of the bed and put his arm around her.

"Patrick," he said.

"Can you think of anything better?" Ellen asked.

He shook his head. He raised the edge of the baby's blanket. He said, "Patrick, you're beautiful."

She closed her eyes and thought: This is a perfect moment, a perfect bond, a small miracle.

RED DRAGON
by Thomas Harris

RED DRAGON

". . . is an engine designed for one purpose – to make the pulses pound, the heart palpitate, the fear glands secrete."
New York Times Book Review

RED DRAGON

". . . is an extraordinary book. A thriller in its own right, with pace, tension, and a capacity to prickle the skin with excitement, but more than this, a superb study of character, seen and understood and created in depth . . . Enthralling, frightening, totally professional. It is quite simply the best of its kind that I have read in twenty years."
Lord Ted Willis

RED DRAGON

". . . simply comes at you and comes at you, finally leaving you shaken and sober and afraid . . . the best popular novel published since THE GODFATHER." *Stephen King*

Over two months on the American bestseller list.

0 552 12160 6 £1.95

THE HUNGER
by Whitley Strieber

Miriam is a ravishingly beautiful young woman . . . but when the hunger grows . . . no man dares to touch her . . .

No-one believes in Vampires any more. But they are still living among us . . . Like Miriam Blaylock who has lived for thousands of years, feeding on the human blood that is her life force . . .

Whitley Strieber, the man who unleashed THE WOLFEN, now unfurls THE HUNGER

0 552 12125 8   £1.75

PEREGRINE
by William Bayer

Circling high over the city is a peregrine falcon, the most awesome of flying predators. She awaits a signal from her falconer. It is given: the bird attacks, plummeting from the sky at nearly 200 miles an hour, striking a young woman, killing her instantly.

So begins a series of brutal slayings, orchestrated by a psychotic madman. . . . So begins the nightmare of a woman enmeshed in his bizarre and deadly scheme . . .

So begins a heart-stopping story of madness and erotic desire which

"Defies readers to stop at any point no matter how horrified they may be."   *Publishers Weekly*

0 552 12096 0   £1.50

PSYCHO
by Robert Bloch

THE STORY THAT ALFRED HITCHCOCK MADE
INTO HIS MOST SPINE CHILLING FILM.

She stepped into the shower stall. She let the warm water
gush over her. That's why she didn't hear the door open. At
first, when the shower curtains parted, steam obscured the
face. Then she saw it . . .

A face peering through the curtains. A headscarf concealed
the hair, and glassy eyes stared inhumanly. The skin was
powdered dead white and two spots of rouge were centered
on the cheekbones.

She started to scream. Then the curtains parted further and
a hand appeared, holding a butcher's knife . . .

0 552 12069 3   £1.25

NO COMEBACKS
by Frederick Forsyth

A rich philanderer plans to kill the husband of the woman he loves in NO COMEBACKS, a skilfully contrived piece with a savage twist in the tale. It is the title story in a marvellously exciting and varied collection by a master story-teller.

To this, his first book of short stories, Forsyth brings the narrative power and the wealth of meticulous detail that have made his novels bestsellers around the world.

"The ten stories vibrate with drama and the shock of the unexpected . . . chillingly effective." *Publishers Weekly*

"A diverting collection of short suspense fiction that should both surprise and delight Forsyth fans." *New York Times Book Review*

0 552 12140 1   £1.95

A SELECTED LIST OF FINE NOVELS
FROM CORGI BOOKS